SERVANT TO A KING

OTHER BOOKS BY SARIAH S. WILSON:

Secrets in Zarahemla

Desire of Our Hearts

Servant to a King

a novel

Sariah S. Wilson

Covenant Communications, Inc.

Cover photography by McKenzie Deakins. For photographer information please visit www.photographybymckenzie.com. Background cover image: *Motive in Teotihuacan* © Gabor Izso, courtesy of iStock.

Published by Covenant Communications, Inc.
American Fork, Utah

This is a work of fiction. The characters, names, incidents, places, and dialogue are products of the author's imagination, and are not to be construed as real.

Printed in Canada
First Printing: July 2008

15 14 13 12 11 10 09 08 10 9 8 7 6 5 4 3 2 1

ISBN 10: 1-59811-572-3
ISBN 13: 978-1-59811-572-7

For Jared and Tina, who know why

Acknowledgments

AS ALWAYS, THANKS TO my publisher, Covenant Communications, Inc., and my editor, Kirk Shaw (for sharing my sense of humor even if we can't use it).

Thanks to Melody Salisbury and Elizabeth Eborn for serving as first readers on this manuscript. My thanks to Jordan Salisbury and Ralph Salisbury for making Ammon and Aaron funny. And a shout-out to Elder Adam Salisbury, whose words about his mission inspired some of Ammon's thoughts and struggles.

Finally, I have so much love and gratitude for my family for their support and belief in me; for Kevin, who helped me physically block out fight scenes; and especially for my daughter, whom I couldn't wait to meet while writing this story.

1

"YOUR FATHER PLANS TO OFFER your hand in marriage."

Isabel held still, disbelieving her maid's words. "Abish, are you certain?"

"I am certain."

Both girls ran to a chest to pull out one of Isabel's most elaborate robes—a soft, green silk tunic. Isabel quickly undressed, and Abish yanked the tunic over Isabel's head. Abish pushed Isabel into a seated position and began to pull at her hair, styling it into a series of elaborate braids and loops tied off with matching green strips of leather.

"Who?" Isabel finally asked.

"They didn't say."

Isabel tried not to wince when Abish pulled her hair even tighter. A thought occurred to her, one almost too frightening to say aloud. But Isabel had to know if her father had gone back on his promise to her, had to know if a horrific fate awaited her. "Is it Mahlon?" she asked in a whisper.

That made Abish stop. Abish's fingers tightened around the shell comb. She looked at Isabel's reflection in the pyrite mirror. "Let us hope not."

Isabel tried to ask her maid more questions about the situation, but Abish didn't seem to know much. She said she had been at her chores when the king's chief servant had started yelling orders for a feast to be prepared. The servant had then commanded Abish to make haste in preparing her mistress, as Isabel would be given in marriage that night.

Something seemed to be worrying Abish, which made Isabel even more anxious. The maid had been with Isabel since they were both young girls, and Isabel considered Abish to be her closest friend. Her only friend.

This could be the last time she would ever see Abish. Isabel would be married to someone at her father's feast and possibly taken to some distant kingdom, never to see her family again.

Not that they would miss her.

Isabel realized the seriousness of her situation when Abish pulled out Isabel's wedding box, the one holding the jewelry her mother had bequeathed Isabel. Isabel had opened the wooden box so many times, playing with the pieces inside as she imagined the sort of husband she would have, what her wedding ceremony would be like. Now that day of reckoning had come so unexpectedly, and she had not even been given the courtesy of being told whom she would marry. Isabel tried not to cry as Abish handed her several heavy spondylus shell necklaces to wear. Isabel's hands shook so badly that Abish took the necklaces and put them on Isabel, fastening them into place. Designed to counterbalance the weight of the necklaces, several long strands of beads hung down Isabel's back. The maid then put bracelets almost all the way up Isabel's arms. A pair of her mother's jade earrings was the final touch.

Abish urged her to hurry. Isabel looked at her own forlorn expression in her mirror. *Someone's wife.* She would lose herself that night. She would become someone's wife, someone's possession, and everything familiar and comfortable in her life would end.

But Isabel lifted her head. She was a princess, the eldest daughter of King Lamoni. She would not shame their family by acting like a coward. She knew what was expected of her, and she would behave as she had been trained.

She kept her hands clasped in front of her as she walked slowly through quiet hallways and empty courtyards toward her father's throne room. Burning incense and smoke combined with the smell of some of her father's precious turkeys being roasted. The scent surprised Isabel. The guest had to be very important to warrant the sacrifice of some of these birds.

Not Mahlon, she thought with each step. *Anyone but Mahlon.*

As she approached the doorway, Isabel heard the booming bass of the drums and knew the dancing had started. She watched the women of the court spinning and swaying in unison until a servant came and covered Isabel's head with a measure of cloth.

"I will discover what I can about him," Abish said to Isabel. Isabel felt her maidservant moving away.

Isabel concentrated on regulating her breathing. She had to calm down. This was what she had been born to do. She had a responsibility to appear in control of herself. Someone took Isabel by her hand and led her into the throne room. She could feel the banging of the drums in her quickened heartbeat. All around her she heard the sound of leather scraping against stone and jingling bells as the dancers twisted and turned. They moved aside to let Isabel pass as she was led to her future husband.

Feeling a slight squeeze on her hand, Isabel understood that she was to stop. She knelt down and tried to rein in her overactive imagination. She reminded herself that her curiosity would be satisfied in a few seconds.

The music suddenly ceased, and everyone around Isabel went silent. From somewhere off to her right, she heard her father speaking.

"Here is my daughter. I would that you take her to wife."

With that, Isabel pulled off her veil, her gaze pointed down toward the floor. She slowly looked up the steps of the dais to where a man sat on thick cushions.

Isabel gasped.

The man in front of her was not a distant relative or any Lamanite king friendly to her family.

The man in front of her was an enemy.

A Nephite.

He was dressed strangely and had no adornments of any kind. He wore his brown hair short, with no feathers or leather straps. Isabel immediately noticed his unusual eyes. She had never seen such a color—a cross between gray and blue, like the sky on a stormy day. He had the audacity to smile at her, as if amused by her studying him. Isabel looked away, embarrassed at her loss of decorum.

Was this how little her family cared for her? Had she so little value that they would give her to a Nephite? Isabel closed her eyes against the hot, stinging tears.

She would retain control. She would not dishonor herself or her family in front of this Nephite. She forced herself to meet his gaze. He still smiled at her. Isabel didn't know whether to feel irritation or outright anger at his impudence. The man stood, still looking down at Isabel.

Then he did something completely outrageous.

He winked at her.

Isabel couldn't help herself. She put her hand over her mouth in shock at his behavior. She looked about her. No one else seemed to have noticed his impertinence.

"You have already been incredibly generous to me, King Lamoni," the man said with a slight, strange accent. His voice was deep and tinged with what sounded like *laughter*. Isabel shook her head. She was going through some sort of nightmare, barely holding on to her façade of calm, and this Nephite found it . . . entertaining?

"And as much as I appreciate your offer, I must respectfully decline."

Decline? Isabel knew what the word meant, but it suddenly felt like a foreign term. Decline? He was declining to marry her? How could that be? Isabel squared her shoulders and lifted her chin. She was a princess. She was above him in class and lineage, and he was declining to marry her? How dare he!

"Instead, I will be your servant."

Utter, total humiliation. This Nephite had just announced to the entire court that he would rather be her father's servant than marry her. With a hot, furious rush, her blood snapped and sizzled inside her. Isabel had never felt such anger before.

She heard the outraged whispers of the crowd gathered all around her. Surely her father would not let this go unpunished. Surely this man would be stretched over an altar and his still-beating heart removed before the sun had risen.

But King Lamoni didn't look angry over the offense. He didn't even look surprised. He was smiling.

"Then you shall be my servant, and I welcome you to my household." King Lamoni indicated that the music should start again. The drums and flutes immediately began in response to the king's silent command.

Isabel still knelt on the floor, too stunned to move. She needed to get up, to get out of this room. But humiliation overwhelmed her. She had been publicly rejected by a *Nephite* who had chosen a life of servitude over her. Isabel directed her gaze downward, too shamed to witness the pitying expressions she knew the others wore.

A pair of sandaled feet appeared at the corner of her vision. Isabel looked up to see the Nephite standing directly in front of her. He still wore that infuriating smile. He held out his hand to her as if to help her up.

Isabel would have died rather than take any assistance from this man. She hoped he could see the hatred in her eyes. She loathed him for what he had just subjected her to. She leaned away from him.

She had only a moment to note the confusion on the Nephite's face before Abish ran up to them. Abish looked as angry as Isabel felt. The maidservant placed herself between the Nephite and Isabel and helped Isabel to stand.

Wrapping her arm around Isabel's shoulders, Abish led her from the throne room, past the mocking glances and teasing words.

Some part of Isabel reminded her to feel happy. She had escaped marriage. She could go on with her life as she wished.

But the mortifying disgrace crowded out the relief of her escape. All of this reminded her how quickly marriage could come and how little control she would have over it.

Or perhaps she didn't have to worry. What worthy man would want to marry her now that a Nephite had passed on marrying her?

Isabel wondered how much time she had until this piece of gossip passed through every palace under her grandfather's control.

She realized that Abish was speaking to her and focused on the maidservant's words, hoping they would distract her from her own painful realizations.

"His name is Ammon. He and his companion were found at the borders. They were bound and brought before your father. Your father asked him if he wanted to dwell in Ishmael. Ammon said that he wanted to live here for a time, possibly the rest of his life. This pleased your father, and Ammon was released. He offered you as a wife then and there, but Ammon told him that he desired to serve your father instead. Tonight they formally cemented their pledges."

Isabel hadn't thought it possible for her suffering to increase, but it had. Her father knew that this Ammon would say no to marrying her, and he still had forced her go through such an indignity. Had no one thought to inform her beforehand? Isabel realized again how little she mattered to her family. Regardless of how she felt, though, why had he turned down marriage?

"Did it not occur to anyone that the Nephite might be a spy?"

"It occurred to everyone," Abish said. "But I think that his saying he would stay here until death was his way of announcing his desire to become one of us. I think that made your father feel more at ease. For some reason the king seems to believe this man."

How could anyone be so naive? Isabel felt shocked. It was obvious to her that this Ammon meant to spy on them. How could anyone trust someone who was a descendant of liars and thieves?

"There's more," Abish said.

More? Isabel didn't know if she could take any more.

"Ammon claims to be the son of King Mosiah in Zarahemla."

"King Mosiah?" Isabel repeated. "Ammon is a prince?" King Mosiah was ruler over all the Nephites. Isabel's grandfather held more land and cities than any other Lamanite king that she knew of, but even he didn't have the same power that King Mosiah did. "It has to be a lie. My father believed him?"

They had finally reached Isabel's bedroom. Abish directed Isabel to a cushion so that she could undo her friend's hair.

"The Nephite brought official documents and books that proved his claim."

This information mollified Isabel slightly. Wasn't it better to be rejected by a powerful prince than a commoner? At least her total degradation now had a royal factor that might offset some of the gossip.

Or that might make things worse. Abish ripped a ribbon out of Isabel's hair, but she barely felt the pain.

Was there a way to rectify this situation? Could she somehow deflect the shame? Isabel couldn't think of a solution; her thoughts were racing too quickly for her to keep up.

One of her mother's necklaces fell into her lap. Isabel picked it up and squeezed it tightly, leaving the imprints of the shells in her hand. Perhaps she couldn't take away her own embarrassment, but she could certainly inflict it in return.

"I'm going to repay that Nephite for what he has done to me." She thought for a while, then laid out a simple plan that would give her some immediate vengeance that night.

Abish nodded. "I will speak to Samuel. This slight against you will not go unpunished."

* * *

"I seem to distinctly recall your father telling you to take advantage of an opportunity like this," Jeremias said as he and Ammon walked away from the throne room. Ammon had been marveling over the sheer size of the palace complex when Jeremias had spoken. The basic design was similar to his father's: multiple plazas and courtyards of varying sizes surrounded by rooms that opened into the courtyard, then long galleries and hallways lined with columns connecting the open spaces. It had the strange effect of feeling familiar and unfamiliar all at the same time.

But Ammon stopped his contemplation to look at his traveling companion, fellow missionary, and cousin. He smiled at Jeremias's steadfastness and loyalty to Ammon's father. The same loyalty extended to him. Even when Ammon had made wrong choices in his life, Jeremias had been constant in his friendship. He had insisted on accompanying Ammon to the land of Ishmael, and despite Ammon telling him repeatedly that he could leave, Jeremias had stayed.

"Opportunity?" Ammon echoed. He knew precisely what Jeremias meant, but he didn't want to discuss it. The night felt full of possibilities, and Ammon was excited to begin this chapter of his life. He didn't want to spend his time discussing what he could have done.

He should have known better.

"Yes, opportunity. Your father specifically instructed you and your brothers to make an alliance through marriage if an offer was made. Now, I may be mistaken, but it seems to me that such an offer has just been extended."

Ammon sighed. "My father isn't here. He doesn't understand the nuances of this situation." He walked over to a stone bench in the courtyard they had wandered into and sat. Jeremias stayed where he was.

"Consider what King Lamoni was trying to do," Ammon continued. "If I had married his daughter, I would have been under his control. A pawn to do his bidding." Ammon stretched his hands up and rested them on his head. He leaned against the smooth limestone wall behind him and went on. "Besides, no one would have taken anything I said seriously. I would have been married to the king's daughter. People would have listened to me out of politeness and then ignored everything I tried to teach them. And that's if the king had even allowed me to preach the gospel."

Jeremias nodded and moved to sit down next to Ammon on the bench. "It sounds as if you've given this a great deal of thought."

Ammon nodded. "I have. The king would have wanted me to denounce my people and my faith in order to join his family. I couldn't do that."

"But you were tempted to accept."

"What?" Ammon said in an incredulous voice. He turned to look at Jeremias. "What makes you say that?"

Jeremias gave Ammon a knowing look. "I saw you tonight when the princess unveiled herself. I've only seen that expression on your face once before."

Ammon began to protest but quickly closed his mouth. His face darkened slightly for a moment, but then he smiled. "Then it is better for me that I didn't accept. I can't go down that path again."

A silence filled with understanding and remembrance passed between the two men. Ammon deliberately refocused his thoughts elsewhere, unwilling to dwell on his past mistakes. He closed his eyes. He had come to the land of the Lamanites to concentrate on his future, and on the future of his Lamanite brethren.

Becoming a servant in the king's household was only the first step. Ammon realized it was not a choice that others might have made, but he knew it had been the right one. Where someone else might see defeat, Ammon saw only great possibilities.

His close friend Alma the Younger had sent Ammon letters regarding his missionary work. He had mentioned repeatedly how willing those poor as to the things of the world were to listen to the gospel message. Alma had had little success with the wealthy.

Ammon had not forgotten Alma's experiences and imagined that his own mission lay not with the king, his family, and courtiers, but with the servants and slaves within the palace. He'd put himself into the best of both worlds—he had the protection of King Lamoni but had unfettered access to the poorest members of the household.

He did not expect that he would meet with immediate success, however. The process would be a slow one. Ammon envisioned it like a mountain spring that started off as a trickle; he would convince one or two individuals of the truth, and then the word would spread and widen to a river that broadened and grew until it emptied into the ocean. He could hardly wait to start.

"Your expression was not the only one I noticed," Jeremias said. "I don't think anyone told the princess how this evening would end."

That made Ammon open his eyes. "I noticed that too. She seemed . . ." Anger was too tame an emotion to describe the fire he had seen in Princess Isabel's eyes. She had clearly wanted to eviscerate him. "A bit upset," he finished.

His cousin quirked an eyebrow at him. "Upset? That's something of an understatement. I half expected her to try and sacrifice you herself."

While Ammon might normally have laughed at Jeremias's quip, he found himself unable to do so. Before her anger, he had seen real pain on the princess's face. He could not make light of her feelings or her suffering.

"I don't think the king told her about the ceremony being a formality," Ammon said.

Jeremias crossed his arms. "That seems cruel."

"I should apologize to her. First thing tomorrow, that's what I'll do."

"I don't know if an apology's necessary. She ought to be thanking the heavens that she managed to escape being married to you." Jeremias laughed.

Ammon nudged his cousin, but it was enough to almost knock Jeremias off the bench. Jeremias's laughter ceased when a tall Lamanite approached them. He looked at Ammon and Jeremias with barely disguised contempt. "My name is Samuel. You are to follow me to your quarters."

"Thank you, Samuel," Ammon said as he and Jeremias stood. The servant did not acknowledge Ammon's thanks, and Ammon tried not to sigh. If he had unintentionally hurt or embarrassed the princess, he realized that there would be many here who would not forgive him for it. Including the princess.

The night air felt extremely cold against Ammon's bare arms. The men here wore cloaks, and Ammon wished he had one. In Zarahemla the air was warm and humid. Here it was cool, refreshing, and clear. No wonder his ancestors had kept trying to return to these lands.

"Do you see the guards trailing us?" Jeremias asked in a low whisper. Ammon had noticed them as soon as Samuel had walked into the courtyard. They were trying to hide in the shadows but were doing a poor job of it.

"I saw them. It's to be expected. I think the king is worried about what I'm going to do."

"Truth be told, I'm a little worried myself," Jeremias responded.

"Don't worry," Ammon said with a grin. "I won't do anything Aaron wouldn't do."

"That worries me even more."

The last syllable Jeremias uttered faded off as they reached a hut that looked as if someone had taken a large stick to it. Ammon took in the disarray of the walls, the roof that threatened to cave in at any moment, the bedding which had been torn and strewn all over the ground, and the distinct odor of manure.

"The chief servant demands that all of the king's servants keep clean and orderly living quarters," Samuel informed them, not looking either man in the eye. "He conducts inspections each morning at sunrise."

The Lamanite servant departed, but their guards stayed behind.

"That smell! Is that . . ." Jeremias asked in a horrified voice.

Ammon finally let out a great roar of laughter, unable to contain his mirth. "Do you think this was the princess's idea?" he asked when he could breathe again. It reminded him of something he and his twin brother, Aaron, might have done when they were younger. He didn't see a reason to be upset. Nothing of value had been ruined, because Ammon kept his copy of the scriptures with him. She was certainly inventive. He had to give her that.

"What are you doing?" Jeremias asked when Ammon walked away from the hut they were to share.

Ammon's eyes danced as he looked back as his cousin. "I have a plan of my own."

2

Abish came in to wake Isabel, but the princess had been up since before sunrise. She had not been able to sleep much the night before, consumed as she was by thoughts of the Nephite and her public humiliation. But her maid's arrival meant that Isabel could stop speculating. Abish would have news for her.

"How did our spy sleep?" Isabel asked. "Not well, I hope."

Abish didn't meet Isabel's gaze as she shook out Isabel's thick rabbit-fur blanket and laid it straight.

Something had happened. Something Abish didn't want to tell her.

While her maidservant smoothed out invisible wrinkles on the blanket, Isabel put her hand on top of Abish's to stop her. "What is it?"

Letting out a great sigh, Abish straightened and said, "He did not get in trouble."

"Why not?"

"Because not only did he repair the damage to his own hut, but he spent the night cleaning and fixing the huts of all the servants. While they cleaned up after the feast, Ammon did their nightly chores for them so that they were able to sleep."

This infuriated Isabel. Why was Ammon trying to make friends with the servants? What endgame did he have in mind? She seized on the only logical explanation. Ammon must be trying to turn the servants against her father. Her father had to be warned.

"Does my father know?"

Confusion flitted across Abish's face. "Your father? What does the king have to do with any of this?"

The king had everything to do with Ammon's treachery. Isabel left the room but kept herself from running to her father's throne. She had to show some decorum as she walked through the hallways and courtyards. Abish followed close behind her.

Isabel went as fast as propriety would allow, hurrying to kneel at the bottom of the dais where her father and his wife sat on plush cushions. She ignored the courtiers, sure they would learn of her message soon enough. It was impossible to keep secrets in the palace.

"Isabel!" her father said in a welcoming tone tinged with a hint of surprise. "What brings you here this morning?"

While last night's feast had been a time for formality in clothing and behavior, and Isabel would never have approached her father this way in a more ritualistic setting, the morning permitted this sort of familial approach.

"That Nephite. That spy," Isabel said from where she knelt on the floor. "Last night he cleaned all of the servants' quarters."

"A servant, cleaning?" the king asked, one corner of his mouth rising up in amusement. "Whatever will he do next?"

Isabel balled her fists up in her lap. "I think this is an obvious ploy on the Nephite's part to turn your servants against you."

"I wish I could share in your concerns, my daughter. But I don't find the young man to be a threat to us. Perhaps he was just trying to be kind."

Kind? Isabel knew her father to be more perceptive than this. Why was everyone being taken in by this enemy? It seemed so obvious to Isabel that the Nephite intended to harm them. She wondered why no one else seemed concerned. It was as if they had all been bewitched.

"Fine," Isabel said, trying to keep the anger from her voice. After all, it wasn't her father she was angry with. "But someone must watch over the Nephite traitor."

Her father exchanged a look with his wife, Kamilah, before he turned back to Isabel. "You should do what you feel must be done."

Isabel heard the patronizing dismissal in his voice. He never took her concerns seriously. Isabel sighed. She was only a woman after all. Her opinion would hardly matter to the king. Even if she was his daughter.

Isabel would simply have to catch Ammon on her own. If her father wouldn't protect himself, then it would be up to her to do it. Isabel imagined how sweet her vindication would be.

Isabel stopped envisioning her future success long enough to see Kamilah nudge Lamoni with her elbow before continuing on with her embroidery. "Oh yes," her father said, then cleared his throat. "Isabel, you seemed upset last night."

"Upset? Why would I be upset, Father?" Isabel aimed for an even tone. She hoped she had achieved it. "I know that I have obligations and duties to fulfill and that I will marry at any time that you deem appropriate."

Her father looked uncomfortable. His expression seemed odd to Isabel—she couldn't remember ever seeing it before.

"Last night was meant to be a formal ceremony of the covenants that Ammon and I had already exchanged. You were to be told beforehand."

That should have made Isabel feel better, but it didn't. Apparently, one of her father's lackeys had failed to inform her. It was not an announcement that her father could have bothered to tell her in person. A thick lump formed in Isabel's throat. She would not cry. She would *not.*

"I was not told." Despite her best efforts, Isabel couldn't keep her voice from wavering slightly.

She turned her gaze to the south wall, unable to look at her father any longer. Isabel heard her father getting up. She looked back to see his hands outstretched toward her. "Isabel, my daughter, I would not want you to feel as if—"

"I must go," Isabel whispered. She jumped to her feet. She would not be able to retain her composure for even a moment longer.

As Isabel fled, she reached out her hand behind her and Abish took it, as Isabel knew she would. Abish squeezed it softly in support.

Distracted, Isabel slammed into what felt like a solid wall. A man's hands grasped her shoulders to steady her so she wouldn't fall. Before she could even open her mouth to say she was sorry, Isabel realized who she had just had the great misfortune of running into.

The Nephite.

He smiled at her in that infuriating way of his. "In a hurry?"

Isabel wanted to strike him. But she didn't. She put her shoulders back, lifted her chin, and walked away from him. She didn't need to respond to him or his condescending smirks. He could act smug and arrogant now; Isabel would discover the truth of his intentions, and then she would be the one laughing.

* * *

Over his shoulder, Ammon said to Jeremias, "If you're keeping a tally, that's twice now I've managed to chase the princess out of a room."

Ammon knew why he made the jest—to ease his own conscience. Again he had looked at the princess's face and seen real pain there. Something or someone had hurt her very deeply, and Ammon worried that he had been the cause of it. As soon as he stood in front of the king, he found himself asking, "Is the princess . . . ?"

Ammon let his words trail off deliberately, suddenly realizing how inappropriate the question was. He didn't have any right to ask after her. Particularly not to her father, the king.

Fortunately, King Lamoni didn't seem to take offense and offered, "She will be fine."

Grateful for the reprieve, Ammon changed the subject. "You sent for me?"

"Yes, I heard that you have been very busy."

A smile hovered on Ammon's lips. "News travels quickly, I see."

The king inclined his head to one side as if agreeing with Ammon. "I also wanted to see whether or not you had changed your mind about your decision."

A picture of Isabel flashed in Ammon's mind and he hesitated. When he realized why he had paused, it only made him more resolved. "No, King Lamoni. I am as committed as ever."

"Very well. The day after tomorrow we will have a tournament of arms here at the palace. Many guests and family members will be traveling here. There is much to be done to prepare for it."

"I am here to serve."

The king nodded. "I have full confidence that you will be of great use to me."

Something in his tone struck Ammon as odd, but he ignored it. He hardly knew the king and was in no position to make any judgments about whether or not his words had a hidden message. King Lamoni trusted him; the least Ammon could do was return the favor.

A courtier interrupted them, begging the king's forgiveness and saying he had a list the king needed to look over. King Lamoni dismissed Ammon.

"What now?" Jeremias asked.

"I should go find Isabel," Ammon replied.

Ammon felt a tug at the bottom of his tunic. "What do you want with my sister?"

A small girl, probably four or five years old at most, looked up at him with a superior, haughty expression that made Ammon hold in his laughter. Yes, this certainly had to be Isabel's sister.

Ammon crouched down so that he was at eye level with the girl. "What is your name?"

"I'm Princess Naima. And you didn't answer my question."

"I think I hurt your sister's feelings last night. I wanted to apologize to her. Do you know where I might find her?"

The little princess held a cornhusk doll in her arms and hugged her toy tighter as she regarded Ammon. "She ran away."

A maid came up behind Naima and hurried her away before Ammon could question her further. Ammon straightened up. Ran away? Had he really had that much of an effect on Isabel that she would leave her family?

"Do you think she really ran away?" Jeremias asked behind him as they left the throne room.

"I'm not sure," Ammon said. "Maybe the little princess was mistaken."

Jeremias clapped a hand on Ammon's shoulder. "I'm going to see what chores the chief servant has in mind for us today. Meet me after you've apologized."

Sometimes it was eerie how well his cousin knew him. Jeremias had correctly guessed that Ammon wouldn't be able to concentrate on other tasks until he had made things right, as well as the fact that Ammon would prefer to make such an apology in private.

The king's palace was situated on higher ground than the rest of the land of Ishmael, and from the courtyard Ammon now stood in, he could see Isabel running away from the palace. She ran so fast that small puffs of dirt raised up behind her.

How had she gotten out of the palace so quickly? It had only been a few minutes since she left the throne room. And why was she running that hard?

Ammon's protective instincts kicked in. She had to be in danger. He ran out of the palace and took up the path behind her. "Princess! Princess Isabel!"

He kept calling her name, but she didn't respond. Ammon looked to his right and left to discover who pursued her. He didn't see anyone else. "Isabel!"

He had to get her to stop. He couldn't protect her if she kept running. She needed to hold still, and then he would fight off whoever was trying to hurt her. Ammon applied a burst of speed to close the gap between them. Pushing off from the ground, he grabbed her around the waist and pulled her down. They tumbled and rolled several times before they came to a stop.

"What is it?" Ammon asked as he held her down. "Who's chasing you?"

With a disgusted look, the princess pushed Ammon away. "An insane Nephite."

"Why were you running?"

"I like to run," Isabel said. She stood and wiped the dust off of her tunic.

Here in the sunlight, this Princess Isabel looked completely different than the creature he had seen last night. That princess had had her hair pulled back into something Ammon thought women probably considered stylish. Someone had painted her face with different designs and colors to indicate her stature. She had worn a costly tunic and so much heavy jewelry that Ammon had been amazed at her ability to stay upright.

But today . . . today the princess looked reachable. Like a normal person. Her face had been scrubbed clean, and there was a simple beauty he hadn't seen last night. What Ammon noticed most was her hair. She had woven it into a single braid, one that reached to the small of her back. Several strands had escaped the braid, and while last night Ammon had thought her hair to be a dark brown, today he realized that "dark brown" was a wholly inadequate description. Her hair was laced with strands of gold and red that shimmered and gleamed in the sunlight. Ammon had always harbored a pathetic weakness for women with beautiful hair. He wondered if it felt as soft as it looked. He stood and took a step toward her.

She moved back. "What are you staring at?"

"Nothing—I just . . ." Ammon tried not to stammer like a child being scolded by his mother. Perhaps an explanation would be best. "I saw you running, and I thought someone was after you. I was trying to help."

With a look that Ammon had seen just a few minutes earlier on Princess Naima's face, Isabel said, "I have nothing to fear in my father's lands. There is only one person here who would dare hurt me."

"Oh, you mean me?" Ammon asked with a grin.

Princess Isabel shook her head and looked like she wanted to stamp her foot. She settled for putting her fists on her hips. It made Ammon's smile wider. She reminded him of a dormant volcano—its outside appearance belying its internal activity. She seemed calm and in control, but even Ammon could tell that everything was boiling and simmering inside, threatening to explode. He had to stop vexing her. This was complete foolishness on his part.

"How dare someone like you speak to someone like me that way," she demanded.

So the princess thought him beneath her. "But I'm—"

"I know who you *were*," she cut him off. "But that's not who you are now. You're just a servant."

For some reason the idea that Isabel had bothered to find out more about him pleased him immensely. "You know that I'm a prince? Been checking up on me, have you?"

Unfortunately this only served to irritate her further. Ammon half expected to see puffs of smoke coming from her ears. "I'm the only one who sees you for who you are."

"I promise to prove to everyone who I really am, Princess."

Her eyes narrowed at him. Ammon knew he had to defuse this situation and try to calm her down. An apology wouldn't go over well if she stayed this angry.

"When I saw your father and mother this morning—"

"She's not my mother." The princess bit off the words as if they caused a sour taste in her mouth.

"You run very fast." Ammon immediately saw the need to change tactics. Perhaps a compliment would work better.

With a barely perceptible lift of her chin, the princess said, "I am the fastest runner in the land. I have never been bested in a race. My father made me stop racing his men, because no one could win against me."

"I think I just did." The words left Ammon's lips before he could catch them.

But to his surprise, Isabel didn't erupt in anger the way he expected her to. She took a couple of deep breaths and said in a low voice, "I wasn't really trying to beat you. If I had been trying, you would never have been able to catch me."

Ammon pressed his lips together to stop his laughter. She had looked like she was trying pretty hard to get away from him. But it wouldn't serve his cause to tell her that. Although a morbidly curious part of him wondered whether or not he could push her into a full tantrum by pointing it out.

"Don't you have something to clean?" Princess Isabel had folded her arms across her chest and seemed to be smirking at him.

"Ah, yes. You are the one responsible for the work I've had to do so far, aren't you?"

"What makes you think I'm responsible for it?"

"Very clever. It sounds as if you're denying it, but you aren't. That's not what I expected from you." She kept surprising him. The princess never seemed to say what Ammon thought she would. Besides, he had to admire anyone with such a devious mind. Aaron would adore her.

"I don't lie, nor do I owe you an explanation."

"You're right. I'm the one who owes you an explanation." That seemed to confuse her. "I came here to apologize to you for last night."

"Apologize? To me? Do you think the words of a servant have any value to me at all?"

That time Ammon couldn't help his laughter, although he did cut it off quickly. "The circumstances of our births do not make us better than anyone else."

"Actually, that's exactly what they do."

"Even a prince can become a servant." Ammon mimicked the princess's stance and folded his own arms. "And you are not the snob you pretend to be. I have seen you with your maidservant, both last night and this morning. You treat her like a friend. You love her."

"You don't know anything about me!" the princess retorted, her face flushed.

"Not yet," Ammon said with a half smile. "And as much as I would enjoy continuing this enlightening conversation with you, I do have a great deal of work waiting for me at the palace—until our next race where I beat you."

Ammon gave a half bow and then walked away, whistling a merry tune. He heard her yell to him in frustration, "I wasn't making a true effort!"

He turned around and stopped. "I think we both know that I could catch you any time I wanted to. All I'd have to do is try."

It was the closest he had come that morning to seeing Isabel lose control. With an infuriated cry she looked around for a rock to throw at him. She even picked one up, but at the last moment she restrained herself, which intrigued him even further.

But now he really needed to extricate himself from this situation. He knew he was getting too close to the fire. And Ammon knew all too well from experience what would happen if he insisted on embracing the dangerous heat. The flames would consume him. *Never again.*

Of course, he knew why he did it. With Isabel's stern disposition, she was practically begging to be teased. Not that it made his actions right.

He found Jeremias in the stables, where the king's animals were kept. Jeremias was piling up loads of manure and mumbling to himself. "Don't know why I have to be a servant. I didn't agree to it. I would marry the princess if someone asked me to." Jeremias stopped his complaining when he heard Ammon approaching. "How did it go?"

"She wanted to throw something at me."

"Did she do it?"

"No." Ammon didn't feel the need to explain to Jeremias that he found her behavior fascinating. The princess was unlike anyone he had ever met. Shaking his head as if to clear it from further thoughts of her, Ammon continued on. "I went to apologize and ended up provoking her instead."

"Why?"

"I don't know." But he did know that he had to stop. Ammon told himself that he had to stay away from the princess. She was a distraction he didn't need. He had a mission to fulfill.

3

THE NEPHITE HAD REDUCED HER to acting like a child.

No one had ever managed to push her to the very limits of her control that way. It irritated her. And, if Isabel was being honest with herself, it even scared her a little. She had thought herself stronger. She never let anyone past the walls she had constructed around herself. How had this spy managed it?

He had only added to her annoyance by disrupting her morning run. It was the part of her day Isabel looked forward to the most. There wasn't anything she loved more than running. She couldn't think of anything more exhilarating than running down the slope of a mountain so fast that it felt like her feet left the ground. Isabel closed her eyes letting her imagination go. It was almost like flying.

She wouldn't let anything get in the way of her favorite ritual. Not even a deranged Nephite.

After she returned to the palace and got dressed, Isabel faked a cough and managed to escape Kamilah's daily embroidery circle. Embroidery was the queen's passion, so Kamilah required the women of the household to join her every morning so that they could all embroider together. Isabel had spent the last ten years devising various methods to avoid the activity, but, unfortunately, she still went more often than she missed.

But having freed herself from any obligations today, Isabel spent the day following Ammon around. Ammon did nothing but work. It made Isabel tired just watching him. She decided that the next time she found her own life tedious, she would remember how much worse things could be. But Ammon never seemed weary. He smiled, laughed, and whistled as he went from one task to the next. He started several conversations with the other servants, but Isabel noted with satisfaction that no one responded to his overtures. The Nephite's plan wouldn't work—he wouldn't be able to turn the household against her father.

Late in the afternoon Ammon was sent to fetch water for the cook, and since he hadn't seemed to do anything especially treacherous yet, Isabel decided to take a break and fill her rumbling stomach. She had her evening meal in her room, as she always did. Isabel preferred to dine this way. The formal meals in the throne room took far too long and had too much pomp and ceremony. Tonight Isabel wanted to eat and be done with it so she could get back to watching over the spy.

Isabel hurried back to the kitchens and discovered that Ammon had already delivered the water. She panicked at the idea that she had lost track of him. He could be executing his plot right now. She had to find him.

It didn't take her long. Isabel found Ammon on the east side of a gallery surrounding a larger courtyard in the guest quarters. He was scrubbing the tall columns that encircled the courtyard with a rag and limewater. And he was still smiling. Always smiling. No one could possibly be that happy all the time. Clearly, he was insane.

Isabel had only a moment to wonder why someone would give Ammon a job that was usually delegated to female servants. Turning, Ammon said, "Princess Isabel, I didn't expect to see you out in the open like this. Don't you prefer skulking around in the shadows to spy on me?"

So he knew. Isabel tried not to flush from embarrassment at her inability to stay hidden. "You have a very active imagination," she informed him.

"Again, a denial that's not really a denial." Ammon grinned. "At least you're consistent. So it must have been someone else that just happens to look exactly like you?"

He was doing it again. Why did everything he said sound as if meant to tease her? And why did it vex her so much? And why couldn't she ever gain the upper ground against him? There had to be something that would get to him, something that would wipe that perpetual smile off of his face. Isabel just had to discover what it was.

"How are you enjoying doing women's work?"

Ammon shrugged. "The work has to be done. I'm happy to do it."

Isabel couldn't understand his behavior at all. He was a prince. It should bother him to be doing such menial, mindless tasks. But before she could reply, Ammon spoke again.

"Now, I might have resented it when I was younger. But I learned from my father to work. My father didn't believe in accumulating wealth. He rules the entire Nephite nation, but there are noble families who have bigger homes and more wealth than he does. And my father," Ammon said with a chuckle, "insists on earning everything on his own. He wouldn't tax the people for his own profit."

Isabel didn't know what to say. She had never heard of such a thing. Every king Isabel knew lived off of the tribute and taxes from his own people, or from smaller tributary kingdoms. It was truly beyond her comprehension.

Ammon dipped his rag back into his bowl, wrung out the water, and went back to cleaning the column. "I was ten years old when I came across my mother, queen of all the Nephites, scrubbing the floors. I was humiliated. I told her to get up, that we had servants for that." Ammon stopped his movements, and he looked toward the horizon as he remembered. "My mother got so angry with me. She said, 'What kind of queen would I be if I didn't take care of my own palace?' Then she made me wash the floor with her. I swore I'd never do it again."

"What changed your mind?"

Ammon gave her a quick, mischievous grin. "That's a story for another day."

Why did the Nephite always act like he had a happy secret or knew a funny joke? It was so annoying. Isabel frowned.

"You are very serious, Isabel."

"And you are very *un*serious," she retorted.

That made Ammon stop. His smile faded. "I am serious about the things that matter."

"And washing columns—is that one of those things that matters?"

Ammon resumed his scrubbing, his smile returning. "Do you know how to do it?"

"What a ridiculous question," Isabel said. "Anyone could wash columns."

Ammon offered Isabel the rag. "Prove it."

She snatched the rag out of his hand. She put the rag into the limewater as he had done and slopped it against the column. Small rivers of water ran down the sides.

"No, you have to wring it out first."

"I know," Isabel snapped. She squeezed the excess water out and went back to the column, rubbing the rag against it the way she had seen Ammon do.

"You don't have to be so rough," Ammon admonished her. "What did that poor column ever do to you?"

That made Isabel scrub harder. If he could do it, so could she.

"You've made a valiant effort, but it is obvious that you won't be able to do it as well as I can. Better give that back to me."

Isabel couldn't stop herself from growling, baring her teeth like an animal. And Ammon apparently couldn't stop himself from laughing at her. Isabel grew tired of being a constant source of amusement for the Nephite. She could clean better than Ammon could. She was not a helpless, sheltered creature. She would show him.

* * *

Ammon was enjoying the sight of the princess trying to clean. He knew he should have some pity on her and take the rag back. She so obviously had no idea what she was doing. But she seemed determined. He liked that about her.

Before he had a chance to once again scold himself for thinking of the princess in anything other than friendly terms, a servant approached and said that the king had asked for him. Ammon told Isabel he would return in just a moment, but she ignored him.

Ammon followed the servant back to the throne room where he found the king, the queen, and two boys and two girls, one of them Princess Naima. He assumed the children were Isabel's brothers and sisters. They were having their evening meal.

Why wasn't the princess here with her family? "Did you want me to go and fetch Isabel?" Perhaps on the way back Ammon could convince the princess not to tell her father that he had tricked her into cleaning. He didn't know how King Lamoni would take that.

The king looked uncomfortable. "Isabel rarely joins us for meals."

"Why is that?" Ammon knew he shouldn't have asked. He reminded himself of his new position, that such impertinence would not be tolerated. Ammon cursed the insatiable curiosity, which had done nothing but get him into trouble his entire life.

King Lamoni stopped eating to glare at Ammon. Ammon put his hand over his heart; he liked having it in his chest and hoped Lamoni didn't have other plans for it.

"My daughter has never gotten over the death of her mother and prefers to keep her own company." And then, before Ammon could ask another inappropriate question, the king continued. "Her mother died while giving birth. Neither she nor the baby survived. It was very hard on Isabel. She was just ten years old."

Ammon had never lost anyone close to him, but he felt an immediate sympathy for Isabel's loss. It had the unfortunate effect of making him want to seek her out to offer comfort. Comfort, he reminded himself, that she had not asked for and would not want.

He remembered something Isabel had said to him earlier that day. She had bristled when he had referred to the queen as her mother. Ammon looked at the children in front of him. If he had to wager a guess, the oldest boy was probably eight or nine years old. That would mean her father had remarried immediately. Ammon wondered if this was the cause of some of Isabel's unhappiness. Because he didn't think he had ever met anyone as unhappy as the princess.

"But this is not why I sent for you," the king said as several servants began to clear away the platters of food laid out for the family—so many platters that most were untouched. Such waste. It was not something his own father would ever have permitted, but Ammon kept quiet and instead moved to help the other servants. But the king asked him to stop. "I brought you here to tell me a tale."

"A tale?" Ammon echoed. He knew that he intrigued the king, and that was the reason he had been permitted to become a servant in the first place. But something felt amiss. Ammon couldn't quite put his finger on it.

"Yes, tell me more of the Nephites."

Tell him nothing.

King Lamoni seemed simply curious, but now Ammon understood it went deeper than that. He recognized the warning he received and resolved to be very careful in everything that he shared with the king.

"What would you like to know?"

The king settled back onto his jaguar-skin cushions. "Why don't you choose something to entertain us? Whatever you wish to share."

Ammon sorted among his memories until he found one the young princes and princesses might enjoy. "Well, there was the time when my brother Aaron and I first learned of the plagues of Egypt in the land of our forefathers."

* * *

Isabel couldn't decide if Ammon was very smart or very stupid. Her natural inclination was to believe that he was an idiot, but she didn't want to rush to any conclusions. He didn't seem unintelligent.

But he couldn't be too bright—traveling with only a single companion into the heart of enemy territory. Isabel stopped her scrubbing. What if he hadn't come alone? What if there were others?

Isabel didn't like the idea that things might be worse than she had initially imagined. Particularly since the only way to gather any information would be to get it from the Nephite. It meant she would have to stop sneaking around, waiting for him to implement his plan. She would actually have to talk to him—without making him suspicious. If he had people lying in wait to attack her father's kingdom, Isabel alone would have to figure out a way to stop it from happening. She didn't want to interact with the Nephite at all. She just wanted to prove that he was a spy and have him imprisoned for life. Having to make conversation with him, to pretend she was interested in anything he had to say . . . Isabel returned to her cleaning with a vengeance, pouring all her frustration out in long strokes.

Someone approached, making Isabel panic. She wasn't ready to face Ammon yet. She needed time to prepare before she saw him again. Isabel's shoulders slumped with relief when she saw it was only Abish.

"What do you think you're doing?" Abish asked.

"He said I couldn't clean the columns as well as he could." Isabel wiped sweat from her brow. She didn't know how long she had been out here or how many columns she had cleaned. She felt an odd sense of satisfaction in what she had accomplished. In this one area at least, she had triumphed. She'd proved that she could do it, and no Nephite would tell her differently.

Her contentment was short-lived.

"I suppose you showed him—doing his chores for him."

Realizing that the Nephite had tricked her, that he had made a fool out of her, Isabel threw the rag to the ground and kicked over the bucket of limewater. She wished she could dump the contents on his head.

Ammon was craftier, more manipulative and treacherous than Isabel could have imagined. He had just shown her how easily he could dupe her. It would take real effort to outwit him.

"This ends here," Isabel told her maidservant. "I will not let myself be taken in by him again."

This time she meant it.

* * *

Isabel pricked her index finger with the bone needle, causing it to bleed all over the cloth she had been working on. She stuck her finger in her mouth and tried not to look as sullen as she felt.

All around her women chatted and gossiped as they embroidered the queen's pattern onto a cloak for the king. Isabel had to suffer the humiliation of working on a different project with Naima. She didn't need to be told that the other women thought Isabel would ruin the cloak—with or without her bleeding finger.

She also knew that if she had been absent from the circle, she very likely would have been the main topic of conversation. The gossip in her father's court had been unending and almost more than she could stand.

Someone laughed, and Isabel looked up to see little Sarala running around the room stuffing bits of cloth into her mouth. One of the queen's maidservants followed Sarala around and forced her to spit them back out.

Kamilah fondly watched the antics of her youngest child. "Do you remember when Naima used to do the same thing?"

Isabel realized that the queen's question had been directed at her. She shrugged and looked down at her cloth. She tried to wipe away the blood but only smeared it further into the fabric. Isabel decided it gave the work character, and since it would undoubtedly be joined by many other bloodstains in the future, she embroidered around it.

"Last night I told Ammon about the time we found Naima cramming her mouth full of jewels."

Naima put down her piece of cloth and in an indignant tone informed her mother, "I still don't believe it."

"I'm quite serious. The servants had to follow you around for days afterwards to make certain that you expelled everything of value."

"When did you speak to Ammon?" Isabel demanded.

An expression Isabel couldn't interpret flitted across Kamilah's face. "Last night. Your father asked Ammon to tell us about the Nephites."

That gave Isabel some comfort. Finally someone had their senses back. Her father must have intended to gather intelligence about the Nephites. Perhaps Isabel wasn't alone in her quest to uncover Ammon's motives.

But Kamilah's next words wiped away Isabel's hopes. "We in turn told him many things about our family." Kamilah pulled the needle through the cloak until the thread went taut. "He is quite the entertainer. There is something disarming about that young man."

Whatever plan Ammon had, it seemed to be working. Isabel had seen firsthand how Ammon's "easygoing nature" could encourage the sharing of confidences. The Nephite pretended to be charming and caring. He seemed so open himself—creating a false trust with his victims.

"He has a very pleasant voice, don't you think?" the queen added.

"I hadn't noticed," Isabel responded. What made Kamilah so interested in discussing Ammon? It made her uneasy that they spoke of Ammon at all. She didn't want to invite speculative looks or sympathetic remarks from the other women.

"Last night he regaled us with tales of his childhood escapades with his brother. He told us how he learned of an account of plagues in the lands of our ancestors—"

"You mean from the records that his forefathers robbed from ours?"

"Er, I suppose," Kamilah said with an embarrassed little laugh.

"Then what happened?" one of the maidservants asked, giving Isabel a disapproving look.

"He and his twin brother decided to reenact one of the plagues. I don't remember all the details, but it ended up with a throne room full of frogs." Kamilah laughed again. "I suppose you had to be there. He's amusing and handsome as well."

Several of the queen's handmaidens nodded in agreement, adding their own observations about Ammon.

"He's so tall."

"He has a very charming smile."

"Broad shoulders."

"And such unusual eyes."

As Isabel listened to the discussion of Ammon's attributes, a sudden awareness struck her, and she felt as if the room had somehow become too small. Isabel felt all the air leaving her body as the room closed in on her. He was handsome. Very handsome. On some level she had registered the fact that he was fair looking. She had never thought him ugly. But this was different. Isabel found him attractive. Despite everything she knew of him, everything she suspected him of, Isabel thought him handsome. She was a bit disappointed in herself for entertaining such a trivial matter. She thought herself capable of more depth than that.

Then Isabel heard someone ask, "I wonder if he has a wife and children back in Zarahemla."

Did he? For some reason it didn't seem like something Ammon would do—put his life at risk while leaving his family to fend for themselves. But still Isabel found herself picturing a Nephite wife and several small boys with the same gray-blue eyes. Something caught in her throat, and Isabel couldn't breathe. It felt like someone had hit her in the stomach with a large stick. This was an emotion Isabel knew all too well. She was *jealous.*

"Excuse me," Isabel said as she stumbled from the room. The Nephite had infected her with his insanity. She had to be crazy to even be entertaining such thoughts.

She had to find Ammon. She had to stand next to him, talk to him, and assure herself that she hadn't lost her grasp on reality.

4

AMMON SWUNG THE FLINT AX down. The ax cut the wood chunk with a resounding crack, and the resulting pieces fell to the ground. He selected another large piece and placed it on the stump. With all the frustration he felt, he slammed the ax down again. He had a steady rhythm going and mindlessly picked up his next wooden victim.

He had made no progress with the Lamanites. He hadn't expected immediate success, but he had hoped that people would at least respond to his overtures of friendship. But the only people who spoke to him were members of the royal family and Jeremias. He had prayed, fasted, and asked for direction. He knew he had to give it time, but Ammon had never had any difficulty making friends. People generally liked him.

His frustration increased because of the real love he felt for these people. He knew it might sound strange to someone else, but Ammon had loved the Lamanites before he'd even come to their lands. Being here, his love for them had only increased. He wanted to share all he knew with them. He wanted to celebrate the instant kinship he had felt. He wanted someone to listen to him. Instead, his intentions had been ignored and he had faced nothing but constant rejection.

Perhaps it was just a matter of being prepared. He would have to look for opportunities and recognize them for what they were. He would have to be ready to share what he knew to be true. Until then, he would just have to be patient.

"Are you married?"

The princess's voice so surprised Ammon that he stopped midswing. "What?"

"Are you married?" Isabel repeated. She had her hands clasped tightly in front of her. Her entire body seemed rigid. She looked as if something was bothering her. Ammon could only assume that he was in some way responsible.

"No, I'm not married." Isabel visibly relaxed and came closer. Ammon almost backed up as a sweet fragrance reached him. At first he couldn't place it, but he realized it smelled a bit like scarlet blossom. It made his heart thump. He had to force himself to look away from her and went back to chopping wood. To Ammon's great relief, the princess had her hair up and hidden away. A man could not be expected to withstand quite that much temptation in one day.

"Where is your brother Aaron?"

Isabel stood next to him. Ammon held still and tried not to breathe her scent in. "You suddenly seem very interested in me. I thought you hated me."

The princess moved so that she could face Ammon. She gave him a coy half smile. It made Ammon's nerve endings come to attention. Was she flirting with him? "How could I not be interested in you? A stranger from a foreign land? In a way, I suppose you're exotic. Shouldn't I be interested in what you can share?"

So now she meant to elicit information from him for her father. Had King Lamoni sent her to do so? Ammon fought the urge to feed her false information just to watch her reaction. He had to remember his purpose for being here. Interesting, sweetly-scented princesses were not part of it.

"I have no time for your games, Princess. I have too much work to do."

But instead of responding to the dismissive tone in his voice, Isabel stayed put. "Why are you chopping the wood out here in the fields?"

"Because in addition to chopping wood, I've also been assigned to watch the crop."

Ammon followed Isabel's gaze toward the fields of maize that were nearly ready to be harvested. The long stalks swayed in the slight breeze, their spearlike leaves flapping and rustling so that it sounded like the fields whispered to him.

"Where are the dogs? They're the best at chasing the birds away."

"They weren't needed. Jeremias relocated them for me." Ammon took another big swing, splintering the wood.

"Why?"

Ammon's hand drifted up to rub at the scar that ran from his right temple to his hairline. "I didn't need the help."

"You're not afraid of dogs, are you?" Isabel looked far too delighted at the notion.

"I wouldn't say that I'm afraid. More that I don't care for them. When I was three, one of my father's hunting dogs attacked my brother Aaron and me. No one knew why he did it or why he chose to go after us. The healers weren't sure that either one of us would survive, but we did and still have the scars to show for it. My first memory is of a large dog chewing on my face. So as you can imagine, I don't care for dogs."

The smile on Isabel's face faded, much to Ammon's relief. He had been envisioning Isabel loosing a pack of dogs on him.

The conversation had become far too serious and personal for Ammon's liking. He had inadvertently revealed one of his biggest weaknesses to a woman who despised him. He needed to change the subject before he revealed any other secrets. Distractions usually worked best. He held the axe out to Isabel. "Want to try it? It's very good for when things are bothering you. You can work out that pent-up anger and aggression."

"For some reason this seems familiar." Isabel tapped her finger against her mouth. She had very soft-looking, very pink lips, Ammon noticed. For a moment he began to wonder what it would be like to kiss her, but he was yanked out of his thoughts by Isabel's voice. "Oh, yes. That would be because you already tricked me into doing your work last night. That won't happen again."

"No tricks," Ammon said weakly. He had to stop thinking of Isabel this way. It was wrong and distracting. Wrong. Distracting. Had to stop. What had they been talking about? Chopping wood. Convincing Isabel to try it. Right. "There's nothing wrong with a little hard work, Princess. And there's nothing wrong with trying new things. You're not scared, are you?"

Isabel wavered for a moment before taking the axe. "I'm not scared. What do I have to do?"

Ammon picked out a much smaller piece of wood than he had been cutting. He placed it on the stump and made sure it was seated flat so that it wouldn't move around on her. "First you want to take the axe and hold it directly above the middle of your head with both hands."

Isabel moved to the spot where Ammon had been standing. She raised the axe over her head. "Then what?"

"You want to bring the axe down straight and strong in one smooth motion. Make sure to hit the wood right in the middle. That should split it."

"The axe isn't going to break in my hands, is it?"

"No, the axe is very sturdy. I'd actually be impressed if you managed to break it."

"Since I live only to impress you . . . here it goes."

Ammon quickly saw that Isabel hadn't used enough force, and instead of splitting the chunk, her axe got stuck in the wood. She tugged at it several times.

Concealing a smile, Ammon offered, "Let me help you."

She swiped at him with one arm. "I can do it." The princess kept trying to pry the axe free by yanking on it. Finally she put her foot on the stump to brace it against the piece of wood. She took in a deep breath and pulled.

The small log came with the ax. Isabel stood there with the wood and the axe hovering over her head for a second before they tipped backward, pulling her with them.

How could he resist? Laughter poured out of Ammon in great bursts. He could hardly catch his breath. Isabel lay on the ground, glaring at him. Ammon bent over at the waist, resting his hands on his knees, trying to stop laughing before Isabel took the axe to him.

"Are you all right?" he finally managed.

"I'm glad you're amused," Isabel snapped. She ignored his outstretched hand and got up on her own, wiping the dirt and grass from her tunic. She leaned down again trying to get the axe loose. She was certainly persistent.

"I'm sorry, Princess, but you make me laugh."

"Everything makes you laugh."

He couldn't argue with that. "Life is to be enjoyed."

"Aren't you ever unhappy?"

Ammon went over and easily pried the axe out of the wood, placing both the axe and wood back on the stump. "Sometimes. But the Lord has comforted me and told me that if I would bear my afflictions with patience, He would give me success."

"Lord?" Isabel echoed, looking confused. "Do you mean your father?"

It was the first time Ammon had had a chance to explain his beliefs with anyone in Ishmael, but he realized that Isabel was in no mood to listen to really anything he might have to say. So with an amused grin he replied, "In a roundabout way, yes. And just so you don't think otherwise, I am very aware of my own shortcomings. I simply choose not to dwell on them."

Ammon heard the call of a black-winged bird as it began its descent toward the maize. He removed his sling from his belt, picked up a rock, and fit it into the pouch of his sling. Holding tightly to the long strings, Ammon swung the sling backward in a circular motion, and as the sling came around to the front, he released one of the lines and whipped the rock forward.

The rock zoomed out and nicked one of the bird's wings. The bird screeched in protest but flew away.

"You missed."

"I never miss. I didn't want to hurt him. He only needed a warning." The sling dangled between Ammon's fingers.

"Who taught you to use a sling?"

"My father. He always said you never knew when it would be useful. I never thought I'd be using it to scare birds."

"Your father trained you and your people for battle?"

So that's where this was going. The princess persisted in trying to bait him into a trap. What did she want him to reveal? The Nephites had no plans to go to battle against the Lamanites. He had no great military secrets for her to uncover. He wished he could tell Isabel as much and have her believe him. But he knew there was little chance of that.

"Of course he did. I'll let you in on a secret." Ammon gestured for her to come closer. With an eager expression, Isabel stepped forward. He leaned in so that she had to lean in too. "All fathers train their sons with weapons," he whispered. "Even fathers who aren't kings."

Isabel straightened with a look of disgust. It had been a mistake to beckon her over. Ammon felt assaulted by that scarlet-blossom scent. He needed her to go. "As I mentioned earlier, I do need to work. As always, it has been a pleasure, Princess."

But she didn't leave. Whatever information she hoped to learn, she seemed determined to have it. Ammon couldn't go anywhere else. His duties were here.

Perhaps if he focused on something else, he could avoid thinking about her. If she insisted on staying, he'd never be able to keep chopping wood with her constant questions. Maybe he could engage her in some activity so that she'd stop tormenting him. Not chopping wood—Ammon didn't like the idea of giving Isabel the axe again. That left him with only one option.

Ammon held the sling toward her. "Would you like to learn how to use it?"

"You can't possibly think me stupid enough to fall for that again." The venom in her voice was unmistakable.

"Be careful with that anger, Princess. Who's to say I won't change my mind and tell your father I *will* marry you?"

She gasped. "You wouldn't."

I wouldn't. Would I? Right then, he feared some part of him would. "You can't hurt yourself with a sling. It won't go anywhere near your body."

The princess snatched the sling from his hand. "Fine. Show me."

Ammon found blessed distraction in explaining how the sling worked. He showed Isabel how to fit a rock into the oval-shaped pouch in the center. He told her to loop one of the two strings around her index finger several times and to hold the other string between her forefinger and thumb. Once Isabel had secured the sling's ropes, he instructed her to let the rock hang down. Ammon explained that there were basically two ways to release the rock. If she desired accuracy and control, she should circle the sling around the way he had, and that when the sling came to the front she should release the string not looped around her finger to let the rock fly. Ammon told her that if she wanted power more than accuracy, she should circle the loop around back and come forward in an overhand motion, letting go once she reached the top of the arc.

Ammon stopped his explanation. The easiest way to teach her would be hand over hand to show her the proper way to swing and release, but that would involve a good deal of touching, and Ammon couldn't risk it. He didn't understand why she affected him so much and why he couldn't seem to keep himself calm and collected. Ammon blamed Isabel. *She* was different. Something had changed for her, and he had detected and reacted to it. Today, somehow, she had used her feminine wiles to demand that he recognize her beauty. And to remember that she was even prettier with her hair down. Isabel made him notice her chocolate-colored eyes and her high cheekbones, and to wonder if her cheeks might dimple if she ever really smiled. He logically knew what would happen were he foolish enough to get caught up in a romantic entanglement with a nonbeliever. But logic had no hold on him, and that concerned him. *I cannot be distracted,* he reminded himself for what felt like the thousandth time.

Fortunately, Isabel was intent on learning to use the sling—most likely so she could use it against him.

Ammon had her practice the swing several times until she seemed comfortable with it. He set up a log on the stump and moved her back. "Keep your eyes on your target. Your arm will naturally follow your gaze. Give it a try whenever you're ready. Nice and easy."

He didn't know what made Isabel disregard his words or why she decided to fling her arm with such force, but she did.

"No, not out to the side—" Ammon tried to warn her.

Too late. By swinging the sling sideways instead of straight back or forward, the princess lost control. Ammon's warning must have startled her because she released one of the ropes too soon and at the same time pulled the sling in toward her, which resulted in her lashing herself across her forehead with the loose string.

Ammon knew better than to laugh as she stood there looking stunned. "So, maybe *you* can hurt yourself with a sling."

Isabel gave him a look that would have wilted grass. Now was not the time to point out what she had done wrong. "This sling was designed for me, and you're much smaller. I should have thought of that."

Still she stood there, not speaking. Ammon thought he saw tears in her eyes. *Please don't cry.* He'd never dealt well with crying women.

"Let me help," he said and pulled her hand up so that he could undo the rope she had twisted around her finger. The tip of her finger had started to turn purple. He expected her to jerk her hand away, but she didn't.

"You're bleeding," he said in surprise. Guilt ripped through his insides. Had he been the cause of that?

"I pricked it doing embroidery today," Isabel replied in a dull voice.

"War wounds, eh?" Ammon smiled. "Poor Isabel. Bleeding and bruised."

"Bruised?" she echoed. "Where?"

"Here," Ammon said, as he traced the red outline on her forehead with his fingers.

"It hurts," she said.

"Poor Isabel," he repeated.

And then he did the most idiotic thing he had ever done.

He kissed her forehead.

He had meant for it to soothe her in a brotherly sort of way, but there was nothing brotherly about the way he felt. Ammon had crossed the line he had drawn for himself in the worst way imaginable. The heat that flared up from that one little gesture was enough to consume the fields around them.

Then, to compound his mistake, despite the fact that he immediately removed his lips from her skin, he didn't move away from her. No, like the fool that he was, he stood there and just breathed in her scent and wanted to kiss her again. To really, really kiss her.

He finally did stumble backward after Isabel's hand cracked across his cheek. He couldn't even muster surprise at her reaction. Ammon knew he had deserved it. He deserved worse for his thoughts and for his wholly moronic actions.

"Why do you persist in tormenting me?" Isabel asked in a strangled voice.

"I could ask you the same question," Ammon responded, barely able to contain his own emotion.

Isabel shook her head, her dark eyes sparkling with unshed tears. She didn't walk away from him. She ran. She ran so fast that within seconds she was out of sight.

That was the way it would have to stay. Ammon had to keep away from her. Despite his resolve, despite his past, despite his mission here, he couldn't seem to keep himself on the right path.

His brothers looked up to him. They came to him for advice and to consult with him on spiritual matters. It had had been Ammon's idea to serve missions to the Lamanites in the first place, an idea his brothers and friends had been eager to agree to. He was supposed to be the strong one. The leader.

Ammon let out a weary sigh. All it had taken was one Lamanite princess to make him forget everything and everyone else.

I can't ever let it happen again, Ammon thought.

Not sure he could continue to trust himself, Ammon turned to the one place he knew he would be able to find strength. Ammon knelt down and began to pour his heart out in prayer. He hoped that the Lord had the answers he did not.

* * *

Isabel could scarcely believe what had just occurred. Not once, but twice he had made a fool out of her. When would she learn? Why did she keep letting him affect her this way? She was stronger and smarter than this. But even after she had vowed to make him stop, Ammon had sucked her in again.

He had *kissed* her. No one had ever dared take such liberties with her before. Admittedly it had only been on her forehead, but Isabel couldn't remember the last time anyone had shown her affection besides her mother. No one else would dare invade her personal defenses. But the Nephite had shown no qualms about doing just that.

Why had he done it? Was it part of his plan, to lull her into submission? Her mind raced as quickly as her feet.

She didn't know what mortified her more—that he had kissed her or that she hadn't tried to stop him. Isabel could still feel the imprint of his lips on her skin. It tingled and burned. Not willing to give Ammon any further concessions, Isabel decided the sensation was due to the welt he'd pointed out.

Isabel knew of only one person who had the power to make Ammon disappear, and so she made a beeline for the palace. She entered through the secret passage at the back in order to gain the throne room more quickly. Very few people in the palace knew of the passages, so they were covered in cobwebs and dust. Isabel had found them as a little girl and had never heard anyone else speak of them.

"Why do you let that Nephite stay?" Isabel asked her father, ignoring the single eyebrow he raised in response to her interruption and disregard for courtly protocol. King Lamoni quietly told his advisors to return in a few minutes.

"He is plotting against you. Ammon is here only to gather information for his own people so that they can destroy us. Why can't anyone else see that?" Isabel let her frustration spill forth, not caring who heard or what they thought.

"The kingdom of Ishmael is not a threat to the Nephites. They would have no reason to send spies here. If they were going to send spies, they would have gone to your grandfather's lands."

That made sense, but Isabel was in no mood for the discussion to be over. Nonetheless, her father spoke in such a way that Isabel understood the matter to be closed. He would not be sharing his reasons for letting Ammon remain. But she knew the Nephite had an ulterior motive, no matter what her father thought.

And if her father wouldn't protect himself and his family, then it would be left to her to do so. This was a responsibility for a son, but Laman was only nine. Isabel's urgency to catch the Nephite plotting and spying increased. Despite what had passed between them, she was not about to let Ammon out of her sight.

"Father, I would like a sling," Isabel said.

"A sling?"

"Yes, a sling of my own. One that would be suited for my size."

He looked confused, but the king said, "I will have one sent to you."

Isabel thanked her father. With the tiny bit of dignity Isabel had left, she pushed her shoulders back and left for the comforts of her own room. She hoped the king would send her the sling soon. She would practice every day until she became expert.

And if Ammon ever tried to kiss her again, he'd get a rock in the face as his reply.

5

So far Ammon had done an excellent job of sticking to his resolution. Today he had not seen or spoken to Isabel at all. Granted, the sun had only just come up, but Ammon was still pleased with his progress.

The king's chief cook had sent Ammon out to retrieve fresh water. Instead of having him go to the well as usual, the cook gave him directions to a stream. Ammon had noticed that there was nothing the servants liked better than to give him extra work. Ammon accepted the assignment as he did all of his tasks—with a glad heart and cheerful smile, which always seemed to disconcert the Lamanite servants.

You could turn any situation around by simply finding the good. Yes, he had to make a longer trip today to get the water, but it might give him a chance to really bathe instead of using a rag to wash his limbs down.

Plus, it got him away from the madness that had consumed the palace. The tournament that King Lamoni had mentioned would be held today, and the servants had too much work and not enough time to complete it in. Twice already this morning the chief cook had suffered a fit of hysteria. But once the tournament began, most of the work would be finished. Ammon looked forward to having several hours to himself. He would not participate in the tournament, despite the king's wish that he do so. Instead, Ammon planned to spend some time in quiet meditation and had arranged to meet Jeremias at the marketplace afterward.

Thinking of his cousin reminded Ammon how much he disliked the idea of leaving Jeremias behind to scrub potatoes, but Jeremias had waved him off. Ammon's concern came from the large influx of Lamanite visitors who had arrived last night, and those that continued to trickle in this morning. The current residents of the palace tolerated Ammon and Jeremias, but Ammon didn't know how true this would be of the king's guests.

He had far too many concerns at the moment, Ammon decided. Better to just enjoy this beautiful, princess-free morning. He could simplify his life merely by staying away from Isabel. No more teasing her just to get a reaction or teaching her new skills. No more trying to show her that a world existed beyond her pampered and privileged one. He should probably never be in the same room with her. And hopefully she would feel likewise and avoid him. Their simultaneous avoidance could lead to mutual peace of mind.

His conscience nagged at him to apologize for his inappropriate behavior, but he recalled what had happened the last time he'd apologized to her. Better to work on the mutual avoidance plan and ignore the pangs that tugged at his heart.

Since Ammon's life did not usually work out the way he expected, he should not have been surprised when he came across Isabel soon thereafter.

The encounter was fated as soon as he heard a little girl shrieking. Concerned, Ammon put down the clay vases and entered the thick foliage surrounding the stream. Soft laughter followed. Ammon heard several other voices. They sounded like children.

Ammon hunched down to walk quietly across the layer of dry leaves, wilted flowers, and fallen branches that made up the forest floor. He pushed down a large palm frond and saw a clearing next to the stream. There sat Isabel with her brothers and sisters. The elder boy created twig boats that he let race down the water. The other brother used corncobs to build houses for stick soldiers. The two girls worked on flower garlands under Isabel's patient instruction, although the youngest seemed more interested in trying to shove flowers in her mouth. Isabel laughed at the antics of the girl and playfully chided the littlest princess as she removed petals from the child's mouth.

The children all vied for Isabel's attention, each demanding that she see what they had created. She praised each one in turn, and it was obvious to Ammon that, despite her absences from family gatherings,

Isabel adored her younger siblings just as much as they seemed to adore her. It confused Ammon. Why would Isabel exclude herself when her family obviously loved her?

Wanting to see better, Ammon shifted his weight to lean forward. Causing a branch underneath him to break. He immediately went still, not wanting to ruin the idyllic scene in front of him. He had never seen Isabel smile before.

Everyone turned toward the forest when the branch snapped. The oldest boy pulled out a wooden play sword and looked ready to charge Ammon's hiding spot. Isabel put a hand on the boy's arm to restrain him. "Time to leave," she told them.

The children all moaned in protest, begging for a few more minutes. Isabel stayed firm, telling them that they were missed at home. They gathered their things together, and the youngest princess held out her arms to Isabel. Isabel picked the little girl up and then covered the toddler's head with kisses. The girl sucked her thumb as she laid her head on Isabel's shoulder. Ammon's heart inexplicably twinged as he backed away.

He hurried to his vases and dragged them into the forest. He feared that if the princess found them she might not return to this spot. And Ammon liked the idea of the royal family spending many mornings like this one. He didn't want to be the reason they stopped.

Ammon waited several minutes after Isabel and her siblings had passed before venturing out to fill the vases.

So, the princess was not as cold as she wanted everyone to believe. Ammon wondered why Isabel worked so hard at that image when she was much more warm and loving than even he could have imagined.

Reminding himself that it was not wise to wonder or speculate about her, Ammon found himself worse off now than he had been this morning. He had seen a side of Isabel that he doubted she showed to anyone else. Much to his dismay, his interest in her now increased exponentially.

He had to firmly stick to his resolutions, now more than ever. Ammon also had to erase the image of the princess smiling and laughing, and the fervent wish that had welled up inside him to make her smile and laugh that way himself.

* * *

Isabel returned the children to the palace through the passages so that they wouldn't be seen. She knew her father would expect her for the morning meal because of their guests, but Isabel wasn't ready to face Mahlon quite yet. Abish had informed her that Mahlon and his party had been the first to arrive the previous evening. It made sense—Mahlon's lands bordered on her father's, so it would be a quick journey for him.

She decided to go for her run and take her new sling with her. Her father had kept his word, and late last night, the leatherworker had brought her the sling. Her run could help her accomplish two things at once—she would practice with the weapon and get away from the palace. The tournament was set to begin immediately after breakfast, and Isabel knew she might incur her father's wrath by not going. But attending meant she would be forced to face the two men she would much rather avoid—Ammon and Mahlon.

Abish tried to get Isabel to stay, but Isabel promised to return for the feast that night. Honestly, she didn't much enjoy watching men beat on one another. Outside of a battlefield, it seemed pointless.

Isabel ran in the opposite direction from the ball court where the tournament would be held.

Her mind cleared as it usually did during her runs. That is, until an image of Ammon managed to slip in. The more Isabel tried not to think about him, the more she did. It frustrated her that she still didn't know what he planned, and she tried to focus on that. Tonight at the feast she would keep a close eye on him, although she didn't think Ammon foolish enough to try anything with all the guests here for the tournament. She tried to guess at what he might do but instead kept remembering what it had felt like when he kissed her, when he had stood so close to her. She shook her head to rid herself of the memories, but she couldn't.

Isabel had to concede that what Ammon had done yesterday really bothered her. More than he usually bothered her. She rationalized that it had been the surprise and shock of it all that made her feel this way. She decided it had nothing to do with her somewhat recent discovery that she thought Ammon attractive, and the fact his attractiveness had seemed to increase in direct proportion to his proximity to her.

She found herself back at the scene of yesterday's crime. The memory washed over her again, making her cheeks turn pink. Isabel's first instinct was to flee. But she planted her feet firmly on the ground and pulled out her sling. This was where she would practice, using the wooden target Ammon had set up. She would prove to herself that Ammon did not have any control over her. She stooped down to get a rock.

"Princess?"

Isabel froze, wondering if she had started to hallucinate. But she lifted her head and there, a stone's throw away, she saw him. Ammon had been lying down in the grass, which was why she hadn't seen him. Now he propped himself up on his elbows, his bewildered expression matching her own.

She slowly straightened and tucked the sling back into the wide sash around her waist. Isabel didn't want to give him the satisfaction of seeing her with it. She knew Ammon would laugh and tease her for her desire to learn how to use it properly, or perhaps he'd discover that she had acquired it to defend herself against him. "What are you doing?" she asked first, fearing that he might ask her the same question.

Ammon stared at her for a moment, then a moment more, before he laced his fingers behind his head and lay back down. "Cloud watching."

Cloud watching? Absurd. "Why would anyone watch clouds?"

He gave her a quizzical look. "Haven't you ever just laid outside to find shapes in the clouds?" Isabel informed him that she had not done anything so juvenile and ridiculous. Ammon let out a short laugh and then pointed to the sky.

"Look there. What do you see?" he asked.

Isabel refrained from rolling her eyes as she looked up. "Oh, yes. I can see it. It looks like a caiman devouring a jaguar."

Ammon laughed again. "I thought it looked like a butterfly landing on a flower."

What a waste of time. The Nephite seemed to make less sense every time she saw him. Perhaps he was sinking into some bout of madness, which might make him more easily confess his plans. Maybe this would be her opportunity to try to get him to divulge them.

"Why aren't you at the tournament?" Isabel tried to keep her voice casual.

"Why aren't you?"

"That isn't an answer to my question," Isabel said. She was not the master spy. *She* didn't owe *him* an explanation. She wasn't staying away from the tournament for nefarious reasons.

Isabel walked toward him. His entire body seemed to tense up, but Isabel was sure she must have imagined it. In her experience, nothing ever seemed to upset or stress Ammon.

"I didn't want to see any of the tournament losers put to death."

"It is my father's prerogative to decide what happens to the winners and the losers of the tournament. His word is law."

Ammon shrugged as if it didn't matter to him. His lack of respect for her father's power and dominion upset her.

"My father is king. Whatever he chooses to do is right. In his kingdom he is not accountable to any man."

That smile of Ammon's, the one that made it look as if he knew a secret, appeared. "No, he is not accountable to any *man*."

Despite the fact that on the surface he agreed with her, his response still irked Isabel. She didn't like the way he said it, the way he put the emphasis on the word *man*. As if her father were accountable to someone other than men. The only person who had any hold over her father was her grandfather. What was Ammon trying to imply?

"Besides," Ammon turned on the full strength of his smile, "I didn't think King Lamoni would appreciate it if I defeated all of his best warriors."

Isabel arched both eyebrows at him. "Boasting?"

"No. Just telling the truth. Like you, I don't lie."

She didn't want to, but part of her believed him. Isabel had seen him in action with his sling, and, in a detached sort of way, his muscular physique had registered with her. Isabel folded her arms. Did he mean to frighten her? To paint himself as an undefeatable warrior? He didn't seem like he was trying to be intimidating. Only that he had meant what he said. His words had a conviction to them that didn't allow for doubt.

Ammon got up and nodded his head at Isabel. "I have plans to meet my cousin Jeremias at the marketplace today. If you'll excuse me."

Isabel couldn't very well let him loose in the marketplace alone. It had surely swelled to festival-sized proportions for the tournament today. Vendors and artists would have traveled from all over to try selling their wares to her father's guests. Ammon and his cousin might plan to meet up with his fellow spies there. It would be the perfect time for such a meeting. She had to stay with him. "I will come with you."

"That's not necessary."

"I insist." Isabel fell in step alongside the Nephite. Ammon let out a noise that sounded like a deep sigh as they walked together.

They did not speak, but it wasn't an uncomfortable silence. Isabel didn't feel pressed to say something just to fill in the space between them. Instead, she considered his words from earlier, wondering if Ammon really could defeat her father's warriors in hand-to-hand combat. She noticed his large, slightly calloused hands and thought they could easily wield any weapon. Isabel looked away, but her gaze returned to the muscles in his arms; however, before her thoughts could go any further in that direction, she ordered herself not to look at him, but her eyes refused to obey. They kept wandering back to steal another peek at him.

"Stop it," she whispered to herself.

"Stop what?" Ammon asked with one of his dazzling smiles.

"Nothing," Isabel said, refusing to let his smile have any effect on her. He seemed so charming, so innocent. Except for the part where he was planning to wipe out the entire kingdom. She knew the truth. She knew he had an agenda and could guess at what he wanted to accomplish.

She hated that it became easier every day to believe his lies.

* * *

Finally, something felt familiar to Ammon. As he and Isabel entered the marketplace near the palace, Ammon relaxed. He had a pang of homesickness as he entered the noisy, crowded center. The first thing he heard was the sound of hundreds of women making tortillas. The constant slapping sounded like applause. The smells of roasting meat and corn dough cooking hit his nose and made his stomach rumble in appreciation. Perhaps this had not been the best place to come while fasting.

Jeremias stood near a stela in the middle of the marketplace. The long stone column had an engraving of King Lamoni as well as his genealogy. It stood here in the marketplace to remind the people of the king's right to rule and of his powers. Jeremias looked at Ammon with a surprised expression.

"You have the princess with you."

"Yes, thank you, I noticed," Ammon said with gritted teeth. Fortunately, Jeremias had the sense to speak the language of their people. Ammon doubted that Isabel would be able to understand them. He glanced over at her, but her face gave nothing away as they spoke.

"You seem . . . put out."

"You have no idea."

Jeremias grinned. Ammon hadn't confided his struggles to his cousin, but Jeremias wasn't dumb and knew Ammon far too well. "You know what Aaron likes to say. That which doesn't kill you—"

"—usually makes you wish it would."

Ammon saw the princess clamp a hand over her mouth as if disguising a smile. Ammon's stomach dropped. "You understood that?"

Isabel's eyes danced with merriment. "Yes."

"How is that possible?"

"I was my father's only heir for many years. He thought it would be a waste not to educate me."

"So, you're intelligent and educated. Another hidden trait," Ammon said thoughtfully. She always surprised him. But now he and Jeremias would have to be more careful about what they said. He didn't know who else might have the ability to listen in on their conversations.

Isabel narrowed her eyes at him. "'Another hidden trait'?" she repeated. "Are you compiling some sort of list?"

Yes. "No."

Ammon had spent these last few years working hard to overcome his imperfections and weaknesses. He wanted badly to make up for them, to prove to the Lord how sorry he was for the decisions he'd once made. And now he couldn't bear the thought of another person suffering the way he'd suffered, so he'd come here in hopes that he could save his Lamanite brethren from the same fate. But in order to do that he had to keep his eye trained on his goals and stop letting Isabel interfere.

"The mission, the mission," he reminded himself under his breath.

But Isabel had ears like a fox. "What did you say?"

"It's a shame you're *missing* the tournament. I'd hate to be the reason you're staying away from it."

Despite all of his hints, the princess still did not leave. Instead she turned to Jeremias and gave him something that looked like a smile, though it didn't reach her eyes. "Earlier Ammon bragged to me that if he competed in the tournament he would win."

"He wasn't bragging," Jeremias told her. "He's probably right."

Isabel gave Ammon a speculative look that implied she still didn't believe it. It didn't matter if she doubted his abilities. Ammon knew what would have happened if he had competed. He had decided that if he did win he ran the risk of embarrassing King Lamoni in front of his peers, relatives, and people. Ammon didn't think that would be the best way to make friends.

"What brings you to the marketplace today?" Isabel's question was again pointed to Jeremias.

"We heard that your father is well known for his love of sculptures and thought this would be a chance to view some of them."

"I'm sure you have other things to attend to," Ammon told Isabel but his resolve to stay away from her was fading quickly.

"My father does have excellent taste in choosing sculptors. I would love to show you some of their work."

Ammon shrugged off his wish that Isabel would speak so sweetly to him and followed behind Jeremias and the princess. Isabel explained to Jeremias that sculptors from all over resided here to work because of her father's patronage.

As they came around a corner, Ammon saw a large stone plaza elevated above the marketplace. Columns nearly twice the length of a man ranged ten across and ten deep. They stood like perfectly organized stone trees. Behind the plaza rose a small temple, like a mountain reigning over a forest. Ammon stopped to fully appreciate the sight; he had never seen anything quite so elaborate.

They walked among the rows of tall columns that had been engraved with pictures of King Lamoni and his father, King Laman. They moved as a group through the available pathways with the columns on either side of them. Ammon had never seen so many sculptures in one place before and commented as much. Isabel replied that her grandfather's collection was even more extensive, and that her father worked to increase his. Ammon watched some of the artisans that were working on a new row with their flint chisels and hammers. Others covered already-carved stone with stucco and painted the stones in reds, oranges, blues, and greens. The princess continued on until she found sculptures of the king's family. "This is you," Ammon said to Isabel.

She nodded. "How did you know that was me?"

"Well, it does have your name on it," Ammon pointed out with a smile. "But while it's a good likeness, it doesn't do you justice. You're much prettier."

Ammon could have kicked himself. Isabel looked at him with wide eyes and made a choking sound. Jeremias stepped in to save him by asking Isabel about the sculpture next to them.

Here he was, running off at the mouth again. Ammon wondered why he never had this problem when he spoke about the gospel. In those situations he always knew what to say, but the rest of the time he routinely said things without thinking first, like a spring shooting forth water.

"Where is this Aaron I keep hearing about?" Isabel asked in a deceptively innocent manner.

Fortunately, Ammon didn't have to give Jeremias a warning look. Jeremias had not been beguiled by Isabel and answered, "I'm not really certain where he is now. We went one way; he went another. Did you know that he and Ammon are identical twins?"

"Are you the eldest?" This time Isabel pointed her question to Ammon. Ammon knew the implication behind her words and why she desired to ferret out which twin was older.

"Yes," Ammon said just as Jeremias replied, "No."

"Yes and no?" Isabel looked confused. "How can that be?"

"No one is sure which one of us was born first. My father believes Aaron was born first; but my mother thinks I'm the oldest. My mother didn't know she was having twins, and there was a great deal of confusion at our birth. You can imagine her relief that she had two babies instead of one giant one. But in the chaos, the midwives neglected to tag us with a ribbon or marking that would tell them which one of us had been born first. But it doesn't matter what everyone thinks, because I am the eldest."

"If you asked Aaron, he'd tell you that he was the oldest," Jeremias interjected with a grin.

"So that's why you're named Ammon. 'The hidden one,'" Isabel said.

"Again, I think that depends. In the written language, that is what it means. But in the ancient tongue of our forefathers it means 'teacher' or 'builder.'"

Isabel ignored his explanation and asked another question. "And this confusion over the birth order, does it cause discord with your brother?"

Ammon laughed. He didn't know if he'd ever met anyone quite so tenacious. She was certainly determined to uncover secrets he didn't possess.

"No, it doesn't cause discord between us. I love my brother despite his delusions. I'm sure you can relate."

"I can relate?" Isabel repeated. "What is that supposed to mean?"

"I saw you this morning—at the stream with your brothers and sisters. You love them. You want everyone to think you don't care, that you're indifferent. But I saw you," Ammon confided in a conspiratorial tone. "It's all right. I suffer from the same affliction myself."

Isabel's lower jaw fell open, and Ammon had the small pleasure of finally seeing the princess speechless.

"Isabel! Princess! We must go at once!" Abish, Isabel's maidservant, came running over to them. The frantic pitch of her voice let all of them know that something was very wrong.

"What is it?" Isabel asked. Abish shook her head, looking at Ammon and Jeremias. Whatever news she had, the maidservant didn't wish to share it with them.

"We must leave. Right now."

"Why? And how did you know I was here?" Isabel asked in a perplexed tone. Ammon thought it a good question—the market had thousands of people milling about.

Abish reached out and grabbed Isabel's hands. "You're with the only two Nephites in the marketplace. *Everyone* knows you are here."

"Everyone?" Isabel repeated in a whisper. Ammon saw her swallow hard.

"Yes. I wanted to reach you first. We must return to the palace."

Without any sort of farewell, Isabel hurried away with her maidservant. This concerned Ammon more than it should have. Something had frightened Isabel in a way that he wouldn't have imagined possible. She had never struck him as the vulnerable type, but he was sure he could see her shaking. His protective instincts roared to life. Ammon had to force himself not to chase the young women or demand to know who had scared them. He reminded himself again that it was not his place to worry over the princess. He shouldn't have these sorts of feelings for Isabel.

So why did he want nothing more than to run after her and offer to always keep her safe?

6

AMMON HAD LOST COUNT OF how many trips he'd made to the celebration in the throne room. He had initially spent the afternoon watching over the flocks, as had become his custom since his arrival, but he had then been wrangled into kitchen duty with almost every other servant in the household. He had been assigned to help with the meat dishes and had brought in platter after platter of turkey, deer, iguana, peccary, and fish, all spiced and grilled to perfection. There were so many people to look after.

But he had not seen Isabel. He had thought about her so much that day and had expected to see her as soon as he entered the celebration. He wondered where she was.

As Ammon left the feast with another empty tray, he heard someone exclaim in vexation. He hurried along the gallery until he found Abish. She was trying to balance a large platter in one hand and an oversized wine jug in the other. She was in danger of dropping both. Putting down his own tray, Ammon hurried over and took both the jug and the platter from her. "Here, let me help," Ammon said.

"Thank you," she replied. "I thought I could carry them both but . . ." Abish's words trailed off as she realized who had saved her. "Oh."

"Where should these go?" Ammon asked, deciding to overlook her newfound displeasure at the rescue.

"I'll show you," Abish said. "Follow me."

They entered the throne room, and Ammon ignored the jibes and jeers from some of the very drunk Lamanites. Loud burps sounded all over the room from guests who had finished and wished to properly show their appreciation for the fine meal that King Lamoni had provided. Ammon trailed behind Abish and set the things down on a low table that she'd pointed to.

A man sitting on a cushion at the table stared openly at Ammon. From the high, green-feathered headdress he wore, the jaguar cloak and spondlyus-shell necklaces, Ammon could tell the stranger was of the noble class, perhaps higher. He might have been a king himself, although he looked to be approximately the same age as Ammon. Ammon had hardly registered the curious looks from the guests that evening, but there was something different about the way this man stared at him. It was predatory, as if the man wished to kill Ammon and needed only a slight provocation to do so.

Ammon fought back the urge to return the look with a challenge of his own. He did not fear this man, but King Lamoni would have certain expectations of Ammon's behavior. Fighting the king's company would most likely not be appreciated. Ammon turned away.

"Is there anything else I can help you with?" he asked Abish. He was rewarded with Abish's tentative smile.

"No, but thank you again for your assistance."

Ammon felt excited that he had finally made some headway with someone at the palace. For the first time his offer of help had not been rebuffed or scorned. Abish actually seemed grateful. Ammon had almost forgotten what that felt like.

The man on the cushion suddenly rose and strode across the room. Ammon saw that the man was not a king. His cloak, tied over his left shoulder, reached the middle of his shins. Only kings were permitted cloaks that fell to their ankles. Ammon looked up to see what had caused the man to quit his party.

Isabel.

Her hairstyle was more elaborate than Ammon had ever seen before; in addition to strips of green leather, she had green quetzal feathers hanging from her hair and dozens of pearls embedded in her braids. She again wore more jewelry than any woman should have been forced to endure, but she sparkled brightly, like one of the pine-pitch candles in the room.

Face paint and markings covered the princess's face, much as when Ammon had first met her. He preferred her without them, but she was dazzling.

The throne room had been decorated with garlands of bright purple, pink, and white flowers, palm leaves, pine branches and needles, but the beauty of the room paled in comparison to Isabel.

As if feeling his gaze upon her, Isabel looked across the room to see Ammon. And she stumbled. It was only a little stumble, something no one else would notice, but it gave Ammon far too much satisfaction to think he affected her that way.

But he also knew that there couldn't be a relationship between them. Ammon would not fall in love again.

Earlier today he had realized that they could be friends. It was silly not to be. He'd been so busy trying to close himself off to her that he didn't recognize that this could be one of the opportunities he'd been waiting for and that there might be another way to deal with her. Yes, the princess was very attractive. Beautiful when she smiled. Ammon could admit that. But it didn't need to stand in the way of a friendship, and he had to stop letting it.

He had resolved to treat her like he would one of his sisters. He could cease worrying about avoiding her. He could maintain his purpose, keeping it foremost in his mind, and befriend the princess. Besides, it certainly seemed that Isabel could use a friend. Especially now that Ammon realized that the man who appeared to hate him had gotten up to talk to Isabel.

Ammon clenched his jaw. He didn't want the nobleman speaking to her. He didn't want that man in the same room as Isabel. Or the same kingdom. "Who is that?"

"Mahlon," Abish said in a low voice that had just a hint of disgust in it. "He's an Amulonite. Half Nephite, half Lamanite, all bad. He is, unfortunately, Isabel's cousin."

Isabel tensed up when the man stood in front of her, and Ammon saw her eyes dart back and forth as if looking for an escape route. "She's afraid of him," Ammon said, trying to keep his anger at bay. Was it this man who had been the cause of Isabel's fear earlier that day?

"As well she should be," Abish replied before moving toward them.

There would not be much that Abish could do to stop this Mahlon from addressing Isabel. But Ammon could put an end to it.

And, he told himself, he would do so out of the protective instincts of a friend. Not jealousy, of course.

His new friend needed his help.

Ammon grabbed a cup off one of the tables, disregarding the protests from the cup's owner. He walked up to Mahlon and "tripped," causing the golden wine to spill all over the exposed portion of Mahlon's *ex,* an elaborately decorated ceremonial wrap.

"Clumsy fool!" Mahlon roared.

"I am so sorry," Ammon said. "Please, you must allow me to clean it. Perhaps you can return to your room and change into another."

Ammon had only a moment to see the look of gratitude in Isabel's eyes before he put himself bodily between Mahlon and the princess.

Several servants, presumably belonging to Mahlon, rushed over to care for their master. Mahlon accepted a rag from one of them and began toweling off the excess wine from his loincloth. Mahlon handed the rag back and waved his servants off.

His predatory gaze focused on Ammon. "You must be the one they call Ammon."

"That's what my father named me."

Mahlon's mouth curved up into a half smile at Ammon's retort. "You came here in ropes, and yet you could have had a Lamanite princess as a wife. And now you are a servant."

Ammon said nothing, quashing down his anger. He detected the bitterness in Mahlon's voice when he spoke of Ammon having a Lamanite princess as a wife. But he didn't have long to dwell on this as all of his instincts were distracting him with the message that Mahlon was dangerous; he had to tread carefully. Nonetheless, Ammon would not let Mahlon hurt the princess, and if it meant incurring the man's wrath, then Ammon was fine with that.

Mahlon waited for some response, and when he realized that none would be forthcoming, he said, "You were not at the tournament today."

"No, I was not." Ammon refrained from sarcastically praising the other man's powers of observation.

"I find that interesting, since all the men of King Lamoni's household were supposed to be present for the show of arms."

"That was my understanding as well."

Mahlon's smile faded and was replaced by confusion. He apparently didn't know what to make of Ammon agreeing with him and not offering excuses for his absence. "I had hoped you would come. I've heard much about you and wanted to try you on a battlefield, to see for myself the inferiority of the Nephite fighting methods."

He clearly meant to provoke Ammon into making the first move, maybe to cause a confrontation in the throne room that would be blamed on Ammon. If Ammon had been foolish enough to respond, his death would have been certain. King Lamoni would never tolerate such an insult to a guest. So much to Mahlon's surprise, Ammon laughed. "Perhaps one day you'll get your wish."

Mahlon's eyes narrowed at Ammon and at the threat Ammon had implied. "Perhaps I will."

"I look forward to it. Especially since it would be such a short fight," Ammon told him, unable to keep himself from provoking the arrogant Lamanite. Mahlon swore and pulled back slightly, like a snake coiling up before an attack. Ammon responded by bracing his body to prepare for the impact. Surely the king couldn't be upset if Ammon fought only to defend himself.

But whatever Mahlon had planned was thwarted by the king's chief captain calling out that the awards and gifts for the tournament winners would now be handed out.

"Fortunately for you, I have a prize to collect," Mahlon said.

"Then you should go get your prize, since it will be the only one you will collect this evening."

Mahlon waited for several moments, his gaze shifting to the princess. "We shall see."

He left, and Ammon made certain that Mahlon was safely across the room before he turned to check on Isabel. Ammon heard Isabel's sigh of relief, seeing the way her body relaxed as the fear left her. "Are you all right?"

Isabel straightened. "How did you know that I was here?" she asked in a whisper. "No one else besides Mahlon ever notices whether I'm here or not. They don't see me."

Ammon heard the pain in her voice. He couldn't help but respond to it. "I know you're here, Isabel. I see you. How can I not?"

Isabel swallowed several times, shook her head, and then fled the room. Abish moved away to return to her duties, but not before she gave Ammon an appraising look.

He would be Isabel's friend, tamping down any other emotion he might feel for her. He had only threatened Mahlon out of a friendly concern for Isabel's well-being.

Ammon continued to assure himself that friendship was his goal as he went to find the princess.

* * *

I see you.

The words echoed in Isabel's mind as she ran to the courtyard designated solely for her family's use. It held a beautiful garden for the family to enjoy and relax in. Pausing to calm down, she began walking through the avocado and fig trees, inhaling the sweet scent of the allspice blossoms and vanilla vines. She came upon the cluster of cacao trees and plucked several of the scarlet blossoms, her favorite flower. She fingered the petals as she walked over to the pond her father had ordered installed just after he married Kamilah. The moon reflected in its still surface. Mahlon would not disturb her here. He wouldn't leave the throne room at all if she knew him. He was far too greedy to pass up on the wealth and gifts her father would distribute.

I see you.

Of course he saw her. The man was in possession of two functioning eyes.

But it bothered her that he had meant something else, and that she had understood it. The way he had said it, the inflection in his voice. . .

"Of course he saw me," she repeated out loud. "I was standing right in front of him."

She was adept at making herself invisible, at being in a room and having no one take notice. But Ammon had seen her.

The night air felt crisp and cool on Isabel's exposed arms. She wished she'd thought to bring a shawl but didn't want to go find one. She wanted to stay here and regain her composure.

Fireflies danced in the night like little glowing flames. The stars overhead shone down, and Isabel was reminded of the story her mother had told her about the fireflies who flew too high and became stuck in the sky, glowing forever.

Isabel held still until her tears dried, letting the beauty around her calm her. After her father's first refusal to Mahlon, Isabel had thought Mahlon would stop persisting in trying to wed her. But if tonight was any indication, Mahlon did not plan to stop. Isabel could not marry him. She had heard too many stories of what Mahlon did to men in battle and what he did to women and animals within his palace. She had actually seen the female servants from Mahlon's household, the ones with missing ears, missing fingers, scars all over their faces and arms, and burn marks on their necks.

She wondered if Ammon had any idea what he had stepped into this night. Mahlon did not take lightly the sort of threats Ammon had issued.

No one had ever stood up for her before or tried to stop Mahlon. Why had Ammon?

Isabel heard soft footsteps behind her. She smiled. It had to be Abish, coming to check on her. She turned to thank her maid for the concern. Instead Isabel saw Ammon, and her breath caught in her chest.

He was more handsome than normal here in the moonlight. Isabel could only stare at Ammon as he moved away to sit on a stone bench. He gave her one of his inviting smiles that tended to make her heart skip a beat. That he smiled at her this way was infinitely vexing. That she found him so attractive when he smiled this way annoyed her even further.

Isabel reminded herself to breathe so that she wouldn't faint. Before she could speak, Ammon said, "Do you know what this night reminds me of? It took my brothers and me a long time to reach your lands. We had to travel up through the mountain passes, which we knew could be treacherous. We tried to be careful. But one beautiful clear night, just like this one, we made camp, set up our huts, and had settled around the campfire to read and tell one another stories. Suddenly, from a bush behind us came a large crashing sound. A deer burst out of the forest and ran through the middle of our camp, running straight through the fire. We had barely recovered from that shock when a few seconds later a black jaguar ran right after the deer—ignoring us—in pursuit. Then there was total silence. I'll never forget what it looked like to see a jaguar leaping over a fire. I don't think any of us will. Nobody was able to sleep that night," he finished with a laugh.

Isabel understood that feeling of ambush, of sitting by while a predator ran through your life, of being unable to stop it. She wondered if that was why Ammon shared the story or if he had another reason. She had been trying so hard to find out more about him, about why he had come here, and now Ammon had freely shared a tale of his travels.

She didn't know how to respond to his story, so she turned her attention back to the firefly stars.

"Why aren't you with your family?"

"It's complicated," Isabel said without looking at him.

"You can tell me. Who am I going to tell? No one here talks to me," Ammon joked.

She didn't know if the trust she felt came from Ammon's earlier actions to protect her, or if it was the anonymity of the darkness and the way the paint on her face and the jewelry on her body felt like a mask she could hide behind, but Isabel found herself saying, "My father did not want to marry my mother. He had grown up loving Kamilah, and he wanted to marry her. But my grandfather wouldn't allow it. Kamilah was the daughter of the palace cloth maker. My grandfather demanded my father make an alliance in his marriage. So my father did as he was told."

Isabel looked over at Ammon. "I know many husbands don't love their wives. But some have affection. Or at least respect. My parents didn't even have that. I know he didn't care for her. She knew it too." Isabel took a shaky breath. "A few weeks after she died he married Kamilah. My grandfather was furious, but when Laman was born, all was forgotten."

"I'm sorry. That must have been difficult for you."

"I'm the only one here who loved my mother. If I spend time with them, if I become part of their family, I betray her."

"I think your mother would have wanted you to have a life filled with love. It's not a betrayal."

"Yes, it would be," Isabel said. "I don't belong with them."

"Where else would you belong? They are your family."

"You couldn't understand. You've always been close with your family."

Ammon let out a cynical laugh. "No thanks to my own actions. I have done some terrible things in my past, and my father had every right to never speak to me or any of my brothers ever again after what we did. But they still loved me, still wanted us to be a family, just like your family wants to be close with you. When I saw you with your brothers and sisters, I saw how much they love you."

"You don't know what you're talking about. You don't know what it's like to be an outcast."

This time Ammon's laugh was loud and genuine. "Oh, I think I understand better than anyone what it means to be an outsider."

"That's different," Isabel retorted. "You didn't have to be. My father offered you a way to become part of his family. You deliberately choose to be an outsider."

"So do you," Ammon responded quietly.

Isabel folded her arms together as if she could shield herself from Ammon's words. She wanted to deny them outright, but even she could see some truth in what he said. Nonetheless, it all felt like too much to sort out right then.

"While I have you here, I want to apologize for my behavior yesterday."

Isabel's cheeks flamed in response, knowing exactly what Ammon referred to. "It seems you are always apologizing to me for something."

Ammon's laughter filled the courtyard a third time. "I suppose that's how it is between friends."

"We are not friends."

"Yes we are. You just don't know it yet."

Ammon stood up and walked over to Isabel before she could give him a proper explanation of his very misguided notions. They were not friends. They were enemies.

But when Ammon stood close to her like this, Isabel found herself unable think sensibly. She could only stare up at him.

"I like you, Princess Isabel. I like you, and there's nothing you can do about it."

Isabel opened her mouth to say something. Anything. Hopefully something that sounded regal and intelligent. But nothing came out.

"Princess? Your father requests your presence." A servant had approached so silently that Isabel jumped in surprise.

Gaining her composure, she wordlessly followed after the servant. She reentered the throne room where the celebration still continued. The raucous laughter of the drunken guests echoed off the limestone walls. Someone threw their wine at one of the many small fires, causing it to flame up. For a moment, it consumed the room with light and heat, and then the flames settled back down. The scent of smoke, one so familiar and comforting to Isabel that she usually no longer even detected it, nearly overwhelmed her now.

Coughing, Isabel made her way to her father's dais. She bowed her head, clasping her hands in front of her. "You wanted to see me?"

Something distracted King Lamoni, and Isabel looked over her shoulder to see what her father looked at. She tried not to flush again when she saw Ammon come in. King Lamoni directed his gaze back to Isabel, then again to Ammon. The king frowned.

"How goes your progress of watching over our Nephite friend?" he asked.

Isabel couldn't very well tell her father she'd had no success yet and that despite watching over him closely she still hadn't uncovered Ammon's plans. "Things are going as well as can be expected. I did discover that he fancies himself a great warrior."

"Really?" King Lamoni asked in surprise.

"Yes, he claims he could have bested all of the participants in your tournament."

The king tapped his fingers against his leg as was his custom when deep in thought. The long green feathers in his carved headdress swayed back and forth as he continued to watch Ammon walk around the throne room. "Perhaps we should test that," he murmured.

"How?" Isabel asked.

But her father did not respond. "That is not why I called you here. Mahlon has a gift for you."

Everything inside Isabel froze. She wished the ground beneath her would open wide and swallow her up—anything to avoid this situation. Then her heart came back to life and thumped so heavily in her chest that she couldn't breathe. She tried not to shake and did what she could to keep her voice steady. "I hardly think I'm worthy of . . ."

Mahlon appeared next to her along with several of his men carrying a large wooden box. "I hope this will be the first of many," he told Isabel.

The first of many? Isabel's stomach twisted. That could mean only one thing: Mahlon still intended to marry her. The giving of elaborate gifts would declare his intentions to everyone in the kingdom, and if her father accepted them and reciprocated, she would be forced to marry Mahlon. Isabel could not imagine a worse fate.

A strange sound came from the box as it was set down. Mahlon pulled back the cover, and inside, Isabel saw a baby jaguar. It mewed and cried in the worst way, and Isabel knew just how the cat felt. Mahlon picked the jaguar up and carried it over to Isabel. "My men and I went hunting the other day and killed the mother. I thought you might like to have the baby."

"You killed its mother?" Isabel repeated. The little jaguar now cried even louder, and Isabel saw Mahlon's hands tighten around the cat, nearly suffocating it in order to keep it quiet. It was too much for Isabel. Protocol, responsibility, and duty fled, replaced only by a numbing fear. She didn't even care if she embarrassed her father. She had to do what she could to stop Mahlon.

"This is much too lavish a gift for me, and I'm afraid I cannot accept it."

Mahlon's visage darkened, frightening Isabel further. Mahlon took the cat by the scruff of its neck and handed it off to one of his men. The servant took the jaguar over to the king, who accepted it. Seeing that her father had been distracted by the cat, Isabel quickly decided to flee. She would be publicly humiliating Mahlon as most of the room watched with interest. She understood the danger she would put herself in, but she had to get away from him.

Isabel turned to leave, but Mahlon's hand snaked out to grab her wrist. He yanked her toward him so that he could growl in her ear. "I don't like being told no. I always get what I want. I never lose. Remember that."

Out of the corner of her eye, Isabel saw someone moving toward them. Ammon. Mahlon would kill Ammon if he interfered again.

Isabel managed to pull her arm free, though her wrist throbbed in pain. "No is the only answer you will ever have from me," she whispered back.

"I'm afraid all this excitement has tired me," Isabel said loudly. Her father looked up from the cat. The baby jaguar had stopped crying and lay sleeping in her father's lap. "With your permission, I would like to go to bed."

Her father indicated that she should approach. Isabel walked up the steps and then knelt down to kiss her father on his cheek.

"You know that if Mahlon asks for you, I can't tell him no again," King Lamoni said in a low voice. Isabel froze.

"You have had a reprieve of four years. It cannot go on indefinitely. I am sorry for that."

Isabel didn't know why her father seemed so fearful of Mahlon—why he was willing to agree to the marriage. But she did know that her father would not offer any explanation.

"Good night, daughter," the king said loudly for the court's benefit. At least her father had permitted her to delay the inevitable for one more night. Mahlon could not prevent her from leaving now. Isabel walked as fast as she dared until free from the throne room. Then she ran, worried that Mahlon might follow.

Abish waited in Isabel's bedroom. She helped Isabel to bathe and to arrange her hair in a single braid. Isabel hated how long everything took, as she desperately wanted to go to sleep so that this night could be over.

Isabel didn't dare speak. Typically she used this time to tell Abish of her day and her concerns. But tonight, if she spoke of what had happened, she might start crying. And if she cried, she might never stop.

Abish broke the silence. "I think that we might have misjudged Ammon. He seems much kinder and more caring than we had thought. He seems to be a good man."

"Not you too," Isabel moaned. Everyone seemed bewitched by Ammon. Even Isabel herself. She had hoped Abish would have more sense than Isabel currently possessed.

"He helped me a great deal this evening, and I think he helped you a great deal as well."

Isabel recognized what Ammon had done for her. He had come to her rescue once, and it seemed that he planned on coming to her rescue again. Perhaps Ammon didn't appreciate the risk he was taking, but Isabel did.

Abish finished with the braid, tying off the end. Isabel went to her bed and settled onto her pallet, pulling her thick blankets over her to ward off the cold.

"Here," Abish said as she handed Isabel a woven drawstring pouch. Isabel sat up slightly to open it. Inside she saw her worry dolls.

"I haven't used these since I was little," Isabel said, emptying the pouch's contents into her hand. They had been her mother's worry dolls. She still remembered when her mother had given them to her. It had been the night of a terrible thunderstorm, and Isabel hadn't been able to sleep from all the noise. Her mother had told her that she had only to whisper her worries to a doll and place it under her pillow. The doll would take away her worry while she slept.

Isabel lay back down, still clutching the dolls. She heard Abish softly call good night before she left. Isabel realized that she had more worries than she did dolls. She thought of Ammon and how he'd been unable to sleep after he'd seen the jaguar leap through the fire. Isabel feared sleep would elude her as well with all the jaguars surrounding her.

7

Early the next morning the chief servant came to Ammon and Jeremias's hut to make assignments. The servant sent Jeremias to clean out the animal pens again, but Jeremias didn't seem to mind. Ammon couldn't help but notice the happy tunes Jeremias hummed and the way his face lit up when he received his task. Ammon had to assume there was a woman, because only a woman had the power to make such a fool of a man—as he knew from personal experience.

The chief servant informed Ammon that King Lamoni desired to see him. Ammon arrived at the throne room in time to see several black-sashed priests being dismissed. They carried books and scrolls, and Ammon wondered what information they had been required to share.

He sensed Isabel in the room, and sneaking a glance at a group of women doing embroidery, he saw her there. She flushed when she saw him and promptly pricked her finger with a needle. Ammon bit the inside of his cheek to keep from grinning. The princess shot him an exasperated look and bent her head back down.

"I am told that yesterday you traveled a distance to fetch water for my cook and that you did not try to leave." King Lamoni's voice boomed out, and Ammon turned his attention to the king.

"As I said earlier, my wish is to stay here with you and your people. I have no plans to leave," Ammon replied. Something felt off. He noticed that everyone else in the room avoided looking at him.

"Today I want you to watch over my flocks at the waters of Sebus."

Why had the king felt it necessary to give him this task here in the throne room? Surely the king's chief servant could have conveyed this information.

"And then what would you like me to do once I have finished with that?"

The king looked startled for only a moment before his composure returned. "You can come back to feed the animals and prepare my chariot for the journey to my father's lands. You may report to me when this is done."

Ammon had heard that King Lamoni's father, King Laman, had planned a tournament and feast of his own on a much larger scale than the one King Lamoni had just given. Many of the king's guests had already departed for King Laman's lands, although some remained to journey with King Lamoni. Like Mahlon.

He was glad that Mahlon was not in the throne room this morning. After all he had witnessed last night, Ammon wanted Mahlon to stay far away from Isabel and her family. He didn't trust Mahlon. Abish had mentioned that Mahlon was Isabel's cousin, and Ammon suspected that this was the only reason the man's presence was tolerated.

King Lamoni spoke to some of his men while Ammon waited to be dismissed. Thinking of Mahlon reminded Ammon of the jaguar gift last night. He briefly wondered where it was before he recalled Isabel's reaction to the cat. He knew that some warriors and nobility liked to keep jaguars as pets, but Ammon had seen that such a predator could never truly be tamed. It might lash out at any moment. It was not at all the sort of gift you'd give to someone you hoped to court.

Ammon's gaze wandered back over to Isabel, who had been watching him. Ammon smiled at her, and she ducked her head again. Ammon could see her lips moving as she muttered angrily to herself.

The king finally told Ammon he had permission to leave. Ammon found the other servants waiting near the stables. The calls and cries of the king's many animals made conversation impossible; the turkeys gobbled loudly, the peccaries grunted and squeaked, the kinkajous whistled as they jumped in their cages, and the green and scarlet parrots squawked and called out words they had learned. If they sounded bad, they smelled worse. Ammon put the back of his hand over his nose to ward off the stench—a mixture of spoiled food, manure, and the combined animal scents.

He saw Jeremias happily mucking out pens. A young woman bringing water to the servants who labored with the animals caught Jeremias's eye and gave him a shy smile before she moved on. Ammon sighed. He knew it.

Jeremias at least had the decency to look embarrassed when he saw Ammon. But Ammon didn't have time to speak with his cousin, as the peccary herd he was to help watch over was led out of their pen.

The sun shone brightly in a clear blue sky, but Ammon would have been able to follow the peccaries even without the light. As a group they emitted a pungent, musky scent that would have made it possible for Ammon to find them anywhere, anytime. But as they moved away from the palace grounds toward the waters, the smell became more manageable.

The peccaries moved at a maddeningly slow pace. From experience, Ammon knew that peccaries were causal, unhurried creatures—unless frightened or threatened. For instance, when your twin brother had the idea of letting a small pack of peccaries loose in your sister's bedroom. He'd had no idea peccaries could run that fast.

But Ammon didn't mind the time it took and enjoyed watching the animals. The adults were dark gray in color with mottled black striping along their backs, while the young ones ranged in color from russet to a yellowish brown. The peccaries continuously bumped their long snouts against one another and called out in raspy bleats and grunts to each other.

The animals knew where the waters were and naturally went in that direction. Ammon and the others could not have hurried them along to their destination, as neither the Nephites nor the Lamanites had ever figured out how to tame or domesticate these creatures. Peccaries could be far too aggressive when provoked. But that didn't stop anyone from trying to keep and fatten up the flocks. Ammon had passed through many villages where the people laid maize kernels outside of the city to encourage deer, turkeys, and peccaries to come close enough to be caught.

Ammon had noted that once peccaries had been fed by humans and become accustomed to them, the animals lost their fear and tended to ignore the people around them.

As Ammon traveled through high grasses and pink-and-purple wildflowers in mountain meadows toward the waters of Sebus, the wildlife of the forest sounded muted and far off. Here the only sounds were a gentle breeze that blew the long grass, and the call of the peccaries talking to one another.

Ammon heard the waters before he saw them. It wasn't too long before they came upon a small, clear lake with a spring bubbling up in the middle of it. The lake had several offshoot streams that led the water away from the center. On the opposite side of the lake Ammon saw many other large flocks of animals, flocks that included deer, peccaries, and turkeys. Lamanite servants that Ammon didn't recognize tended these flocks. Ammon waved his arm in a greeting, but no one returned it.

The peccaries spread out to look for grubs and roots and to drink from the waters. Ammon grinned. It was a perfect spot for reflection and meditation. He would have to bring his scriptures here to read when he had a free moment.

He thought back to earlier that morning when he and Jeremias had studied the scriptures before setting out for their daily tasks, as was their custom. A desire to share what he had read that morning seized him, and Ammon approached one of his fellow peccary watchers.

"Beautiful day, isn't it?"

"There's nothing good about it," the man snapped gruffly before he walked away.

Ammon felt his spirits flag in the face of yet another rejection. He tried to remember to stay positive. Sometimes he felt overwhelmed with doubts and fears. There was a dark voice at the edge of his consciousness that whispered that he should just go home, that he would have no success here, that he wouldn't touch anyone's life for the better. Sometimes it seemed too hard.

He had known it would be hard. He had done everything he

could to prepare for this mission, but he still had moments like this where it felt as if everything was conspiring against him.

At times like these Ammon recalled the words of the Lord's promise to him, that if he would be patient and long-suffering in his afflictions and be a good example, the Lord would make Ammon an instrument in His hands.

He had to trust. And try again—if for no other reason than the love he felt for the Lamanites in Ishmael. His father had been right—he did love those he served. And Ammon would never turn his back on someone he loved. He decided he should take advantage of his current situation. Here he was isolated with the other servants, their only task being to watch over the animals. He had a chance to get to know them better, to befriend them.

Smiling, Ammon approached a young man barely out of boyhood. The young man sat on the ground in a heap with a decidedly sad face.

"Is everything all right?" Ammon asked.

The boy looked up at him, blinked several times, and then asked, "What did you do to make the king mad?"

The sense of unease—the growing dread—he had felt that morning with the king returned. Ammon wanted to ignore the feeling, but this time he couldn't. This was a warning, and he knew it.

"I didn't do anything that I'm aware of," Ammon said in reply. He looked around him, across the lake to the foothills behind it that blocked his view. The landscape made him uneasy; an enemy could attack them and they wouldn't even see it coming.

The young man gave a hoarse laugh. "You don't have to know what you did to end up here—we're all dead men."

Now Ammon really looked at the other servants with him. They all shared the young man's miserable expression, as if they expected something horrible to happen and didn't plan on being able to stop it. They were men who had given up.

Ammon quickly assessed the situation. He was in an unfamiliar, flat, open place that he could not defend. His fellow servants did not look as if they were willing or able to fight. And he had no weapons.

For the first time Ammon temporarily regretted the decision he'd made to bring only hunting weapons to the Lamanite lands. Ammon and Jeremias had wanted to show the Lamanites they had come in peace. All Ammon had with him now was his sling and a hunting knife.

"Something's going to happen, isn't it?" Ammon prompted.

The young man stared blankly ahead and didn't respond. Ammon scanned the area for a weapon. Plenty of stones surrounded the lake—more than enough ammunition for his sling. He hated that he didn't know what to prepare against. A dangerous animal? The flocks would certainly serve as an attraction for predators. Soldiers? Thieves? Ammon looked back across the lake. Were those servants over there also at risk?

There. Ammon found a servant near him who had a long drawstring pouch that held a sword. The presence of a real weapon eased his mind somewhat. He might be able to fight off whatever danger existed long enough for one of the other servants to run back and get help.

"We have to stand together. We can fight." Ammon hoped he sounded more confident than he felt.

"You don't understand," the man said in a broken voice as he looked up at Ammon. "The king sent all of us here to die."

* * *

Isabel's mind wandered from one subject to the next as she deliberately tried to do anything except think of Ammon.

She sighed, giving up. Perhaps a change in scenery would help. She put her embroidery on the ground and walked over to the open gallery that overlooked the large western courtyard. When not in attendance to her father in the throne room, the courtiers gathered here in the courtyard to gossip and enjoy the sun's rays.

And there was always something new to gossip about. Isabel had felt gratitude when the gossip had stopped being about her. The days immediately after Ammon's rejection had been almost more than she could endure.

Isabel stood behind a column to stay in the shade it provided. From her vantage point, she saw King Lamoni with his chief captain. Her father's face looked intent, serious. Curious, Isabel moved closer to them. Neither man took notice of her.

"Mahlon grows bolder, my king," the captain said. "I think it will not be much longer until he challenges you outright. And if he has your father's blessing to do so . . ."

The captain's words trailed off. The expression on King Lamoni's face did not change and Isabel felt an overwhelming wave of panic. While she didn't have the particulars, just that one statement conveyed everything she needed to know. Mahlon planned on challenging her father for the throne. Mahlon—who had more men, and who had spent most of his life currying her grandfather's favor. In all of her worst-case scenarios, Isabel had never imagined that Mahlon would try to become king by deposing her father.

"I believe the harassment of your flocks to be only his first step," the captain continued.

"He means to embarrass me," King Lamoni said in a voice laced with anger. "The only way I could save my reputation among my people is to put those who herd the flocks to death."

While Isabel had heard that the servants who watched over the flocks had been put to death, it had never registered in her consciousness as being important. Servants were routinely executed for a variety of offenses, and losing part of the king's flocks seemed as logical a reason as any; it cost the king a great deal of his wealth to be deprived of his animals. Isabel had thought thieves responsible for the loss, but now she realized the truth of the matter. Mahlon and his men meant to make a fool of King Lamoni by publicly stealing his flocks, and the king had shifted the blame from Mahlon to the servants who were charged with the task of protecting the flocks.

But why wouldn't her father respond outright to Mahlon's actions? Why not send his armies to protect the animals? Or at least arm the servants he sent?

Isabel's chest constricted as she realized that her father feared Mahlon. If King Lamoni sent soldiers or ordered the servants to defend the flocks, it would be tantamount to declaring war against Mahlon.

Mahlon would win, and her father knew it.

And the king also could not afford to publicly acknowledge that Mahlon was stronger or that he feared his nephew. He had to retain his people's respect and belief in the king's own near divinity. Otherwise they would overthrow Lamoni themselves.

"Are you sure they will scatter the flocks again today at the waters of Sebus?" Isabel heard her father ask.

"I am certain of it," the captain replied.

"Hmm . . . well, so are the priests. I had them read the charts, and they proclaimed today to be the most auspicious day for me to change the fate of my kingdom."

"That is why you sent the Nephite?"

"Yes. The spy will be killed and perhaps aid in frustrating Mahlon."

Isabel's mouth went dry. Her father had deliberately sent Ammon. If Mahlon's men did harass the flocks today, one of two things would happen. Either Ammon would manage to kill some of Mahlon's men, as he had earlier bragged himself capable of doing, and then get killed in retaliation. Or Ammon would do nothing, and when he returned without the flocks, Lamoni would put Ammon to death.

And if Ammon did manage to take some of Mahlon's men with him in a fight, her father could simply shrug the entire situation off while privately enjoying the disrespect to Mahlon. Certainly Mahlon would discover that her father had personally given Ammon his task, but how could King Lamoni be expected to control the actions of one crazy Nephite? Anything Ammon did would reflect only on himself and not on the king. And if Ammon had to be put to death for failing to fulfill his duties, could Ammon's father blame King Lamoni? In one stroke her father had prepared for and guarded against all eventualities.

"One way or another," the king said as the two men moved away, "the Nephite will not be my concern much longer."

Ammon was a spy. He meant to destroy her father's kingdom. Isabel was sure of it.

Or she had been sure of it.

She shook her head. No, she couldn't let herself fall under Ammon's spell. She had to remain vigilant. She should be glad that her father had finally acted so wisely and eliminated the problem.

But all Isabel could think of was how Ammon had so willingly come to her rescue, and the danger he had put himself in to protect her.

Her feet moved of their own volition, and she found herself running from the palace toward the waters of Sebus.

But Isabel didn't know whether she ran to save Ammon or to act as a witness to his destruction.

THE ATTACK HAPPENED SO QUICKLY Ammon had no time to prepare.

One minute Ammon faced toward the city they had just left, wondering if King Lamoni would send guards after them, and the next he was surrounded by a maelstrom of dogs and men.

The dogs barked loudly, and Ammon froze for a moment, unable to react. He shook his head to wipe away the memory. He was no longer a helpless child. He couldn't let the dogs scare him. He had to help the other servants.

But the dogs did not attack Lamoni's servants. Instead, they ran through the flocks, snarling and snapping at the peccaries. The larger male peccaries clattered their teeth and tusks loudly, barking sharply in response. The females and younger peccaries scattered, many into the lake waters where they swam away from the chaotic scene.

Men yelled to further scare the peccaries. Ammon realized they were the ones he had seen across the lake. They had crossed the streams with their dogs and were even now trying to encourage the peccaries to come over to their side.

Ammon called out to them, "What are you doing?"

The men laughed and, having scared the animals, fled back across the streams to their own animals which they had left on the opposite side of the lake.

The men meant to steal King Lamoni's flocks when the ruckus was over. Ammon couldn't help but scowl. It wouldn't happen while he kept watch.

The young man Ammon had spoken to earlier still sat on the ground to Ammon's left. He had not moved at all during the attack.

"Now the king will slay us, just like he did our brethren when their flocks were scattered." The young man began to cry—great big choking sobs that only served to make Ammon angrier with the men across the lake.

All around him King Lamoni's servants wept and cried out over their imminent deaths. Ammon realized that this had happened before. The king's servants had come out here with the peccaries, the animals were scattered and stolen, and King Lamoni had put his servants to death.

Ammon could stop it. He would stop it. Not one of these men would die.

The air around Ammon crackled with an energy he recognized; he was filled with the Spirit. This was it; this was the opportunity he had prayed and fasted for. His heart swelled with an indescribable joy at the chance he would have to show these men the power of the Lord. He would restore the flocks to King Lamoni, and these servants would survive. Surely that, if nothing else, would soften their hearts so they would listen to Ammon and his message. He had come to consider King Lamoni's people his brethren, and just as he would have given his own life for Omner, Himni, or Aaron, he would protect these servants. And now he had the reassurance that the Lord would help him in the course he chose.

Ammon called for the servants, asking them to gather around him. His voice reverberated with joy; it seemed that his fellow servants' curiosity over how he could be so happy with death on the horizon motivated them to join him.

"Do you celebrate our impending deaths?" one of the men asked scornfully.

"No, because none of you will die. We have nothing to worry about. Let's go find the flocks, gather them together, and bring them back here. That way King Lamoni will not slay us."

The look on the servants' faces indicated that this logical idea hadn't occurred to any of them. Perhaps their conviction that they would die had rendered them unable to think of a way out of their situation. Ammon thought his suggestion would be easy enough to execute—the larger male peccaries had stood their ground, and it wouldn't take much to convince the females and younger ones to return to the heads of their flocks.

Ammon and the other servants ran swiftly for the water, where a majority of the animals had fled. They were quick enough and managed to get in front of the peccaries. At the sight of Ammon and King Lamoni's men, the peccaries decided to return to their side of the lake.

The male peccaries called out for the rest of the herd, which encouraged the animals to swim even faster. Ammon and the servants followed behind them to make certain that there were no stragglers.

Not all the peccaries had run for the water, and Ammon and the servants used the animals' distinct scent, now even more prevalent given their fear, to track down the stragglers.

Within an hour they had restored the flocks. Several of the servants cheered; many came over to pat Ammon on the back and thank him. Ammon couldn't stop grinning. This was it. With the Lord's help he had finally done it. He was no longer just an outsider, a stranger to be ignored. The servants treated him like one of them.

He should have known that it would not be that easy.

Ammon heard a commotion behind him. He turned to see the men who had just caused so much heartache returning to finish the job. This time they did not run, as they had already launched one surprise attack and could not hope for another. The men sauntered over as if they had all the time in the world. Their casualness and obvious delight in their wicked intentions further infuriated Ammon. As the men walked, their dogs barked and bared their teeth, straining against the rope leashes their masters had put on them. Ammon could see now that each one of the men heading toward them carried multiple weapons. King Lamoni's servants were as ill-equipped as Ammon for a fight.

"They won't fail this time," the young man whispered at Ammon's elbow.

Ammon shouted for King Lamoni's servants to encircle the flocks so that they wouldn't flee again. The servants rushed to obey his command. Then Ammon went over to the man he had seen with the sword and, without even asking for permission, tugged the drawstring loose and yanked the sword out. He held the weapon up to inspect it. The wooden center was strong and without cracks, and the rectangular obsidian blades encircling the outer edge were adequately sharp. It would do.

"Now what do we do?" one of the servants asked.

"Stay here. I will go and deal with those men."

"Alone?"

"Alone," Ammon confirmed. In addition to the sword he had just appropriated, he pulled his sling out, made sure he had easy access to the hunting knife in his belt, and headed for the lake.

The dogs seemed nearly as tall as the men, though Ammon knew they weren't. He counted five dogs and approximately twenty-five men, although in the commotion earlier he would have sworn they were much greater in number. *I am not a child. I am not afraid.* He had to bite back the fear he told himself he didn't have.

"The Lord promised my father that I would be kept safe," Ammon said quietly to himself as the men and their dogs advanced.

Ammon put the sword down on the ground next to him and picked up a handful of heavy stones from the lake bed. They were smooth, which he knew would make them fly straighter. He stuck them into an open pouch at his waist. "The Lord will deliver me from all danger."

He kept one stone in his hand and fit it into his sling. "Turn back!" Ammon called to the men. None of them stopped. Ammon let the rock fly so that it nicked the ear of the man closest to him.

Ammon sent another rock flying through the air, and another, and another. Each time they whizzed past the men, grazing a scalp or an upper arm. "Those are warning shots!" Ammon called out. "This is your last chance to go back. Next time I won't miss."

The Lamanites laughed at him. "You've missed every shot so far!" one of the men taunted him.

"Turn around and leave this place!" Ammon replied.

The men did stop their advance, but to Ammon's dismay, they halted only to let the dogs loose. The distinct command to "kill" reached Ammon's ears. Apparently the Lamanites had decided that fighting Ammon was beneath them, and they were sending their dogs to finish him. The dogs sprinted for Ammon, the sounds of their heavy panting crushing Ammon's senses. All Ammon could see were five sets of blindingly white, sharp teeth.

Dogs. He clenched his jaw. *It would have to be dogs.*

"I have no reason to fear," he whispered with a mouth that had gone dry.

Ammon retrieved the sword he had left on the ground and put his sling away. He dug his heels into the earth. Here he would make his stand. His heart thumped loudly in his chest, and his breaths came quick and shallow as he prepared for the fight.

"I believe all the words of my father."

Two of the dogs ran faster than the others. They headed straight for Ammon, growling as they came. The two frontrunners got within striking distance and both leapt at him.

Ammon took his sword and swung it with all his might. The sweeping motion hit one of the dogs into the other. The sound of the dogs' skulls crashing together was unmistakable, and they fell to the earth with yelps of pain.

The third dog was nearly on top of him. Not having enough time to swing his sword again, Ammon dropped it to the earth and whipped his hunting knife out of his belt. Ammon crouched down just as third dog jumped at him, then reached up and thrust his knife into the dog's soft belly. He used the dog's momentum to push the dog behind him, where the animal landed with a whimpering thud.

The other two dogs skidded to a halt at the sights and sounds of their fallen friends. Their ears and tails drooped. Instinct overtook training, and the dogs ran away from Ammon, ignoring the calls of their masters.

Ammon stood slowly, trying to control his labored breathing. He had hoped that this defeat would be enough to turn the men back. He saw that it was not to be. The Lamanites were angry with him, though perhaps a little wary after watching Ammon take down the dogs. They pulled out their slings and shot missiles at Ammon.

None of them even came close. Many of the rocks fell just short of him and landed on the ground or in the streams with a thud.

So this was how it would be. One rock whistled past his ear, but Ammon held his ground. He took his own sling out again as a strange calmness overtook him. His limbs stopped shaking, and his breaths now coming easily. A sense of power, of strength, coursed through him. He had given them every chance to turn back.

These would-be robbers and murderers were now responsible for their own fates.

* * *

Isabel had arrived at the waters of Sebus and stopped short when she saw a pack of dogs racing straight toward Ammon. She'd tried to call out, to warn him somehow, but her throat had closed up on her.

But in a few seconds Ammon had defeated the dogs. She remembered the story he had told her of his fear of dogs and could only wonder at his ability to face and dispatch them so quickly.

Now a band of men shot at Ammon with slings. There had to be at least two dozen of them. And all of them were slinging rocks at Ammon. One man could never overcome so many. Isabel took a single step forward and then fell to her knees. They would hit Ammon with their rocks, and once he had been knocked down, they would finish him off with their swords. Ammon would die, and she could do nothing to stop it.

Those were Mahlon's men. She recognized the two brothers who acted as Mahlon's second in command, Mocum and Mulek. Mahlon had once punished them horribly. But he'd spared their lives, telling them that since they shared one brain, they could share one set of eyes. Both men had mirror scars on their respective missing eyes. The brothers were as vicious and horrible as Mahlon.

Ammon wouldn't survive.

Isabel tried to stand back up but found that she had no strength. Some distant part of her mind finally registered her terror. She didn't want Ammon to die. But Mahlon's men would slaughter him.

With great surprise, Isabel found herself crying. She let the tears burn a path down her cheeks.

Her eyes fixed on Ammon as rocks rained down around him. She only saw him from behind back, but nothing in his posture indicated that he was afraid.

"Run," she whispered. "Run, Ammon."

It was what any sensible person would have done. The odds were too overwhelming.

But Ammon didn't run.

Instead he pulled out his sling and fit it with a rock. With precise movements, Ammon whipped the sling around and sent the stone soaring.

The rock found its mark, and one of Mahlon's men fell to the ground.

Ammon let loose another rock. He didn't hesitate. He didn't slow down. And every rock felled one of Mahlon's men.

The men Ammon struck were not merely injured. They were dead. Even from this distance Isabel could see the unmistakable stillness of death settle on them. It didn't make sense. Warriors used slings to immobilize or disable. She had never known anyone capable of using a sling to take a foe completely out of the battle.

How was Ammon able to do it? How did he know where to hit them? How could anyone be that strong, that accurate? She had the slightly hysterical thought that Ammon had not been lying when he said that he never missed with his sling.

Six Lamanites fell before Mahlon's men realized that Ammon would pick them off one by one. So they threw their slings down and pulled out their clubs and swords. Then they ran toward Ammon, swearing at him and yelling oaths to take his life.

Isabel's heart beat as hard and fast as a rabbit fleeing a jaguar. She couldn't catch her breath. The ground beneath her seemed to rumble from the men as they ran screaming that they would drink Ammon's blood.

Ammon dropped his sling and calmly picked up his sword. He held still and waited for the coming onslaught.

Isabel wanted to close her eyes. She couldn't watch. They wouldn't all rush him at once—not only did they risk injuring their comrades accidentally, but there would be little honor in a fight where a warrior was so obviously outnumbered. But they would tire Ammon out one by one. He would only be able to hold on for so long.

Just as Isabel had expected, Mahlon's men came at Ammon one man at a time. Isabel gasped on the first man raised his club above his head, and Ammon smote off the arm holding the weapon. The man's arm fell to the earth as he howled in pain. Another man stepped forward to avenge his fallen friend, and Ammon blocked the man's swing. So the Lamanite lifted his club to bring it down on Ammon. Another arm fell to the ground.

Every man who lifted his weapon against Ammon soon found himself missing an arm. The air was rent with the shrieks and cries of those who found themselves literally disarmed.

"Enough!" one of the missing-eye brothers called out. He stepped forward. It was Mocum. "I will finish this Nephite," he growled.

In one hand, Mocum held a sword in front of him. Ammon didn't move as Mocum stepped into the circle surrounding them. Isabel felt indignation at Mocum's cowardice, waiting until Ammon was too worn out to fight back. But when she looked at Ammon, he didn't seem tired. Ammon had turned to watch the leader, and Isabel saw his profile. Ammon held perfectly still as Mocum taunted him, making jabs in the air with his weapon to provoke Ammon into making a mistake.

But Ammon simply waited and watched while Mocum circled him. Mocum darted around Ammon, intending to attack him from behind. Ammon seemed to have expected this and turned quickly with his sword in front of him to block the blow. Ammon pushed Mocum away with great force.

Isabel could see that Ammon said something to the other man, but she couldn't hear it. Ammon let his sword drift down to his side. She wondered what Ammon was doing. He pointed toward the hills. Did he plan on letting the other men leave?

But Mocum ran at Ammon again, and Isabel heard the sound of wood cracking on wood. He swung wildly at Ammon, who met each hit with careful exactness.

It was like watching a child trying to fight his father. Isabel knew that Mahlon's men had extensive battle training and were all experienced warriors, but there was nothing Mocum could do to get past Ammon's defenses. Ammon moved too quickly, almost too fast for Isabel to track.

And while Mocum looked to be weakening, Ammon still showed no signs of fatigue as he fended off all of the Lamanite leader's advances.

Again and again their swords met, and Ammon deflected each thrust, each lunge, much to Mocum's great frustration. Ammon pushed him off again, and Mocum yelled something angrily at Ammon. Isabel heard the words "kill everyone." Ammon's countenance immediately changed at Mocum's words. Mocum ran at Ammon with his sword held overhead. Ammon raised his sword in response and turned his weapon so that the obsidian blades sunk into the wooden base of his enemy's sword. The swords stuck together, and, before Mocum could react, Ammon reached up and grabbed the other man's wrist.

Ammon tugged his own sword loose and threw it to the ground. He pulled Mocum's arm across his body so that the other man was forced to bend at the waist. With his now-free hand, Ammon grabbed the hilt of the leader's sword and yanked it from the man's grasp.

Isabel saw Ammon swipe the sharp edge of the sword across Mocum's stomach and watched as the man fell down in a crumpled heap.

Mahlon's men stood in silence until Ammon turned to face them. Isabel could see that with their leader now conquered, they believed the gods were on Ammon's side. Mahlon's men must have displeased the gods somehow. Having chosen Ammon, the gods would ensure that the other warriors lost their lives.

So Mahlon's men did the only thing they could. They fled.

Ammon stood still, holding Mocum's sword at his side. He didn't chase after the fleeing Lamanites, as another might have. Instead he let them go. But he did not give up his vigil until each man had run over the foothills and out of sight. Still Ammon waited—perhaps, Isabel thought, to make certain that they wouldn't return. She couldn't imagine that they would.

She didn't know how much time had passed, but her legs had gone numb. Ammon finally turned, and Isabel could see blood all over him. He had been hurt!

Isabel tried to stand, but the pricking and tingling sensation in her legs was too painful for her to move. She looked around for spider webbing to stop up his cuts.

But as she watched Ammon move easily to the lake and begin to wash himself, she realized that Ammon had not been injured. The blood she saw on him was from the other men.

Her legs felt normal again, and where a moment ago she had wanted to run to him and care for his wounds, a different feeling now overcame her. Isabel swallowed several times, trying to push the overwhelming despair down.

She had thought Mahlon to be the greatest threat to her father's kingdom.

But a man who could do what Ammon had done, who could fight the way he had and emerge unscathed from such a battle, was a man to be feared. Her father's kingdom was lost. He was a man who could destroy them all.

Isabel had to warn her father.

9

ISABEL TRUDGED BACK TO HER father's palace. Her feet felt as if she had waded through knee-deep mud. She hadn't left right when she'd intended to. She had stayed to see what Ammon would do next.

Was he even human? How could he be? No man could do the things he had just done. Isabel didn't know what she had expected to see—her mind filled with the possibilities of how he might further show his power.

But in this Ammon had disappointed her. After he'd rinsed himself off, he'd returned to the servants and the peccaries. The animals had nervously watered themselves, and when they'd had their fill, they turned of their own accord to return to the king's pastures.

The other servants had avoided Ammon, who, for the first time, seemed weary. He sat down and put one hand against his forehead as if it were too heavy for him to support without help. She saw that Ammon didn't notice when some of the servants went back to the site of Ammon's battle to collect the arms that lay all over the ground. From here they looked like misshapen branches. It jarred Isabel to remember exactly what they were and what they represented.

The servants must have intended to bring the arms back to her father. Isabel saw the logic in that—how else would they convince anyone of this tale? They now had the proof they would need.

When the animals left, so did Isabel. She did not follow Ammon and the servants any further. She wanted to go to her father's throne room so that she could corroborate the story the servants were sure to tell.

Only now did Isabel begin to consider the possible outcomes of this revelation. Would her people have to leave? Or would they stay with Ammon as their king? Was he some sort of otherworldly being that would require the Lamanites to worship him?

It felt strange to even think it. The Ammon she had come to know was very much just a man. An annoying, teasing, and exasperating sort of man—a man that she had suspected of harboring treasonous plans, but still a man. *One man?*

But Ammon was not here alone. She thought of Ammon's brothers, how they had spread throughout the Lamanite kingdoms. Were they as dangerous as Ammon? Would the entire Lamanite nation fall? Her steps faltered, but she forced herself to push on. Her father must be told, even if it was too late for any of them.

Isabel felt as if she stood at the edge of a great precipice with the wind howling all around her, pushing her closer and closer to the edge. It would only be a matter of time until she plunged over the side, never to be the same again. The change was here. It was the way she had felt the night before her mother died. She wasn't sure how she had known it would be her mother's last day, but she had known. Just as she now knew that everything in her life, in all of their lives, was about to change forever.

She wrapped her hands around her upper arms to ward off the chill that overtook her. It surprised Isabel to find herself at the palace, and she made her way to where she knew her father would be.

Upon entering the main throne room, she plodded toward her father's dais. The conversations around her went silent, and courtiers stared at her as she passed.

King Lamoni and Queen Kamilah rose with mirror expressions of alarm upon seeing Isabel. "Daughter!" her father called out with more concern than she had ever heard from him. "What is it?"

Isabel realized that she must look the way she felt. "Ammon."

Her father seemed to relax a bit at that one word. "Is he dead?" he asked.

"No, not dead," Isabel whispered. Why was it so cold in here? Didn't anyone else seem to feel it?

"Not dead?" King Lamoni's voice sounded strangled. "What do you mean not dead? And where are my flocks?"

She stopped moving as her teeth began to chatter. Her hands felt cold and clammy. Her heart started pulsing quickly in her chest, and her breathing became rapid and shallow. She closed her eyes as the image of Ammon fighting Mahlon's men returned to her. All of her strength seemed to leave her in that moment as the enormity of what this meant settled firmly on her. Isabel was only vaguely aware of Kamilah ordering a blanket to be brought for Isabel and a fire to be built. She felt the soft material being wrapped around her and opened her eyes long enough to see that Kamilah was leading her toward the fire.

Her father followed behind them, demanding that Isabel explain herself. Kamilah managed to quietly defuse Lamoni's anxiety while tending to Isabel. "There will be time for that in a moment. Let her collect herself."

Isabel let Kamilah administer to her as if she were still a child who needed a mother. Kamilah said soothing things and brushed the loose hair from Isabel's face. She struggled against the inviting warmth, against simply closing her eyes and sleeping. Perhaps she would awake later and find that this had all been a dream. But she could not sleep yet. She still had to warn her father. "Send for the servants," Isabel croaked softly to Kamilah.

Kamilah seemed to understand the importance of this statement and relayed the information to her husband.

King Lamoni called out for the servants who had watched over the flocks to be brought to him. Ripples of excitement filled the room, and Isabel knew that those around her anticipated another round of executions. Those people were about to be greatly disappointed.

The servants arrived, all except Ammon. Where was Ammon? Isabel wondered. Why hadn't he come with the others? She felt an inexplicable need to see him, to rest her fingers against his upper arm to reassure herself that what she had seen earlier could not have really happened, that Ammon was a real person and that she was just being foolish.

But, the servants entered carrying large blankets. With a sinking sensation in her stomach, Isabel knew what they contained. Her father paced across his dais as the servants recounted the tale of Ammon's success against the would-be robbers and how he had single-handedly protected all of the king's animals. Their words overlapped and rose in chaotic confusion as many tried to tell the fantastic story of how Ammon had saved them from the punishment of death.

Isabel shut her eyes again when the servants let their blankets fall open to prove their report. She heard the gasps and cries of the courtiers and felt Kamilah stiffen next to her.

She opened her eyes to see her father's mouth drop open, his eyes widening in disbelief at the gruesome evidence. He took a single step down the dais and stopped. "Surely this is more than a man." Her father went silent for several minutes and then said, almost to himself, "He was opposed to the death of my servants . . . Could he be the Great Spirit, who sends a punishment on this people because of their murders?" Her father's thoughts followed her own, but Isabel hadn't considered the possibility that Ammon might be *the* Great Spirit.

Her grandfather had spoken to her about the Great Spirit, just as her father had. And while it was clear that both men respected and believed in this being, the king still had absolute power in his kingdom. Everything he did was right and just, because he was king. But if Ammon was the Great Spirit . . . He had said he did not like the killings in this kingdom. What if her father wasn't always right? What if there would be consequences for his actions? Isabel trembled again to think of what Ammon could do to her father.

A scraggly, unkempt man whom Isabel had seen speaking with Ammon before the fight stepped forward. He kept his eyes pointed respectfully downward, as if he feared to look directly at his king. "We spent much of the day discussing this. Whether he is the Great Spirit or a man, we don't know, but this much we do know, that he can't be slain by the enemies of the king; neither can they scatter the king's flocks when he is with us because of his skill and great strength. We do know that he is a friend to the king." From the man's intonation, Isabel knew he wasn't done speaking. The last part had been said as a reassurance, a softening blow that was yet to come. The servant cleared his throat, glancing up once before looking down again. "Yet we do not believe that a man could have such great power, for we know he cannot be killed."

King Lamoni considered this testimony. Moving to sit, he did not choose his cushions but sat on his formal throne. Isabel focused on the stone bench attached to the floor and the wall painted in shades of red and white. The glory that surrounded her father might end. King Lamoni tapped his fingers against his leg. Isabel thought it looked like the feathers in his headdress were shaking slightly.

"Now I know that it is the Great Spirit, and He has come down to preserve your lives, that I might not slay you as I did your brethren." Her father spoke quietly, a slight tremor in his voice. Isabel could only hear him because the rest of the room had gone still at the servant's revelation.

She also saw something she had never seen before—a look of absolute terror in her father's eyes. If the Great Spirit had come to punish him for putting all those servants to death . . . Isabel couldn't finish the thought.

"Where is this man that has such great power?" King Lamoni asked. The servants exchanged glances until finally one spoke. "He is feeding your animals and preparing your chariot."

Isabel's thoughts flashed back to that morning when her father had personally given the instruction. Ammon had been told to watch the flocks and then to prepare for the journey to King Lamoni's land of Nephi to attend her grandfather's tournament and feast. After what had happened, Isabel would never have expected Ammon to still fulfill his tasks. He had done something spectacular, and yet he still worked as if nothing out of the ordinary had happened.

King Lamoni seemed equally astonished. "Surely there has not been servant among all my servants as faithful as this man. He remembers all of my commandments and executes them."

Isabel winced at the king's choice of the word *execute,* as she feared that was exactly what would happen to her father when Ammon arrived. For surely Ammon would arrive soon. Her father had told Ammon to report to him once his tasks had been completed. And as Ammon did the jobs previously assigned to him even now, it seemed unlikely that he would fail to carry out the final request.

Murmurs spread throughout the room, and Isabel heard one of the soldiers say, "Can he really be the Great Spirit?"

King Lamoni must have heard as well, for he replied, "I know that this is the Great Spirit." He paused again for a long while before finally saying, "I want him to come to me, but I don't dare send for him."

Isabel understood all too well the panic in her father's voice. She too wanted Ammon to come, to give an explanation that would help all of this make some sort of sense, but another part of her wanted him to stay far away, because she was terrified of what he might do. To her father. To all of them.

But she knew he would come. They could only wait. And worry.

* * *

Other than the peccaries, Ammon found himself alone. The other servants had all disappeared after the animals had been taken back to the pasture.

Ammon had moved on to his other chores to ready the king's animals and chariot for the journey to the land of Nephi for King Laman's feast. It was another task he performed alone. Part of him wondered where everyone else had gone.

He had the sensation of being tired and weary, yet he did not feel this physically. It was more of an emotional or even spiritual exhaustion. Ammon tried not to recall the events of the day. He wondered what he had set in motion. Surely there would be some sort of retribution for his actions. Would King Lamoni be angry? From what little he had been able to gather from the other servants, the robbers had been acting on behalf of someone powerful. Had Ammon caused unnecessary trouble for the king? Not to mention the fact that he had thwarted the king's plans—King Lamoni had intended to slay them for losing the peccaries. What would he do when he found his flocks intact?

Ammon did not doubt that the part he had played would be told to the king. Perhaps the servants would try to save their own lives by giving up Ammon's. He sighed. It was a risk he'd been willing to take earlier that day and one that he was still willing to take. His father had always taught them that while they could control their actions and decisions, they could not control the consequences of their choices. Ammon had only his faith to sustain him, the belief that the Lord would keep His promise to protect him.

He heard someone calling his name. Ammon looked up to see Jeremias hopping toward him, his hands behind his back. Ammon ran to his cousin, realizing with a sick feeling that the Lord's promise had been extended only to the sons of Mosiah. Nothing had been said about those that traveled with them. Now he could see that Jeramias had been tied up, which spurred Ammon to go faster.

Ammon pulled out his hunting knife and first cut the ropes behind Jeremias's back before getting the ones around his ankles. "Who did this to you?"

"I don't know. I was collecting manure, which, as you know, is one of my favorite tasks," Jeremias began wryly as he rubbed his wrists, "and two soldiers grabbed me and tied me up. They told me they were taking me to the prison. When I asked why, I got a fist in the face as an answer. We got as far as the palace before another soldier came running up to them with some sort of news, and the three left together. Then I came to find you." He clasped Ammon on the shoulder. "I'm very glad you're not dead. I thought you had gone and gotten yourself killed."

"The day is still young." Ammon grinned back. His smile quickly faltered when he realized the danger he had put Jeremias in. Ammon considered telling Jeremias to leave and return to Zarahemla, but he knew Jeremias wouldn't. Ammon resolved to keep his cousin close to him from now on. Unfortunately, that might mean putting Jeremias in more danger when Ammon went to report to the king as he was supposed to.

Ammon explained to Jeremias all that had happened that day, telling him of the political situation he had created, and what he now thought the king might do.

Since Jeremias seemed confused about the reason he had been tied up, Ammon explained that the king had meant to execute Ammon and the other servants, so the king must have decided to execute Jeremias along with Ammon.

Jeremias's eyes widened at this revelation.

"Or else they tied you up because they were afraid you'd want revenge as soon as you saw my dead body."

This made Jeremias relax and grin. "They don't know me very well, do they?"

Ammon shared in the humorous but fleeting moment before telling Jeremias the rest. "I have to go see King Lamoni. But you don't have to—"

"Then I will go with you."

Ammon didn't need to ask if Jeremias knew what he was committing to. He could see that Jeremias understood the seriousness of the situation. "Why?"

"Your fate is my fate. It has been since the day I cast my lot with yours."

Ammon gulped once, swallowing back the emotions that threatened to overwhelm him. "You have always been a good friend to me."

"Yes, I have," Jeremias said with a smile. "Now let's go face what the king has planned for us. I'm sure we'll be fine."

"Are you trying to convince you or me?" Ammon asked as they walked toward the palace.

"You. One of us should go into this meeting not completely terrified."

There were no guards at the entrance to the palace. Nor did Ammon see any servants. It struck him as very strange, and caused his uneasy feeling to increase tenfold. He again thought about trying to convince Jeremias to leave, but he knew the determined look on his cousin's face too well.

They arrived at the king's throne room. A sea of people stood between the south entrance and the king. In addition to the usual courtiers, musicians, poets, entertainers, scribes, artisans, relatives of the king, soldiers, and priests, Ammon saw many of the servants he served with. Everyone turned when Ammon arrived. He took a tentative step into the completely silent room. People stepped aside, creating a path from the doorway to the king.

King Lamoni sat so still, he almost looked like one of his statues in the marketplace. He looked at Ammon, and Ammon knew something had changed. The expression on his face . . . Ammon didn't know what it meant. The king's eyes flickered over to Jeremias, and Ammon stepped in front of his cousin. Obviously the king knew what Ammon had done. It seemed as if everyone knew what Ammon had done. Ammon quickly decided to leave. He could deal with the king at another time—alone, to keep Jeremias from any further harm.

"Let's go," Ammon murmured to Jeremias. He turned to leave, but one of the king's highest-ranking servants approached him. "Rabbanah."

Ammon looked behind him to see who the servant addressed.

"I think he's talking to you," Jeremias whispered.

"Rabbanah, the king desires you to stay."

Now he would have to stay. If the king desired it, Ammon had to do it. To walk out now would be more than just insulting. It would be an act of open defiance and rebellion against the king's power and position.

Ammon ventured further into the room with Jeremias close behind him. He walked to the king, made a slight bow, and asked, "What would you like me to do, my king?"

Ammon waited for a response. And waited. And waited.

He shifted his weight from one leg to the other. He folded his arms across his chest for a while, let them fall loosely to his sides for a bit, and then clasped them behind his back. He refrained from rocking back and forth on the balls of his feet as he had done when a child.

Something obviously perturbed the king. Ammon could see that King Lamoni was struggling—but with what, Ammon didn't know. He hadn't been acquainted with the king long enough to accurately interpret his moods and feelings. Obviously it must have something to do with what had occurred at the waters of Sebus. Was he trying to decide on a proper punishment? Would he ask Ammon to give his own accounting of the events?

At first his sense of dread and concern for Jeremias's sake consumed him and made him impatient. But as the time went on, Ammon felt a peace that he knew came from only one source. He smiled, welcoming the feeling of knowing that he was not alone.

To determine the position of the sun, Ammon glanced between the pillars that opened onto a large courtyard. Nearly an hour had passed since he had entered this room.

No one around him spoke. No one even moved.

How long would this go on?

"What do you desire of me?" Ammon asked again, feeling a prompting to engage the king.

He wouldn't have thought it possible, but the room went even quieter. Ammon knew the protocol he had just breached. Having already addressed the king, it was his responsibility as a lesser to wait for the king to acknowledge him and respond. But he had felt the prompting, so he had to have faith in the risk he had taken.

The air around him began to hum with the crowd's unspoken anticipation. This was why he had come to Ishmael. This was why he had left behind his family, friends, and his responsibilities, why he had willingly placed himself in harm's way.

Ammon could feel that something important was about to happen.

10

ISABEL HAD FINALLY STOPPED SHIVERING. Kamilah had stayed close by her side, her arms still around Isabel's shoulders. But for once, she didn't mind. She let Kamilah offer her comfort as they watched Ammon addressing her father.

When Ammon spoke to King Lamoni a second time, Isabel almost gasped in shock. Her father would have killed other men for such impertinence.

As Ammon calmly stood there, he seemed different to her. Not just because of what she had witnessed earlier, but because there was a confidence she had never seen before. He'd always seemed sure of himself, bordering on arrogant most of the time, but this was . . . different. She couldn't think of another word to describe it.

Despite Ammon speaking again, her father still didn't answer. Ammon bowed his head slightly, closing his eyes. After a few more minutes, Ammon raised his head and said, "Is it because you have heard that I defended your servants and your flocks, and slew seven of their brethren with the sling and sword, and cut off the arms of others? Is this what causes you to marvel? Why are you so amazed? I am a man, and I am your servant. So whatever you desire which is right, I will do it."

Her father looked shocked. "Who are you?" The king's voice came out raspy, as if he had forgotten how to talk. "Are you the Great Spirit, who knows all things?"

Ammon smiled. "I am not."

"How do you know the thoughts of my heart? You may speak boldly and tell me concerning these things, and also tell me how you smote off the arms of our brothers that scattered the flocks."

This was something Isabel desperately wanted to know as well. What power did Ammon possess? He had just said that he was only a man, but he had done things beyond mortal abilities. If it was something that could be taught, if Ammon could teach her father how to wield that kind of power, the king would no longer have to worry about Mahlon or any Lamanite king again. They would be safe.

"If you will tell me these things, I will give you whatever you desire. I will even guard you with my armies—though I know you are more powerful than all of them. But, still, I will grant you anything you desire," King Lamoni said. He looked earnest and a bit excited at the prospect of learning the secret of Ammon's gifts.

For the first time, Ammon's eyes flickered over to Isabel. She held her breath as his eyes seemed to see right through her as if she could have no secrets from him. Her father had just offered Ammon anything. Could he . . . would he . . . ask for her?

As her heart hammered in her throat, Ammon looked away. No, he would not ask for her. He hadn't wanted her before. Why would he want her now? And more to the point, why was she disappointed?

"Will you listen to my words if I tell you by what power I do these things? This is all I would desire of you."

King Lamoni straightened up. "Yes, I will believe all of your words."

Ammon looked down for a second and Isabel saw a fleeting smile that disappeared when he answered the king. "Do you believe that there is a God?"

"I do not know what that means," her father replied, his eyebrows knit in confusion.

"Do you believe there is a Great Spirit?"

"Yes."

"This is God. Do you believe that this Great Spirit, who is God, created all things which are in heaven and in the earth?"

The king nodded. "Yes, I believe that He created all things which are in the earth, but I do not know the heavens."

"The heavens is a place where God dwells with all his holy angels."

"Is it above the earth?"

"Yes." Ammon smiled. "And He looks down upon all the children of men, and He knows all the thoughts and intents of the heart; for by His hand were all things created from the beginning."

The people in the room moved closer to Ammon and the king. Isabel dropped the blanket that she had been holding on to. She shrugged off Kamilah's arms and stood. Isabel was only vaguely aware of Abish entering the room and whispering to the queen that her youngest daughter needed her. Kamilah tried to say something to Isabel, but Isabel didn't listen. She walked toward Ammon. There was something so compelling in Ammon's voice, something that made her want to get closer so that she could hear him better.

"I believe all the things which you have spoken." King Lamoni's voice had become stronger, surer. "Are you sent from God?"

"I am a man," Ammon reassured her father again. "And man, in the beginning, was created after the image of God, and I am called by His Holy Spirit to teach these things to this people, that they might find knowledge of that which is just and true."

The crowd that had moved near Ammon stayed an arm's length away, keeping a respectful distance. Isabel stood there with them, feeling almost entranced by what Ammon said. She didn't know why it affected her so, why his words seemed so powerful, why they resonated throughout her limbs. They were more than just words.

Ammon explained that it was the Spirit which gave him knowledge and power according to his faith and righteous desires. Then Ammon started at the beginning, recounting the creation of the world and of the first people, Adam and Eve. He told them of the fall and quoted from scriptures and records which he said he possessed, sharing the words of the prophets and even the words of their mutual forefather, Lehi.

Then Ammon spoke of more things Isabel had never heard—how their fathers had traveled in the wilderness, and how they had suffered. Ammon said that her ancestors, the sons of Ishmael, along with Laman and Lemuel, had rebelled against Father Lehi. Ammon recounted all of their rebellions, and while Isabel didn't want to believe him, while this went against everything she had ever been taught, she couldn't help but listen and want to know more. He told of the records he possessed, relaying the histories of both their peoples.

Switching from history to his beliefs, Ammon told them of something called "the plan of redemption" and spoke to them of the Son of God, named Jesus Christ, and told them of God's plans for all of His children.

"I believe you," King Lamoni said suddenly. "I believe your words."

He did?

To Isabel's surprise, her father rose suddenly to his feet and called out, "O Lord, have mercy. According to the mercy you have had upon the people of Nephi, have mercy upon me and my people."

When he finished speaking, King Lamoni collapsed to the floor. Isabel broke through the crowd and rushed over to him. She turned him over and realized that he wasn't breathing. She put her head to his chest. It didn't move, nor could she hear a heartbeat. "We must get him to his bed. Send for the healers and the priests!" Isabel cried out. He couldn't be dead. He couldn't. Isabel didn't know how to live in a world where her father didn't exist. She loved him so much. Giant tears sprang forth, and everything around her shimmered until the tears began to roll down her cheeks. Several of the servants rushed forward to carefully lift King Lamoni and carry him into his bedroom.

Kamilah was in the king's room with Sarala, who appeared to be sick, her face flushed. Kamilah handed the littlest princess to one of the female servants when she saw Isabel's father being brought in. "What happened?" she asked.

Isabel couldn't answer; the tears clogged her throat and made it impossible to speak. The servants laid the king upon his bed and then backed away. Kamilah ran to the king and did as Isabel had done, laying her head on his chest. "Lamoni!" she cried, shaking his shoulders. "Lamoni!"

As Kamilah wailed over her husband, Isabel clapped her hands over her ears. She couldn't stand the pain in Kamilah's voice. Isabel leaned against one of the limestone walls and slowly slid down until she sat in a heap on the floor, her ears still covered.

She felt Naima's arms go around her neck and realized that her brothers and sisters had all come. Isabel pulled the girl into her lap, and Naima's tears wet the front of Isabel's tunic. Isabel mindlessly rocked her, unable to accept what had just happened. One second her father was fine, and in the next, he was dead. It seemed impossible.

The priests and the healers arrived next. The priests performed rituals there in the king's bedchamber, with promises to the queen that they would do more at the temple. The healers administered all kinds of concoctions to the king, putting herbs into his mouth and listening intently to his blood, but nothing seemed to help. They made their deepest apologies to the royal family.

Kamilah sent them away when it became obvious that no one could help King Lamoni.

For the rest of the day, the family kept a vigil at the king's bedside, quietly crying. According to tradition, when night fell they could give full rein to their grief, wailing and mourning loudly. Above the lamentations in the bedchamber, Isabel could hear courtiers in the palace crying for their king.

As the sun rose, the weeping had to be muted once again. Isabel had begun her fast when her father collapsed, as had the rest of her family. She knew that those connected with the family outside the bedchamber would be fasting as well in preparation for the passing of her father's soul.

Several priests came to Kamilah, asking to be given leave to prepare her husband's body for burial. Isabel recalled a few years previous when she'd attended the funeral of one of her cousins, the firstborn heir to her uncle's kingdom. She knew what would happen to her father's body. It would be shrouded and laid on a low table with two candles lit at each end. Ground maize, a special drink, and jewels would be placed in his mouth. He would need to be buried one day after his death in the tomb that he created in the temple.

"Please, my queen. Let us at least gather his scepter and his weapons, the things he will need to be buried with," a priest asked.

Kamilah refused to even look at the young man. "He is not dead. Leave me at once."

Isabel wanted desperately to believe as Kamilah did. Her father's skin felt cold, and he did not seem to be breathing. He didn't move, didn't make any sounds. An overwhelming sadness threatened to consume her. Isabel tried to keep it at bay with denials. Her father was too strong to die. He couldn't leave. They all needed him.

Her thoughts often turned to Ammon. Had he used his powers to cause this to happen? He had told King Lamoni that he was a man and had no special powers. But just by speaking, he had somehow caused her father to collapse and die. For what purpose? She could not understand. She wanted to be angry with Ammon. She wanted to hate him for this. But she found that she couldn't. She did not know if he had done this. Besides that, being angry with Ammon did not lessen the tight pain in her chest.

Abish, in between whatever other duties she had, sat next to Isabel, gripping her hand tightly. Isabel took comfort from Abish's silent strength. At one point Isabel whispered, "Ammon," realizing she needed to know what had happened to him. Any other man would have been immediately put to death for what had occurred.

A strange look crossed Abish's face, one that spoke of discomfort. But the maidservant seemed to understand her mistress's unspoken question and told her in a low whisper that none of the soldiers dared go near Ammon.

Many of her father's high-ranking servants also filled the room to mourn the loss of their king. The number of people in the room made Isabel feel overwhelmed; she wanted to scream at them to go away and leave her family in peace. But it was their privilege to be there as their king's soul left the world. Isabel had to bear it. It made her even more grateful for Abish's quiet presence.

Words came to Isabel from across the room. "If he were dead, I would know it. I would feel it. He's not dead."

Isabel didn't know how many times she had heard Kamilah utter those words now. As day turned into another night and the proper time for her father's burial came and went, Isabel started to despair.

King Lamoni didn't wake up. Somewhere in the middle of the night, as everyone around Isabel moaned and wailed, she realized that her father would probably never wake up.

Isabel's grief was compounded by the unwelcome arrival of Mahlon in the morning. As the king's nephew, he had a right to be in the king's rooms. Isabel felt him walk up behind her. She knelt next to her father's bed on his left side. Mahlon knelt down as well.

"The king has died. He needs to be buried and a new king put in his stead."

Before Isabel could speak, Kamilah repeated her mantra. "He is not dead." She stroked the side of King Lamoni's face with her hand.

"He is dead, and he is starting to stink. He needs to be put into the sepulchre," Mahlon retorted.

Isabel turned her head to look at him. His boldness stunned her.

"Kamilah could be right. Maybe he is just sleeping. He could still wake up."

Mahlon's dark eyes pierced her. "You know as well as I do that your father will never awaken."

Isabel swallowed down a large lump of emotion. Some part of her feared he was right. She looked away from Mahlon.

"I will go to our grandfather to make the necessary arrangements. He must be informed of Lamoni's death, and we must be wed."

That made Isabel glare back at Mahlon. "I will not marry you."

"You will," Mahlon said with supreme arrogance. "Who else will lead this kingdom? Laman? He is still a child. Kamilah? She's not even worthy of the title she holds now. You?" He laughed.

If her father were truly gone, Isabel no longer had any hope of protection. Mahlon could force her into marriage. A choking fear grasped Isabel, making it difficult to breathe.

"My answer will always be no."

He gave her an imperious look. "Your answer does not matter. I would suggest preparing yourself. I will return soon."

Mahlon left, and Isabel found that she had no more tears to cry. He was right of course; she would have to marry him. Her desires did not matter. She knew Mahlon wanted this marriage more than anything; it was the only way her grandfather would make Mahlon king over the lands that Mahlon possessed. Mahlon currently acted only as a steward. King Laman had promised years ago to make Mahlon a king when he married Isabel. Her body nearly collapsed in total exhaustion, physical and emotional exhaustion, unlike any she had ever known. She forced herself to retain her wits.

Isabel had hoped, after her father's first refusal, that Mahlon would give up on her, though she didn't particularly want him to find another wife—she wouldn't have wished Mahlon on any woman. It had been a childish wish, and now it seemed that reality had finally caught up with her.

After Mahlon left, Isabel grasped Kamilah's arm, pulling her out of a trancelike state to repeat Mahlon's plans. Kamilah's face turned paler.

"King Laman will come to Ishmael," Kamilah said, "And he will bury your father even though he isn't dead. We must do something, Isabel."

"We should call for Ammon. Ammon might be able to save him." The words surprised her, although they did make some sense. If Ammon had done this, perhaps he had the power to undo it. She wondered why it hadn't occurred to her before.

"What makes you say that?"

"I'm not sure. But there is no one else."

One of the servants in the room, perhaps excited at the possibility of finding someone who could awaken the king, overstepped his bounds and agreed loudly with Isabel. "Yes, Ammon could help. He has been teaching us about his faith. I believe him to be a prophet, and he has the power to do things in his God's name."

Several other voices joined the first servant's, echoing what he had said.

Isabel saw a small measure of hope in Kamilah's eyes. "Send for Ammon."

11

When he heard that the queen had finally requested him, Ammon went to her as quickly as he could.

Ammon had expected to be put in prison after the king collapsed. It would not have been the first time, nor presumably the last, that he would be incarcerated. But the guards had left him and Jeremias alone.

And by staying out of prison, Ammon found himself able to do just as he'd wished from the moment he'd had the idea to come to the Lamanite lands.

There were many who wanted to know more about what Ammon had told the king. Ammon taught five men at first, all of them among the servants who had gone to the waters of Sebus, and then those men had returned with their families. Word spread rapidly and the size of the crowd who came to listen had grown so large that Jeremias had to teach half the group while Ammon taught the other half.

Ammon had heard whispers and innuendoes that the king had died and that the queen had become crazed with grief and refused to let him be properly buried. Ammon longed to go to them, to give the queen and her children some comfort. He thought often of Isabel, and he wondered how she was doing. He had seen her crying over her father's still body. He had seen how much she loved the king, and he felt her suffering.

So when word came that the queen wanted him, Ammon tried not to mentally berate the slow-moving servant who led the way.

The queen stood in her family's courtyard outside the king's bedchambers. She looked as if she hadn't slept in days. Her clothes were simple, her hair done in a single braid. The royal family's private courtyard was filled with all levels of courtiers, soldiers, servants, and members of the king's family. Everywhere he looked he saw expressions of grief and sadness.

His eyes instinctively sought Isabel out from the crowd. There the princess stood, looking just as weary and sad as the queen. She wore a simple tunic, and her hair was also in a single braid. She should have looked terrible. But to Ammon, she looked beautiful. It surprised him that his arms ached to hold her, to offer Isabel what comfort he could. The pain in her eyes was nearly unbearable.

Ammon wondered for a moment why her suffering affected him more than the others; then reminding himself of why he was there, he asked the queen what she wanted him to do.

The queen's voice was even and clear, despite her obvious fatigue. "The servants of my husband have made it known to me that you are a prophet of a holy God and that you have power to do many mighty works in His name."

She waited for Ammon to respond, but Ammon sensed that she had reasons beyond this for wanting him there, so he waited.

"If this is the case, I want you to go in and see my husband, for he has been laid upon his bed for the space of two days and two nights, and some say that he is not dead, but others say that he is dead and that he stinks and that he ought to be placed in the sepulchre." At last the queen's voice caught, and she blinked several times before she regained her composure and continued in a very soft voice. "But as for myself, to me he does not stink."

Those last words spoke of the great love and affection between the king and queen that Ammon had already witnessed for himself, and it touched him. He was glad for the queen's request for help. He knew the king wasn't dead.

Ammon had seen this happen only once before, when one of his best friends, Alma the Younger, had undergone something very similar. Having spoken to Alma about it many, many times since then, Ammon knew that the king merely slept. The dark veil of unbelief that covered King Lamoni's mind was being cast away. The king was being touched by the light of God, a light that gave great joy, a light that could forever dispel any clouds of darkness, a light that filled the whole soul and would naturally overcome a man. Ammon had tasted a small portion of it before and knew how powerful it could be. King Lamoni had simply been overwhelmed.

Queen Kamilah held out her arm, gesturing toward the king's chambers. Ammon went in the direction she indicated. His steps nearly faltered when he locked eyes with Isabel, so intense was his desire to ease her suffering. Instead he resolutely marched into the king's rooms, knowing that this was the only way to help her.

Ammon did not need to see the king. He came into the room only because of the queen's request. Alone with the king's family and several upper-level courtiers, Ammon walked over to where the king lay. No, not dead. The scene certainly felt very familiar. This was just like Alma.

"What do you think?" Kamilah asked behind him.

The inspiration was quick and definite. "He is not dead. He sleeps. On the morrow he will rise again. Do not bury him," Ammon relayed.

Ammon turned about to look at the queen. "Do you believe this?"

Kamilah lifted her chin, as Ammon had seen Isabel do so many times before. But then she lowered it and reached out to take Ammon's hand with both of hers. "I have had no witness save your word and the word of our servants, but I believe that it will be according to what you have said."

This stunned Ammon momentarily. He had already been impressed with the reaction of King Lamoni. As Ammon had taught the king, he had seen that Lamoni believed his words. He saw in the king's face the emotions he himself had felt when he learned the truth all over again after putting aside his own wickedness.

The king had done more than just believe, though. King Lamoni had acted by praying, and it was that action that had impressed Ammon.

And now the queen was saying she was willing to take Ammon at his word. She had not had a personal witness as King Lamoni had. She had no reason to believe Ammon at all. Yet she still believed. Ammon couldn't remember ever witnessing faith like this before.

"You are blessed because of your exceeding faith. There has not been such great faith among all the people of the Nephites."

The queen nodded and tried to smile. "Will you stay here for a time?" the queen asked as she released Ammon's hand.

"I will."

Queen Kamilah nodded and moved away from him to resume watching over her husband.

Of their own volition, his feet moved him to Isabel's side. He knelt down next to her. She glanced at him several times out of the corner of her eye but did not speak. Ammon closed his eyes to take advantage of the quiet, wondering how Jeremias's current teaching session was going, pondering over what he should next teach the Lamanite people who were willing to listen, and imagining how his life would change when King Lamoni finally awoke.

"Why didn't you come earlier?"

Isabel's words were so quiet, Ammon nearly missed them. "You know I couldn't come until I was sent for."

He looked at her profile, but Isabel did not return his gaze. The scent of scarlet blossoms, the one he would forever associate with her, delicately wafted over to him. He noticed how her long multicolored braid hung over her right shoulder and the way tendrils of hair had escaped the braid. He again wondered how soft it was as his fingers longed to tuck the tendrils behind her ear.

"Couldn't you make him rise now?" Isabel asked, bringing Ammon sharply back to reality.

He cleared his throat. "It isn't my place. We will have to wait for him to awaken in the morning."

Perhaps because he was paying such close attention to her already, Ammon noticed the almost imperceptible way her body shifted away from him and the way her eyes kept darting up to look at him; it was as if she feared him.

"Are you afraid of me?" he asked quietly.

A series of emotions flitted across her face, but surprisingly, she did not answer right away. He had hoped for a quick denial. He sincerely disliked the idea of Isabel fearing him. Ammon waited until she said, "I saw you."

Ammon knew what she referred to, but he'd had no idea that Isabel had witnessed the events at the waters. "I'm sorry you did. I wish you hadn't. But I couldn't let them hurt the servants or cause their deaths."

"I'd never seen anything like it," Isabel said.

In that moment, Ammon realized that he would have said just about anything to ease her fears about him. It worried him that he was willing to do so. The last time he had felt this way for a woman, he had been led down a very dark path. Part of him was tempted to let her go on with her fear, to let her keep her distance. In the long run it would make things easier. But he couldn't be dishonest with her. He had to tell her the truth. "Isabel, you must know that you don't have to be scared of me. You have to believe that. You know that I would never hurt you."

Isabel finally looked at him, her dark brown eyes brimming with tears. "I do know it." She seemed startled by her admission, as if she hadn't expected to say it.

"You believe me?" Ammon wouldn't have predicted that as her response.

"Yes, I believe you," she whispered.

He suppressed a grin. He hoped it wouldn't be the last time she said those words to him.

They lapsed into what felt like a comfortable silence to Ammon. He didn't know if she felt the same. He tried not to mull it over too much.

"How did you know what my father was thinking?"

Ammon didn't know if there was a way to explain, but he sensed that she needed to know. "Through the Holy Ghost. I could see in my mind what worried the king, almost as if he was speaking the words to me." Ammon smiled at her. "Of course, I suppose some might say I could have logically guessed what was bothering him."

That made the corners of Isabel's mouth move slightly upward. Then she looked back over at her father. "Is he in pain?"

Ammon again felt the urge to say what Isabel wanted to hear, but he resisted. "Possibly. Most likely."

Isabel turned to him with an alarmed expression.

"I know just how your father feels. I've been in the darkest abyss," Ammon said, hearing the hollow and flat tone to his voice as he recalled his own repentance, his own suffering for the things he had done.

"You?"

He wished he didn't have to say anything further. "I was the vilest of sinners, Isabel." He didn't know why he told her this. It was as if he couldn't help himself, as if the words took on a life of their own.

"When we first came here to the Lamanite lands, there were many times I wanted to go home. You can probably imagine how we were treated. We were cast out of villages. We were mocked. Spit on. Beaten. Stoned. Bound with cords and put into prison. I remember feeling depressed and wanting to turn around and return to Zarahemla." Ammon took a deep breath. "But I did it. I suffered through all of it in hopes that I could save even one soul. So while I feel sorrow that your father is suffering, if it means that he will know the truth, if it means that I've found one person to help, then I will wait and suffer through it with him."

Isabel looked at him without speaking. "He will wake up, and then, if he is in pain, it will be over soon," Ammon told her. He couldn't read the expression in her eyes. He waited, wanting to know what she would say next. Something important had just happened, although Ammon wasn't sure what it was. The air crackled between them; it was as if every breath he took came from her. He again wished he could reach out and hold her.

Ammon heard a noise from across the room. He saw the queen studying them with a concerned expression, her eyes going from Isabel's face to Ammon's and back again. Ammon could only imagine what the queen thought. It might appear that Ammon had upset Isabel. Kamilah furrowed her eyebrows and then spoke. "I thank you for the time you have spent with us. Will you return in the morning?"

Her dismissal confirmed his idea that Kamilah misunderstood the situation between them. Ammon allowed himself to look at the princess one more time. "Of course."

It took all of his strength to stand up and walk away from Isabel. He reminded himself that the entire room was watching him go. Now was not the time to make a total fool of himself.

He walked out into the bright sunlight, shading his eyes to see better. The king's bedroom had been dark and smoke filled. It had made him think that it was nearly evening when it was only now just going on noon. He should find Jeremias to help him with the teaching.

Ammon felt someone grab the crook of his arm. He turned to see Isabel behind him. "Did you mean that? Do you promise he will awaken?"

"I promise you, Isabel." There was something beyond her concern for her father that tinged her questions. Ammon didn't know what it was, but it bothered him.

"He's all I have, Ammon. I can't lose him."

"He's not all you have." *You have me.* Ammon quickly tamped down the unbidden thought. "And you won't lose him." Ammon put his hand over Isabel's. He let it linger for longer than he should have, feeling the warmth of her skin seeping into his own. His heart started beating faster in response. Isabel looked up at Ammon in surprise, as if she felt it as well. Ammon quickly withdrew his hand and walked away. He couldn't let things become even more serious between them.

A voice inside him whispered that it was too late.

* * *

Isabel felt her eyes drifting shut, her head nodding down. She couldn't remember the last time she had slept, and her body's exhaustion tried to take over to force her to sleep.

Unfortunately, every time she closed her eyes she saw Ammon. She heard his promise, heard herself saying she believed him. Ammon's promises were all she had right now. She knew the consequence if her father didn't wake up in the morning as Ammon had said he would. Her grandfather would arrive, bury her father, and force her to marry Mahlon.

But what if Ammon was right? Despite the fact that she had earlier believed him to be a spy and a liar, she now realized that Ammon hadn't ever lied to her. He had in fact been very open with her about himself and his life. It was why she could believe him when he asked her to.

Abish was again at her side, giving Isabel the comfort that seemed to come solely from the maidservant's presence. Isabel whispered to Abish her plan if her father awoke, and Abish agreed that it was a good one. The maidservant offered to go in Isabel's stead, but Isabel wanted to meet with the messenger personally. She couldn't entrust this job to anyone else.

She also couldn't act until her father had actually woken up. To act prematurely, before she saw whether or not Ammon was right, would only make her life harder.

The curtain that hung over her father's bedroom door had been pulled to one side so that the room's occupants could see when the sun rose. Kamilah had not permitted further mourning for her husband, and the night had passed in almost total silence, making it even more difficult for Isabel to stay awake.

The world outside turned a hazy shade of orange and pink. It was then when King Lamoni suddenly sat up.

Nothing could have surprised Isabel more. King Lamoni held out his hand to Kamilah, a look of such intense love in his eyes that Isabel felt embarrassed to be witnessing it. "Blessed be the name of God, and blessed are you, my beautiful wife." He cupped his hand around Kamilah's cheek, and the queen's tears fell fast and furiously. She reached out to embrace King Lamoni.

That was all Isabel needed to see. She ran from the room to the barracks. Isabel told the guards there that she needed a runner, someone exceptionally fast. The guards went to find their captain, who then went through the process of calling all of his men together to decide which one was the fastest. Isabel nearly died of impatience. Finally a man was selected, and Isabel gave him the message he had to deliver to King Laman—that King Lamoni had woken up. At Isabel's words, the soldiers around her began to cheer, and Isabel had to wait for them to calm down before finishing the message. There would be no need for King Laman to come; it had been a false alarm.

She made the soldier repeat the message back to her twice to make certain he knew it and wouldn't forget it. In the time it took to make the arrangements for the oral message, she could have written everything down for her grandfather to read. She'd had no idea it would take so long.

Isabel then decided to send three runners, having each of them take a different path leading from Ishmael to Nephi. She couldn't afford for the messenger to miss King Laman if he was already on his way here.

Once all three were prepared, they departed. That would stop Mahlon temporarily. Isabel knew it was only a temporary solution, that she would somehow have to convince her father to do what he most dreaded—stand up to his own father. She couldn't spend whatever would be left of her life as Mahlon's wife. She didn't imagine that she would live for very long if Mahlon had his way.

As Isabel stood and contemplated her future, Abish came running up to her. Isabel had never seen her maidservant in such a state. Abish's eyes glowed brightly, almost as if she'd had too much to drink—which was ridiculous, as Isabel had never known Abish to partake of wine.

"You must come quickly, Princess."

Then Isabel saw a large group of people behind Abish.

"What has happened?"

"Come and see," Abish said. "All of you," she called out to the soldiers. "All of you must follow me and see!"

Abish brought Isabel back to the palace, back to her family's courtyard, now overrun with people—not just with palace servants, but villagers, and farmers.

"I went from house to house to gather everyone together," Abish told Isabel.

"Why?"

But again Abish didn't answer. "Look inside."

Isabel went to her father's rooms and pushed aside the curtain.

It looked as if a massacre had happened.

Her father, Kamilah, Ammon, and a roomful of servants lay on the floor. No one moved.

"No, no, no," Isabel moaned. Not again.

She had believed Ammon. She had trusted him, and now they were all dead.

12

"What happened?" Isabel could scarcely utter the words. Her shock at the horrific sight caused her knees to shake and her throat to close in. She leaned against the doorway for support.

Abish quickly recounted the story, and Isabel could feel the people behind her pressing forward as they tried to hear what the maidservant said. She told Isabel that the king had testified of seeing his Redeemer, who would be born of a woman and would redeem all mankind who believed on His name. After the king had made this testimony, he had again lapsed into an unconscious state. Queen Kamilah was similarly overcome.

Abish then related that Ammon, having arrived shortly after Isabel left, after he had seen and heard all this, fell to his knees and prayed, thanking his God for what He had done for the Lamanites, and then he also fell to the earth. After Ammon had gone still, the other servants in the room began to cry out and pray as they had seen Ammon do. They too fell to the floor, one by one, until Abish was the only one still awake.

"Why weren't you affected as they were?" Isabel asked, her hands still gripping the doorway tightly. She didn't want to look into her father's chambers but couldn't help herself. She kept looking at each and every still figure, willing them to move.

A look of fear flashed in Abish's eyes, replaced with a tentative confidence. She took a deep breath. "Before I was born, my father found a Nephite who had been injured in a skirmish with Lamanite soldiers. This was when the Nephites still lived in the lands here, before King Laman chased them out. My father took the Nephite in to care for him, and although the Nephite only lived for a few days, he taught my father many things concerning his faith. The Nephite taught him to pray, and my father prayed to know if what the Nephite had told him was true. He was answered with what he called a vision, like a waking dream, where he saw God. He was converted to the Nephite's faith, and he taught me to believe as he did. I think that because I have felt the Spirit of God many times, it did not overcome me as it did the others."

"So all this time . . ." Isabel felt something akin to betrayal. Abish had believed as Ammon did from the time of their childhood? She had prayed in secret, concealing her true faith from Isabel? Isabel had thought them to be the best of friends. She thought there were no secrets between them. "Why didn't you ever tell me of this before?"

"You know what would have happened to me if I had announced that my beliefs differed from those of your father."

Isabel did know. Abish would have been put to death. It eased her hurt feelings somewhat, knowing that Abish had truly had no choice, but she wondered what it was about this particular god that made Abish and Ammon and now her father seem so enthralled.

"Now everything has changed," Abish said loud enough for those behind her to hear. "I knew it was the power of God that had caused this to happen. I brought the people here to show them what had happened; I thought that if they saw this, it might help them to believe in the power of God."

Abish's words did not seem to have the effect she desired. Isabel heard grumbling and murmuring behind her.

"A great evil has come upon them because King Lamoni allowed the Nephite to remain in the land," Isabel heard a man say.

Other voices disagreed with the first man, saying the king had brought this on his house because he'd killed the servants who had let the flocks be scattered at the waters of Sebus.

There were more protestations, and Isabel turned to see Mulek, one of Mahlon's men. He was the brother of a man Ammon had killed at the waters. He yelled back that the blame did not belong to any Lamanite, but it was the fault of the Nephite. "I say we put the Nephite to death to make certain that he can have no more hold over the king!"

Several people cheered Mulek on as he charged with a look of rage-fueled hatred on his face. Too late, Isabel realized that Mulek had drawn his sword.

She reached out to grab at Mulek's arm but got only a fistful of air. Yelling oaths as he ran, Mulek raced with his sword above his head into the king's chambers. He stopped just short of Ammon. Still growling and yelling oaths, Mulek held his sword with both hands and started to bring it down on Ammon.

Isabel lurched forward, knowing it was too late to save Ammon but feeling as if she must do something. She called out Ammon's name, hoping that perhaps he would awaken. He didn't.

But then Mulek made a gurgling sound in his throat, crumpled up, and fell to the earth as if he had been struck by an invisible foe.

The sword Mulek held smacked against the floor with a loud crack, made even louder by the fact that the entire crowd behind Isabel had gone silent.

"The Nephite cannot be slain!" someone whispered in shock. The crowd backed away from all of the servants in the room, perhaps fearing that if they tried to touch any of them they would die as Mulek had.

"What can be the cause of this great power?"

"What do all these things mean?"

"He is the Great Spirit," one man offered as an explanation.

"No, he was sent by the Great Spirit," another said in reply.

"He is not the Great Spirit. He is a monster sent by the Nephites to torment us!"

"It was the Great Spirit who sent him, to afflict us because of our iniquities."

"The Great Spirit has always attended the Nephites. It always delivers them out of our hands, and it destroys many of our brethren!"

The arguing back and forth among the members of the crowd grew increasingly louder and more intense.

Abish walked into the room and stood next to Isabel. Isabel saw that Abish was silently crying. "This is not why I brought them here. They don't understand. I wish I could help them to understand what this really means."

Then Abish walked forward, stepping over and around the servants on the floor. Isabel realized what Abish was doing. "Abish, no!"

Abish leaned down to touch Kamilah's hand. Isabel held her breath, fearful that Abish would die as Mulek had.

Instead, Kamilah opened her eyes. She quickly stood and said, "Oh, blessed Jesus, who has saved me from an awful hell! Oh, blessed God, have mercy on this people!"

Kamilah clasped her hands together, a look of pure joy and rapture on her face. She continued to speak, but Isabel couldn't understand what Kamilah said. It was almost as if she spoke a different language.

Then the queen walked over to King Lamoni, took him by the hand, and he also awoke and stood on his feet.

The king headed toward the crowd of people; then he stood before them, rebuking them for their contentions and teaching them the words he had heard from Ammon. Kamilah stood next to him, testifying of the truthfulness of what the king said. The people stood transfixed, listening to a king who had died twice.

Abish went around the room, awakening the other servants.

Ammon still lay on the floor, and Isabel went over to him. She crouched down next to Ammon and, after a moment's hesitation, reached out as she had seen Abish do, gently touching Ammon's hand.

His eyes opened slowly, and he blinked several times before he focused on her face. "Isabel," he said with a sleepy and boyish grin. Then Ammon sat up and surveyed his surroundings. His gaze followed the path King Lamoni and Kamilah had taken into the courtyard. He smiled again when he heard the things the king and queen were saying.

"What is all this?" Isabel asked. "I don't understand."

"You will, I promise," Ammon said. "Come and listen for yourself." He stood and offered Isabel his hand.

She slipped her hand into his, allowing him to help her to her feet, and then followed Ammon into the courtyard.

* * *

There were few things Mahlon hated more than being patient.

But just because he hated doing it didn't mean he wasn't good at it.

Perhaps he had become too good at it, since all he ever seemed to do was wait. He waited for King Laman to give him his kingship. Waited for King Lamoni to declare war against him so that he could lawfully depose the king. Waited for someone to make Isabel marry him. He'd always waited.

But then, like a gift from the gods, King Lamoni had died. Well, it was possible that Lamoni had not actually died, but he had been close enough. And Mahlon had determined that being buried in the sepulchre would definitely resolve that question.

After rushing to the land of Nephi with what he hoped was a sorrowful expression, Mahlon had sadly related the tale of Lamoni's death.

Predictably, King Laman had been outraged. He had sworn vengeance on the Nephite and gathered together a sizeable band of soldiers. He'd made plans to leave the next morning.

Mahlon kept his excitement in check, but he was so close he could actually feel the weight of a king's headdress on his brow. He could hear his subjects calling him King Mahlon. He could imagine the wealth he would accumulate when he taxed the people of Ishmael.

He did not sleep that night, his anticipation was so great.

But when the morning came, all of his hopes and schemes had flown away into the fading night; for morning brought three separate messengers from Ishmael proclaiming that King Lamoni lived.

King Laman had doubted the veracity of their statements until one of the soldiers told the king that Princess Isabel had personally sent them.

Isabel.

King Laman had visibly relaxed. Mahlon knew that the king had not wanted to leave his guests, many of them family members who had traveled great distances for the king's tournament and feast. He had called for a celebration for the news about his son's good health.

Mahlon had bitten the inside of his cheek to keep from reacting in front of King Laman. He had bit so hard that he'd tasted blood.

Isabel again stood in the way of his getting what rightfully belonged to him. He deserved to be a king. He was the grandson of

King Laman. Mahlon's own father had been a king for a short time before his death. Mahlon's father, a Nephite nobleman named Amulon, had been greatly esteemed by his grandfather. Amulon had taught the Lamanites to use a written language, had taught them the benefits of trade. He had increased King Laman's wealth.

This had all occurred of course after his father had kidnapped his mother, one of King Laman's daughters. King Laman had eventually tracked down the Nephites who had stolen the Lamanite women from a grove where they had been performing a sacred women's ritual. All was forgiven when Amulon had forced his wife and the other captured Lamanite women to plead for their husbands' and children's lives. It was one of Mahlon's earliest memories—the way his father had put an obsidian knife to his throat to force his mother to comply. Then the future had brightened forever once Amulon had showed Mahlon's grandfather how to multiply his wealth a thousand times over.

Mahlon was meant to be a king. He had wondered many times why no one else seemed to recognize this.

His mother died not long after his father had been killed by his own soldiers. Mahlon had been sent to live with his grandfather, where his life became a struggle for survival. Regarded by King Laman's court as an outsider, Mahlon had to fight daily for attention and recognition. King Laman alone held all the power, and Mahlon learned quickly that if he wanted anything of value in his life, he would have to get Laman's affection. So he lied and cheated and stole and did whatever he had to do to gain his grandfather's favor. He became the king's best warrior and was made famous through his battlefield conquests. But still he remained outside of the circle of power, outside of the family. Mahlon had labored for years trying to find the one thing that would gain him entrance to this world. He had finally exacted a promise for a kingship if he married Isabel. King Laman shared Mahlon's concern over King Lamoni's poor choice in a second wife, and with grandchildren who were the offspring of someone so common, Isabel was the only true heir to her father's kingdom. Their union in marriage would naturally undo Lamoni's bad decision.

A kingship would also make Mahlon a recognized and honored member of Laman's intimate circle. He would never be treated badly again.

Mahlon's men had arrived not long after the messengers. Mahlon had left Mulek and a squad of soldiers to watch over Ishmael with instructions to report to him if anything happened. His men had returned without Mulek and reported the strange tale of Mulek's demise. They told Mahlon of the belief that the Nephite could not be killed, which Mahlon had disregarded. Every man could be destroyed. All one had to do was find their weak spot, and from the stories his men told, Mahlon had begun to suspect that the Nephite's weakness was Isabel.

He only half listened as his men continued explaining what had happened to the royal family, how King Lamoni and his wife now professed a belief in the same god that Ammon believed in, and how they had testified and taught the people in Ishmael.

"And did the people listen?" Mahlon saw another potential problem. If King Lamoni changed his religious infrastructure and the people followed, Mahlon would have to undo it when he became king. It would be time consuming and annoying. Not to mention that the people might try to oust him as king since he wouldn't share their new convictions.

His soldiers told him that while there seemed that many would be converted, there were just as many who were not listening. They told him of Lamoni's servants who claimed that their hearts had been changed and how they had no more desire to do evil. The servants had spoken of seeing angels.

This struck Mahlon as funny and helped calm some of his concern. Visits from otherworldly beings? Seeing gods? It made Lamoni and his household sound insane. It would certainly help Mahlon's cause in securing King Laman's blessing for a marriage to Isabel. He didn't anticipate that it would take much to convince King Laman that King Lamoni would need a rational son-in-law in his household.

And he had to be convinced now. Time pressed down on Mahlon. He saw his grandfather softening toward Lamoni's oldest son, a child named after King Laman. Soon the child would grow old enough to be a serious threat to Mahlon's quest for the kingship of Ishmael. Mahlon had to seize control now, before it was too late.

Mahlon found his way to his grandfather's side. King Laman celebrated with the people around him over his son, speaking of how he looked forward to seeing Lamoni when he arrived for the feast.

Mahlon's men had indicated that King Lamoni seemed intent on converting his people to Ammon's religion. If that was true, and if Lamoni was as caught up in dreams as reported, there was a great possibility that Lamoni would be foolish enough to miss the feast.

Seeing the chance to drive a final wedge between his grandfather and his uncle, Mahlon cleared his throat. When King Laman finally gave Mahlon his attention, Mahlon said, "I hope this means that King Lamoni will not miss the great feast you are giving in honor of all your sons."

King Laman's cheerful expression did not dissipate as he proclaimed, "Of course he will be here! He knows he is expected." With that, Mahlon understood that King Laman would not tolerate such a disrespectful action.

Mahlon pressed his lips together so that he would not smile. "The Nephite in your son's court seems to have an exceptionally strong hold over the king. Perhaps he has convinced him not to come . . ." Mahlon deliberately let his words trail off.

That made his grandfather stop smiling. "Lamoni will be here. And if that Nephite interferes, I will kill him myself. Lamoni will come."

King Laman turned from Mahlon, and Mahlon slowly backed away. To stay away from the feast would be an act of open rebellion. With that insurance in place, Mahlon left the festivities to prepare for the tournament. He would win the tournament, and for his prize he would again ask for Isabel as his wife. He knew King Laman would give her to him, and King Lamoni could not protest this time, particularly if Lamoni missed the feast after the tournament. Once Isabel was his, Mahlon would quickly dispose of King Lamoni and the rest of Isabel's family, and he would test the theory of whether or not the Nephite could be killed.

Mahlon gave a slight smile. *And then I'll teach that woman a lesson about holding her tongue.*

13

Isabel didn't know what to think.

She had been overwhelmed the day her father had awoken. Twice she had believed him dead, and it had simply been too much to try to listen to everything he had to say.

Not that she hadn't had many opportunities since then to better understand what her father now believed. King Lamoni spoke about his newly discovered faith at every turn.

Her father had never lied to her. Never. And now he proclaimed to believe what Ammon taught. Isabel didn't know what to believe. Either her father told the truth and was right, or he mistakenly thought himself to be telling the truth and was wrong. Regardless, Isabel's world had been radically changed.

King Lamoni even looked different. Isabel couldn't adequately describe what had changed in her father's and Kamilah's countenances. But they looked . . . more like Ammon.

The night after her father's conversion, Abish had asked Isabel come with her to hear Ammon speak to the people. Overcome with curiosity, Isabel had to go with her maidservant. Ammon seemed to prefer teaching the people in outdoor settings, most likely because he couldn't find a building big enough to house all those who came to listen.

One visit should have been enough.

But Isabel couldn't stay away. Every time she knew that Ammon would teach the people, she went to listen. Like a fly going to honey, her feet became trapped by his words—words her mind told her she couldn't possibly believe, but words she couldn't forget or let go.

Over the next few days Ammon established a church and began to baptize people. Isabel observed many baptisms, including the very first ones—her father and stepmother.

Initially, Isabel had very much wanted to resist the new ideas Ammon and her father had given her. And then, for the first time, she had recognized her desire to be contrary just for the sake of being contrary. When she realized that she'd lived her life being obstinate, that all of her decisions had been based solely on choosing the opposite of what she thought her father or Kamilah would want, Isabel felt a keen wish to change. She wanted to start choosing things for a better reason—because she wanted them. She wanted to change for herself.

King Lamoni had changed in the way he spoke to his household and the way he treated everyone around him. Now when he looked at Isabel, it disconcerted her. She saw in his eyes the love that she had craved her entire life. Part of her wanted to join those that Ammon baptized, just so that her father would always look at her that way. But her pride struggled against it. If what Ammon taught was true, Isabel wanted to discover it for herself. She didn't want to belong to Ammon's church because her father wished it. Or because Ammon wished it.

Despite not wanting to admit to it, Isabel knew her perception of Ammon had changed. She no longer believed that he was a spy or that he was here to hurt her family. In fact, her family had become annoyingly happy. Ammon had brought nothing but joy to many people around her. How could she continue to suspect him of ulterior motives?

Once Isabel let go of those notions, Ammon became a different man to her. She saw his loyalty to his cousin, to the people of Ishmael. She saw his passion when he spoke of his god. She saw his intelligence as he answered question after question. She saw the love he felt for her fellow Lamanites, despite how he had once been treated. She saw his charm when the girls of the city vied for his attention. She appreciated his humor when he related amusing tales to prove a point.

Isabel didn't want to respect Ammon, but she did. She didn't want to see the good things in him, but she did. And as she saw them, she felt herself drawn to him more and more. She wondered if he ever thought about her now. If he saw good things in her. If he felt drawn to her in the same way. If she meant more to him than another potential convert.

Ammon never even seemed to notice her. Admittedly, she did hang back, keeping to the shadows so as to not call attention to herself when he taught. But Ammon never sought her out. Since the incident, he hadn't spoken to her at all. He seemed to be ignoring her.

One evening, as the fireflies flashed and woodsy smoke from the fire filled the air around her, Isabel again listened in the shadows as Ammon taught. His voice, deep and soothing, lulled her into a sense of security and rightness, as if this was where she belonged.

"May I join you?"

The voice of Ammon's cousin crashed against her like a wave of cold water, like the time many years ago when Abish had emptied a vase on her head because Isabel had refused to get up.

It took several moments before Isabel could nod. She disliked that she had been discovered, and it annoyed her that Jeremias had broken the reverie Ammon had created.

"What do you think of all this?" Jeremias asked.

Isabel did not answer immediately but finally replied, "I'm not certain what to think."

"Understandable." Jeremias sat down next to Isabel. "Would you mind if I told you a story?"

Isabel didn't want to stop listening to Ammon, but she nodded.

"Ammon didn't always believe."

This did not surprise Isabel; Ammon had indicated as much to her. She remembered that he called himself the "vilest of sinners." But he had never expounded on what he'd meant. Suddenly Jeremias had Isabel's full attention.

"Not that he began his life that way. Ammon has excellent parents and was brought up in the truth. When he became a young man, Ammon fell in love."

Jealousy flared to life inside of Isabel, so quick and furious that all she could do was blink in response. She wanted to know everything. Who was this woman? Did Ammon love her still? Did this woman wait in Zarahemla for Ammon's return? Was this why Ammon had rejected her?

"She did not belong to our church and took great pleasure in leading Ammon away from everything he had ever believed. This was made easier by the fact that one of Ammon's best friends, a man named Alma, had also fallen away and married an outsider. Alma's father was the high priest, and Alma spent his time preaching against his father's church and teachings. Alma was quickly joined in his rebellion by the sons of King Mosiah, including Ammon."

Isabel had to know. "Did Ammon . . . did he . . . marry her?"

"No. Ammon's never been married." Jeremias stretched his legs out in front of him. "It took some divine intervention to turn Ammon from his ways." Jeremias chuckled slightly, as if enjoying some private joke. "Ammon is a very dedicated person. When he makes a decision, he carries it through to the end regardless of the consequences. His father has often warned him about his single-mindedness. It's something I know Ammon struggles with. But in this case it worked in his favor. He had committed himself to the wrong cause, and when he realized what he'd done, Ammon walked away from his old life, including the woman. He had a new direction to go in."

A silence passed between them as Ammon concluded his speaking. The people in front of Isabel stood up—some to leave, others to talk privately with Ammon.

"He doesn't talk about it much, but I know that Ammon deeply regrets the choices he made. Sometimes I think he punishes himself more than he should. He thinks it's worse to have the truth and deny it, as he did, than to repent when you didn't know any different. I try to remind him that God's forgiveness extends to us all, even those who know better. And while I know Ammon logically believes it, sometimes I think his heart hasn't been convinced."

A hurricane could have blown through the highlands and Isabel would have ignored it. She savored this opportunity to learn more about Ammon, to understand things about him that he might never share himself, things he might not even realize about himself, the sort of things only a close friend or family member would know.

But unfortunately, Jeremias stood up. "And despite what he might feel for someone, Ammon has dedicated himself to serving a mission among your people. He won't allow himself to be distracted by anything or anyone. Even if he should," Jeremias murmured the last part as he looked at Ammon.

"Good evening to you, Princess." Jeremias joined the crowd, and many people turned to enthusiastically greet him.

Isabel couldn't help but feel a thrill at Jeremias's parting words to her. Given Ammon's history, it would make sense that he wouldn't allow himself to feel anything for her. Perhaps Ammon didn't ignore her because he didn't like her, but because he *did*. It would explain why he seemed to pull her in and then push her away at the same time.

She had to laugh at herself—not too long ago she'd wanted Ammon's death. Now she hoped that he might have feelings for her.

It seemed pointless for her to hope, if Ammon really was as determined as Jeremias described him to be. Better to let Ammon keep the distance between them. Besides, she didn't want any of these burgeoning and unfamiliar feelings to get in the way of finding out for herself whether or not what Ammon taught was true.

Which was much easier decided than done, particularly once Ammon sat down next to her and flashed a bone-melting grin that made all her resolutions collapse.

She could be strong. Surely she was not that pathetic.

Surely.

* * *

"What are you doing?" Isabel looked bewildered.

"Jeremias said you wanted to see me."

"I didn't—" she cut her words short and pointedly looked away from him.

This was the first time in several days that Ammon had allowed himself to be this close to Isabel, to actually speak to her. He liked it far more than he should have.

"He thought you might have some questions about the things you've heard."

"No." Isabel's lips had pressed into a thin line, and she continued to avoid his gaze. "No questions."

He should wish her good night, stand up, and walk away. *Just stand up. And walk away.* It was easy. *Come on*, he urged his legs. He'd been an expert walker for the last twenty-two years. There was no reason for his limbs to suddenly forget how to do it.

"Perhaps I could ask you a question instead."

Isabel inclined her head slightly, which Ammon took as acquiescence. "What does *rabbanah* mean?"

That got her to look at him. "It means powerful or great king. Why?"

Ammon grinned. It would be better for him not to share in what context he had heard that word. Isabel would probably accuse him of arrogance again. But before he could say anything else, Isabel spoke.

"Jeremias told me of the woman you loved."

It was Ammon's turn to look away from Isabel as a series of emotions rushed through him—shame, guilt, regret, embarrassment—followed by complete and total humiliation that she knew.

"At your age, most men are married. Why aren't you?"

Where had this come from? He hadn't expected these sorts of questions from Isabel. At first, he didn't know how to respond.

"There isn't any room in my life right now for a wife or family. I have a mission to fulfill."

"And yet you speak of a Father and a Son. Wouldn't your god want you to also become a father? To have a family of your own?"

For a second Ammon envisioned little girls with Isabel's hair. He squeezed his eyes shut, willing the image to leave his mind. This was not what he needed right now. Ammon had to clear his throat before answering. "I suppose when the time is right, He will let me know."

"What if you're too busy making restitution to notice? You keep speaking of repentance and forgiveness. Jeremias said you haven't forgiven yourself for your mistakes."

That stunned him. "Yes, I have."

"I think Jeremias is right. You haven't forgiven yourself. That's why you push yourself and even deny yourself. If you truly believe that your God has forgiven you, who are you to say otherwise?"

Ammon could feel the lower half of his mouth hanging open at Isabel's perceptions and insights, and he had the sinking feeling that she was actually right. He smiled weakly at her. "Well, at least I know you've really been listening when you come here."

"Yes, I have paid very close attention to everything you've said. And I wonder if you even realize what you're asking of this people. You're saying that everything we know about the world, everything we have ever been taught, ever believed, is completely wrong. You're not asking us to stop believing in one god and believe in another. This is not just a change of religious beliefs. This is changing our entire way of life."

"I know."

"And you, a Nephite, are asking us to believe this. All my life, all I've ever been taught is that your people are the children of liars and robbers, and suddenly you're the bearer of truth?"

Ammon wanted to respond, but Isabel kept talking in an incredulous voice. "And then, that day you all woke up, the servants said they had seen angels. Angels! Is that even possible?"

"I've seen one."

That made Isabel stop.

"I knew the truth. I grew up with it. But I turned my back on everything I believed, everything my fathers believed. You can't imagine how much time I devoted to trying to destroy God's Church. I was in an awful, sinful, and polluted state. When I think about what I deserved, the punishment God should have given me, my soul shrinks at the thought." Ammon sighed deeply, not wanting to revisit those memories. "But instead, God gave me a second chance. Not just me, all of us. My brothers and Alma. He sent an angel to rebuke us, to call us to repentance. Alma fell into a state similar to the one your father entered. He told us of the pain he had endured, the pain we all had to endure as we came back to the Church. I don't ever want anyone else to have to go through that."

"So you came here." She paused. "What does your family think of you being here?"

Ammon had to laugh. "Well, my father didn't want us to come. But we insisted. The people of Zarahemla laughed at us, scorned us. They said we couldn't bring the Lamanites to a knowledge of the truth, that we couldn't convince you of the incorrectness of your fathers' traditions. Some wanted us to come to war against you and destroy you. But I didn't want to destroy anybody. I just wanted to teach what I know to be true. I wanted to share the happiness that I feel."

"I feel that when you teach," Isabel said quietly.

"And what do you feel about me? I mean, about what I teach?" Ammon hoped Isabel would take it as a slip of the tongue. He hadn't meant to say it. Even if he did wonder sometimes.

"I feel . . . comfortable. And . . . peaceful, I suppose. It's strange."

That made Ammon's flagging spirits right themselves. He recognized the chance to help Isabel understand what she felt. "That's the Spirit."

"The Great Spirit?" Isabel sounded confused.

"This would be more like the Great Spirit's messenger. It's confirming for you the truth of what I'm saying."

"But I haven't seen Jesus Christ like my father claims to. I haven't seen an angel."

"What happened to your father and mother is rare. A testimony in Christ is something that usually grows gradually, from experience and prayer. Have you prayed about these things?"

Isabel shrugged but didn't answer. She might not admit it, but Ammon felt that despite her questions and objections, Isabel was starting to believe. He could see it in her face, in the way she spoke. He reached out and took one of Isabel's hands. She looked at him, alarmed. Ammon understood. He felt fairly alarmed himself. He didn't know why he had done it, but now that he had, he didn't want to let go.

"If something makes sense in your mind—and if it feels right in your heart that what you're hearing is true—why deny yourself what your heart desires?"

He *was* still talking about the Church, wasn't he? And he told himself he was talking about Isabel and not about himself. It didn't matter what made sense in his mind or what his heart wanted. He had a mission. "Promise me that you will pray about this," Ammon continued, trying to keep the rawness he felt out of his voice. "And if your mind and your heart tell you it's wrong, I will not ask you about it again."

"I promise," Isabel said, almost in a whisper, apparently as unable to pull her hand away as Ammon was to let it go. "But how will I know if I've received an answer?"

Ammon's legs finally remembered how to stand, so he did. Isabel stood up with him, but still he held on to her hand. He had to let go.

His mind had to command his hand to release hers. His natural tendency to make light of situations that were uncomfortable prompted him to say, "It will be a soft whisper that speaks to your soul, and it will sound like this: *It's true, and Ammon is always right.*"

Isabel laughed in a way Ammon had never heard her laugh before. It wasn't too long before Ammon joined her and their laughter mingled together so that everyone turned to look at them.

Later that night, as he looked back at that moment, Ammon truly did not know what made him say what he'd said next. Perhaps with the tension between them dissipated, he had let his guard too far down. Or perhaps Aaron was right and the fall Ammon had taken out of a tree at seven years old had left his mind addled.

Whatever the reason, once his and Isabel's laughter had died down, Ammon said, "I was wrong."

"Wrong about what?" Isabel asked, the smile still on her face.

"I thought you were pretty. You're not pretty."

Her smile faded, and she looked confused.

He should have stopped. But instead he continued. "Isabel . . . when you smile like that . . . you're not just pretty. You're so beautiful that I forget who I am. It takes my breath away. It's a good thing you don't do it very often."

A shy, sweet smile crept across Isabel's pink lips, and Ammon found himself again seized with an overwhelming desire to kiss her. He might have, had it not been for Jeremias's intervention.

Jeremias cleared his throat loudly as he walked up behind them. Ammon wanted to take back what he'd said. Not because he didn't mean it, but because he did. That information was better off locked inside his heart, and he didn't like the fact that now it walked around freely because he had let it out.

Isabel slipped away without even wishing him farewell. Ammon tried to make sense of what he had just done. What was wrong with him? Would he always be this weak?

"It's not like you to skulk around in the shadows," Ammon remarked to Jeremias.

Jeremias stroked his chin thoughtfully. "You should try it. You learn very interesting things that way. When are you going to tell her?"

"Tell her what?"

Jeremias shot Ammon a look that reminded Ammon of his mother's expression after he and Aaron had done something particularly stupid. "You know what. You might try admitting it to yourself first though. You can't play the fool with me. I know you far too well for that."

Part of Ammon wanted so badly to give in, to chase after Isabel and tell her . . . what? What would he tell her? That he admired her? That he thought . . . that sometimes he thought he might be falling in love with her? Or that he loved her already?

No. He couldn't. "I can't lose control that way again," Ammon said, clenching his fists tightly. "I can't love a woman who doesn't share my beliefs. I can't travel that path again. I can't."

"Have you even bothered to ask her what she believes?"

Ammon said nothing. If he thought of Isabel this way—as someone who believed as he did—it would be too hard to stay away from her.

"Do you still think yourself so weak? You're not. You're one of the strongest men I know. You can love the Lord, teach His message, and love a wife. One doesn't preclude the other."

"Why are you pushing this?" Ammon demanded.

"Because she makes your face light up in a way that I've never seen before. I think, whether or not you'd admit it, she makes you happy. And whether or not you want it, she has a place in your heart."

Ammon again said nothing. It would be too much of a distraction to love her. He and Jeremias were doing such good here in Ishmael. He couldn't risk it.

Jeremias sighed loudly. "I can count on one hand the number of times in my life when I thought you were being a complete fool. And just so you know, this is one of those times."

14

MAYBE JEREMIAS WAS RIGHT. MAYBE he should tell her.

"I don't want to see you miss out on a chance for happiness," Jeremias had told him.

So Ammon had followed the path Isabel had taken back to the palace. His heart raced despite the fact that he walked at a calm and even pace. He tried to think of what he would say, but his mouth had gone dry. It felt as if his tongue were stuck to the roof of his mouth and he couldn't dislodge it.

The red columns he passed indicated that he was nearing the royal family's private courtyard. From here he could see the white water lilies bobbing on the pond and the silvery fish that swam in between the lilies' roots. He knew he could go no further. The night he had followed Isabel here, he had known they would be alone, and that was the only reason he had risked it. He supposed he could find a female servant to find Abish to find Isabel, but perhaps this was a sign. He hadn't overtaken her on the path or found her waiting for him as he had imagined she might be.

"Ammon?"

He turned to see the queen sitting outside on a wooden bench. "What are you doing here?"

What could he possibly say? "I wanted to . . . er, that is, I, uh . . ." His tongue refused to let him speak properly.

The queen gave him a knowing smile as she wrapped her multi-colored embroidered shawl around her shoulders. "Ah, I see."

Ammon wished he could see. He himself didn't understand why he had come here. The queen indicated that Ammon should sit next to her. Ammon sat down, grateful that he no longer had to face her. They sat in a companionable silence until the queen said, "Isabel talks to you."

Her words so surprised him that she might as well have hit him in the head with the wooden bench. Ammon exhaled a deep breath and smiled back. "If by 'talks' you mean yells at me, then yes, Isabel talks to me."

"She talks more to you than she does to anyone else here."

If that was true, it seemed very sad to Ammon. Oh, a small part of him liked the idea of being Isabel's confidant and friend, but the other part of him realized how wide the gap was between Isabel and her family.

"I want so badly to reach out to Isabel, but every time I try, I fail miserably. I know she hates the embroidery I want her to do. But I'm not trying to punish her. I just want to spend time with her. I loved her the moment I came here, because she was Lamoni's daughter. Then I came to love Isabel for herself, for her passion and determination and intelligence."

Ammon, unfortunately, completely understood.

The queen's voice wavered as she continued. "I know how Isabel feels about me. She's made that very clear. She cannot bear to be anywhere near me."

Ammon wondered whether he should say anything. Would he be breaking Isabel's trust? He determined that it was more important to mend the pain in this family and to help if he could. "Do you know that Isabel takes her brothers and sisters out early each morning and plays with them?"

The queen nodded. "I know she does."

"Then why not tell her? Why not tell Isabel that you know how much she loves them?"

"She wishes for us to remain ignorant to it, and I'm afraid that if I bring it up she will stop. I wouldn't deprive my children of their time with her. Perhaps that is the wrong decision. I confess I am often at a loss as to how to deal with Isabel."

Ammon noticed how tightly the queen gripped her shawl, holding it against her body the way a warrior might keep a shield close for protection.

"I'm not very good at any of this—particularly at being queen. I was not raised for it. My father was a cloth maker. He was a very talented man, and King Laman kept him at the palace to make beautiful fabrics for the royal family. I met Lamoni when I was a child. We grew up together, and I can't remember a time when I didn't love him. I nearly died the day he had to marry another. And when he came back into my life . . . I didn't care that I didn't know how to properly address a king or how to perform royal rituals at the temple. Although in time I felt very foolish when I realized that my knowledge only extended to things such as the number of cochineal beetles that had to be ground up in water and the precise temperature needed to produce King Laman's favorite shade of crimson. Not very useful in being the wife of a king, I'm afraid. Or in being the mother of a sad, scared princess."

"I think you're an excellent mother," Ammon interjected. The queen tilted her head to one side, but she did not respond. She sat still, her posture erect, her demeanor calm. But Ammon saw the way the queen's fingers twisted and turned the shawl.

"I also think Isabel cares more for you and the rest of her family than she lets on," Ammon said. "But she's worried that if she admits it she will somehow betray her mother. She told me once that she's the only one here who loves her mother, so she's focused all of her affection on her mother's memory."

"She's wrong." Ammon could hear the queen's voice beginning to crack. "She's not the only one who loves her mother. I love her for giving us Isabel. Naima was named after Isabel's mother so that we would always remember her."

The queen straightened up and shook her head, causing her necklaces to jangle together. She remained quiet for several moments before saying, "I wanted to know if you would speak to Isabel about being baptized. I worry that we're the reason she hasn't been yet. I know she comes to hear you teach. I am not in her confidence, so I'm not certain, but Isabel wouldn't spend any time listening to you if she didn't believe some of what you were saying. Would you speak with her? I thought that perhaps she would talk to you."

"I did speak to her this evening about that very thing. But it is a decision Isabel must make for herself. I don't think that she would base her decision of whether or not to be baptized on you or her family. She's too intelligent for that. Have faith that Isabel will find her own way."

The queen stood and smiled down at Ammon. "I hope you're right."

She wished him a good night and left for her chambers.

So it hadn't been just wishful thinking on his part. He had felt that Isabel had begun to believe, if she didn't believe already. The queen seemed to agree with him. Why was Isabel being so stubborn about it?

That's just Isabel. It startled him that he felt as if he knew her so well that it didn't surprise him in the least that she would react the way she had.

His recent missionary work had taken all of his time, keeping him away from Isabel. But now that she had put herself into that part of his life and he had begun to connect with her on this spiritual level, it added a frightening new dimension to their relationship. Things had irrevocably changed between them.

And to Ammon's dismay, he realized he wanted them changed. He didn't want to only be her friend.

He wanted more.

* * *

Isabel prayed.

And prayed and prayed.

Nothing happened. She didn't see angels. She didn't fall to the earth as if dead. She didn't have some sort of overwhelming experience. She felt more of that happiness, that comfortable feeling, but no voice spoke to her confirming that Ammon's words were true.

Isabel spent a great deal of time thinking over why she was so different, why she didn't receive answers the way everyone around her seemed to. How could she truly know for herself if God remained silent on the subject?

She continued to attend the meetings Ammon and his cousin held. She listened intently, wanting to absorb it all. She felt like she couldn't make a proper decision until she had all the facts. When she realized that she had heard much of what they taught before, Isabel knew it was time to make a decision.

After her morning run, Isabel stopped at a rocky outcropping that overlooked the entire land of Ishmael. She prayed again, the way that she had seen Ammon and Jeremias pray. Again, Isabel heard nothing. And she felt no burning in her chest, as Abish had once described it.

She finished her prayer and looked to the bright blue sky, marred only by a single wisp of gray smoke from a nearby fire. It reminded Isabel of Ammon's eyes. Like gray storm clouds in an early spring sky. She sighed in disgust. She was spending far too much time thinking about something so trivial.

As Isabel walked back to the palace, pondering over what more she needed to do to uncover the truth for herself, the thought suddenly occurred to her that she already knew. Isabel stopped walking. The peaceful feelings she'd had, those were her confirmation! She had received an answer but hadn't recognized it for what it was.

She had expected discovering the truth to be complicated. But suddenly it all seemed so simple. She knew. She believed. Only her own self-doubt had kept her from realizing it.

A sudden, overwhelming joy coursed through her. Isabel ran faster than she ever had before. She had to find Ammon. She had to tell him.

When she returned to the palace, Abish was the first person she saw. Isabel ran to her maidservant and threw her arms around the startled woman. "What is it?" Abish asked in a voice filled with concern.

Isabel laughed. "I know. I know Ammon's telling the truth."

Abish excitedly hugged Isabel in return, laughing in excitement with her. "How did you—"

But Isabel didn't let her finish. "I must find Ammon. Do you know where he is?"

Abish gave her a sort of patronizing smile and an I-know-why-you-really-want-to-find-Ammon sort of look, but Isabel brushed it aside. This had nothing to do with how Isabel felt about Ammon. Ammon had challenged her to find out, and she had. It only seemed right that she tell him as soon as possible.

"I think he's speaking near the waters of Sebus."

Isabel gave Abish one last hug before she ran off to find Ammon. She loved it when he taught at Sebus—the soothing sound of the water, the soft winds that blew all around them, the scent of the wildflowers. It had quickly become one of her favorite spots.

She imagined Ammon's face when she told him. What would he say? Would he baptize her right there at the waters? She was nearly there. Isabel pushed herself to run faster.

Something whipped against her legs, tangling them together. Losing her footing, she smacked into the ground. The air left her lungs. She groaned in pain and turned over to see why she had fallen. Isabel looked down and saw a rope weighted at both ends by heavy rocks. It was the sort of thing hunters used to bring down bigger animals, like tapirs.

Isabel did not have to wonder for long why someone would use the device on her. A group of men blocked the sun as they crowded around her. She attempted to scream, but one of the men quickly tied a gag on her mouth.

She tried to calm down, to breathe normally through her nose. The dirty cloth bound tightly against her mouth made her feel as if she would throw up. She struggled, but the men quickly tied her at the wrists and ankles.

The men then slid a pole between the two sets of ropes, subjecting Isabel to the humiliation of being carried like an animal.

They took her away from Ishmael, away from the waters of Sebus. A full-blown sense of panic overtook her. She started to sweat, so much so that her tunic was soon wet with perspiration. She shook so hard that she caused the pole to wobble back and forth. These men could do anything to her. Anything. And she could not defend herself. She was helpless.

Isabel squeezed her eyes shut, wishing desperately that this was some horrible nightmare she would wake up from, something her worry dolls could take from her while she slept.

But this was all too real. Isabel reminded herself that her only way out of this situation was to retain her wits. If these men were going to violate her, they most likely would have done so already. She wore nothing of value for them to steal. But if they didn't want her for those reasons, why were they taking her toward the jungle? Isabel realized that they were taking her somewhere—to someone. A kidnapping?

Perhaps someone wanted to ask her father for a ransom. But who would do such a thing?

Her only recourse would be to talk her way free. And in order for that to take place, she had to stop her teeth from chattering. Her lungs hurt from her panicked breathing. *I have to calm down,* she thought again. If she couldn't control her current situation, she could at least control her reaction to it.

Unfortunately, her mind's logic didn't convince the rest of her body to comply. Isabel strained against the ropes, trying to see if she could wriggle her way free. She counted the men around her. Six. She could outrun them if she could just get loose. She'd have to be sure to run side to side to keep them from using the weighted rope on her again.

But it was hopeless. The ropes had been tied too well. Despair closed in on her until Isabel remembered that Abish knew where she had gone. She would be missed. When Ammon told her family that Isabel had never arrived at the waters, she would be looked for. Ammon would find her. And then he would singlehandedly defeat every man here.

That gave her some reassurance, some strength to stay calm. These men weren't even trying to hide their tracks. They would eventually be discovered. Isabel just hoped it would be soon.

The group continued their trek through the forest. Fern fronds slapped across her body each time the pole swung slightly, and thorns from prickly shrubs cut through her tunic and pierced her skin. The vine-draped ceiba and oak trees overhead only let small patches of sunlight in. At last they came into a clearing where several huts had been set up. The men brought Isabel to the largest one in the middle and unceremoniously dumped her to the ground so that she landed with a thud. Someone from behind her removed the gag. She held her wrists up, expecting the rope to be cut, but instead she was tossed into the hut behind her.

She blinked several times as her eyes adjusted from the bright sunlight outside to the darker interior.

Isabel cried out when she realized who had captured her.

Mahlon. He sat on a thin pallet where he watched her with a malicious grin.

Mahlon fed off of weakness. It would make things worse for her if she showed him how scared she was. She had to appear strong, even if she was terrified. "How dare you!" She hoped he couldn't hear how her voice faltered. "When my father hears about this—"

"Your father will not hear about this, because you will not tell him," Mahlon interrupted. He held an obsidian dagger in his hand, angling the shiny black blade back and forth to catch the sunlight.

Not tell her father! It would be the very first thing she would do as soon as she found a way to get free. Mahlon must know that. So why the confidence that she wouldn't? Horrible scenarios flooded her mind as she imagined what Mahlon might do to ensure her silence.

"Do you think you can threaten me?" *There.* Her voice had finally regained the regal detachment that wouldn't betray her fear.

"Your father's power has been diminishing for some time. I think I can do whatever I wish to you and there will be nothing your father will do in response."

Mahlon sounded far too confident. Isabel tried to match his tone. "Untie me."

He gave a slight chuckle. "You don't give the orders here, Isabel."

"You will address me by my title."

That made Mahlon laugh out loud. "Now, Isabel, is that any way to talk to your future husband?"

Isabel swallowed hard. She tried to stand. Her terror wiped out her reason. If she had to hop all the way back to the palace she would. Mahlon must have a reason for being so bold. He must know something she didn't.

"You can't keep me here," she said, feeling dangerously close to tears. All she could think was that she had to get away.

"Enough talk from you. Sit down, be quiet, and listen."

"I will not—"

"You need to learn your place and do as you're told. I will not tolerate defiance."

As she struggled to get up, still hampered by the ropes, Mahlon suddenly rose and pushed her back down. Isabel fell hard and noticed the look of pleasure it gave Mahlon to hurt her. She went still, not wanting to give him a reason to continue.

"That's better." Mahlon stood over her for moments that felt like hours, forcing Isabel to anticipate what sort of aggression he would unleash on her. Finally he sat back down, and Isabel sighed in relief.

Mahlon picked up his dagger and again turned it back and forth in the available light.

"There have been two times in your father's life when he has stupidly defied his own father." Mahlon's voice made Isabel jump; she'd been so busy watching him with his knife, wondering what he might do with it, that his speaking surprised her. "The first was when he married Kamilah. You know he didn't have permission."

Mahlon looked at her expectantly, and Isabel swallowed, recognizing that he was waiting for a response. "He had already married my mother as my grandfather ordered him to."

"Yes, and after your mother's tragic death, King Laman had another woman in mind, another alliance to strengthen."

Isabel had not known that. Her grandfather had selected another wife for her father?

"Your father lost a third of his kingdom as punishment for his misbehavior."

Something else Isabel had not known. Suddenly, things began to make sense to her. She had often wondered why Mahlon possessed land on the borders of Ishmael. Her grandfather had taken land from her father and given it to Mahlon. It must have been some sort of reward for his accomplishments in battle. It was rumored that her grandfather gave Mahlon special attention because of the love he had for his daughter, Mahlon's mother, who had gone mad before she died. It had been whispered that Mahlon's father, Amulon, had been the cause of her madness.

And as Mahlon sat before her with that eerily calm expression, Isabel wondered if that madness had been handed down to him.

"When I asked your father for your hand, he foolishly refused me—even when he knew that King Laman desired the match."

"Then why didn't my grandfather force me to marry you? He could have overridden my father's objection."

"Your father managed to convince him that you should be given some time to become accustomed to the idea. But Lamoni was still punished for his disobedience in again going against our grandfather's wishes. King Laman couldn't have anyone seeing him as weak. So your father lost another third of his kingdom to me."

When her father had initially denied Mahlon's marriage request, he had warned Isabel not to ask him to defy her grandfather again.

Now she understood why, and the enormity of what her father had lost for her sake hit her. She'd had no idea what it had cost her father to stand up for her. He had to know that he would lose the rest of his kingdom if he said no to his father again.

"Now I am King Laman's tournament winner, and for my prize, I asked for you again. What do you think the king said?"

From the gleam in Mahlon's eye, Isabel knew exactly what her grandfather had said. "No." she whispered the word. She would endure anything but that. She couldn't be Mahlon's wife. She thought again of his mangled servants, of a life filled with torture that she couldn't begin to imagine.

"You have no defenders left," Mahlon informed her. "Your father won't say no this time. If he refuses his father, he will lose everything. King Laman will strip him of all of his lands. Think of it, Isabel. Think of your family with nowhere to go, no home to live in. How will you survive? You can agree to the betrothal. You can keep your family safe and let your father retain what he has left of his lands, or you can watch each member of your family die from starvation. No one would go against our grandfather and take your family in."

"Why are you doing this?" Isabel couldn't stop the tears from filling her eyes at the image Mahlon had put into her mind. The thought of little Naima or Sarala going hungry, of having to watch them suffer and knowing it was her fault, was more than Isabel could take.

The smile faded from Mahlon's face. "My reasons are my own and are not for you to question. All you have to do is answer. Yes or no." His voice began to rise. "You cannot delay this any further."

Her thoughts flitted from one alternative to the next, like a bird hopping from branch to branch. The choice was herself or her family. Either she would sacrifice herself, or she would sacrifice them all.

"A decision, now!" The walls seemed to shake from Mahlon's rage, and Isabel flinched.

As she had a briefly thought of Ammon, something inside her shattered like a thousand clay pots breaking all at once. "Yes," she whispered.

Mahlon relaxed and then stood up. "I was hoping that would be your answer." Mahlon held his obsidian dagger in front of him as he stalked his way over to Isabel.

15

Isabel's eyes went wide with the terror she felt. She put her hands out in front of her, as if that would stop Mahlon from harming her. He grabbed her wrists, but instead of carving up her arms, he cut the bonds and then stooped down to cut the ropes from her ankles. When he finished he reached out and with one hand grabbed Isabel's upper arm so tightly that she had to bite her lip to keep from crying out. He yanked her to a standing position. Isabel slumped slightly, having to lean against him as her feet had no feeling in them.

Mahlon forced her to walk, and the prickling sensation in her feet let her know that she would soon have full use of them. She gritted her teeth against the pain as Mahlon shoved her outside into the light.

He did not release his hold on her as his men encircled around them. Isabel's heart raced as she wondered what he would do next, and her upper arm throbbed beneath his tight grip.

She again realized her precarious situation. As Mahlon had said, she had no defenders left. She was alone.

Again an image of Ammon entered her mind. Ammon would defend her if he could. But even he could not stand against her grandfather, the most powerful king in the Lamanite lands. Even Ammon could not save her.

"She must be returned to the palace. See that it is done."

So she would be given this one reprieve. He would not harm her now. She realized that Mahlon couldn't afford to do so before any marriage took place. If he offended her father by hurting her, and if her grandfather chose to be upset by it, then Mahlon would not be allowed to marry her. Perhaps she could provoke him into making a mistake. If he left her bruised and bleeding . . . She would gladly endure a beating now if it meant avoiding a lifetime of them. Her mind grasped hold of the one thing she knew would infuriate Mahlon.

"You may have power over my father, but there is one man you will never control. If Ammon finds out, he can stop you."

A black rage twisted Mahlon's features, and his grip became even tighter on her arm. Isabel prepared herself as best she could to be hit. She screwed her eyelids shut and waited. Nothing.

She slowly opened her eyes to see Mahlon studying her with what, on anyone else, would be a pitying look—mixed with what looked like jealousy. She didn't know what to make of it. "You will not tell Ammon. He seems to have some misguided sense of honor, and if you told him, he might very well try to stop me. But if he comes after me, King Laman will order his death."

Mahlon was right. He still had her grandfather's protection as one of his favored stewards. If Ammon challenged Mahlon and won, King Laman would kill him in retribution. Ammon had fought mightily at the waters of Sebus. He had won a battle against many men. But not even Ammon could stand against the full strength of her grandfather's armies. She couldn't let him die for her. And if he did somehow stand against the king's armies, Isabel knew she would be responsible for all those deaths, now that she knew the truths Ammon taught. She couldn't tell him anything.

It worried her that Mahlon seemed to have thought through every eventuality, that she couldn't surprise him. Isabel had never dared provoke him as she just had, and he still hadn't responded. He must have known what she was doing.

"You know, Ammon and I both want the same thing."

Isabel's breath caught. Did Mahlon think Ammon wanted to marry her too? Could it be possible?

"What?" she finally asked.

"Eventual control of Ishmael. We're simply employing different tactics. I am being honest about it by marrying you. Ammon is far more devious."

"That's not true. Ammon would never—"

Mahlon laughed at Isabel's spirited defense. "What happens if Ammon succeeds in instituting his religion? Do you think King Laman would ever allow that to happen?"

Isabel tried to move away from Mahlon, but he held fast to her arm. "Ammon's not like that. You don't know him. That's not why he's here."

"Then why is he here?"

Isabel knew she could never explain Ammon's reasons to a man like Mahlon. And suddenly she truly understood the isolation she would live in. She would not be able to be baptized. She would not be permitted to pray or attend any of Ammon's or Jeremias's gatherings or go to the church that Ammon and her father were building.

She would have to practice Mahlon's religion, as Mahlon would now become a king over her father's stolen lands. As his queen, she would have to participate in bloodletting rituals. She would have to witness sacrifices. What had once seemed normal and commonplace now filled her with disgust and despair. She had turned away from those beliefs, from that lifestyle, and the thought that she would now have to continue living something she knew to be against what God wanted filled her with intense pain.

"It was rather foolish of him to come to the Lamanite lands by himself," Mahlon remarked, interrupting her thoughts.

Any slight against Ammon felt like a personal slight to Isabel. "He didn't come alone. He came with his brothers."

Mahlon shrugged as if the entire conversation bored him. He thrust Isabel toward one of his men, repeating his instructions for her to be returned to the palace. "You will say nothing," Mahlon warned her again.

Isabel's upper arm pulsated with pain. She didn't need the reminder. The only way to keep her family safe and to protect her father's remaining lands would be to keep her mouth shut. For their sakes, she would do it.

* * *

"How can you be so certain the girl will not talk?"

Elam, the man Mahlon had selected as captain after Mulek's and Mocum's deaths, was surprisingly mouthy considering how Mahlon had dealt with his predecessors for similar missteps.

"I'm certain," Mahlon said. Isabel was not quite as foolish as most women, but he believed that he had sufficiently scared her into submission.

Now that Isabel would belong to him, Mahlon found that her defense of the Nephite bothered him. He already owed the Nephite a long and painful death after what Ammon had done to Mulek and Mocum. Mahlon did not like his people or his things being taken from him. The Nephite had taken two of his best men and, apparently, the affection of his future wife.

Mahlon returned to his hut and from a woven basket pulled out the folded parchment that contained the maps of his lands. There, in the middle of his portions, lay the piece that still belonged to Lamoni.

Elam had followed Mahlon into his hut and stood waiting in case Mahlon had any commands for him.

As Mahlon traced the outline of the land that represented the kingship he would soon attain, he realized he did have need of Elam's services.

"She said that the Nephite had brothers that came with him. I want them found. Send twenty of my best trackers after them. Whatever kingdom you find them in, promise the king any favor if he will imprison them."

Elam had a questioning expression, but Mahlon didn't care to elaborate. His spies had told him of the changes in King Lamoni's behavior, and how he professed to believe in the Nephite's religion. He might object again to Mahlon marrying Isabel. And despite currently having his grandfather's favor, Mahlon knew the old man's whims could change from one moment to the next. Mahlon could find himself landless and cast out of the Lamanite lands if King Laman decided tomorrow that that's what he wanted.

So Mahlon had to walk a delicate line. He had to keep himself in favor with his grandfather and accomplish his goals without King Lamoni getting in the way. As soon as Isabel had said that Ammon had brothers in the Lamanite lands, Mahlon had started to form a plan. If Ammon's brothers were imprisoned, surely the Nephite would go himself to free them.

Then Ammon would be imprisoned as well. And Ammon's imprisonment would necessitate King Lamoni personally retrieving the Nephite. This would give Mahlon time to marry Isabel at King Lamoni's palace in front of all the witnesses and without interference. By the time—or if—Lamoni and the Nephite returned, it would be too late.

"I will find the Nephite's brothers, but I still don't understand how that will help you become king of Ishmael when Lamoni and his eldest son still live." Elam was apparently still there. Mahlon would have to make certain that in the future that Elam obeyed more quickly, but for now the man could speak; Mahlon's delight in his own cunning moved him to tolerate Elam's disobedience at this particular moment.

Mahlon carefully folded up the parchment. "King Laman does not intend for Isabel's half-brother to become king. He doesn't recognize Lamoni's second marriage. Isabel is his only heir."

"You are content to wait until Lamoni dies to become king?"

Mahlon chuckled at Elam's naïveté. "Lamoni will not be alive much longer."

* * *

How had the day begun with so many possibilities and ended up so horrifically? Isabel wished she could start the day over and do everything differently. But even if she could, Mahlon would have found another way to get her, to threaten her into compliance.

She wanted to go to her room, to curl up on her bed and cry until she fell asleep, although she doubted that sleep would give her any respite. She knew nightmares of Mahlon would follow her there.

She stopped short when she reached her family's courtyard. She had expected everyone to be either in the throne room or at the formal courtyard adjoining it. It surprised her to see them all here.

Her heart constricted when she saw Ammon in the midst of them. He crawled on all fours and had Sarala and Naima on his back. They laughed and giggled as he chased after her brothers, who tried to hold the beast off with their wooden play swords. Ammon reared up suddenly, and the girls shrieked with delight.

She absentmindedly wiped away the tears that suddenly appeared. Just as she had known this morning that what Ammon taught was true, she now knew that she loved him. She loved him, and she could never have him. She had always kept such a tight grasp on her heart. She didn't know when it had slipped away from her keeping to find a new home.

Isabel would have to stay away from Ammon. It would be too hard to be near him, to have him smile at her the way he did, when she knew that her future had been sealed. She tore her gaze away and backed up. She would have to cross the courtyard to reach her room, and she feared that if she had to talk to Ammon she would want to confess everything to him. She was not strong enough to see him yet.

As she turned to go, Isabel nearly ran into Abish.

"I'm so sorry, I didn't see . . . what's wrong?" Abish demanded.

"It's nothing," Isabel whispered as she tried to brush past Abish.

"Don't tell me it's nothing. I know you far too well for that," Abish said. The maidservant reached out to take Isabel by the arm. Isabel cried out in pain. Abish's eyes narrowed, and she pushed up the short sleeve on Isabel's tunic. Abish's eyes then went wide at the purple bruise on Isabel's upper arm. "Who did this?"

Isabel pulled herself away and pushed the sleeve back down. She didn't trust herself to speak.

"Who did that to you?" Abish again asked.

"I can't tell you."

"You can and you will," Abish said. The concern in her eyes made Isabel want to start crying all over again. "Or I will tell your father."

Isabel considered trying to remind Abish which one of them was the princess and which one was the maidservant, but she knew it would be of no use. Abish had always been her best friend despite the roles they were supposed to have. Isabel pulled Abish away from the columns that bordered the long gallery and sank down with her on a nearby stone bench.

"If I tell you, you must swear to me that you will tell no one else."

Abish nodded her agreement, and Isabel found it a relief to share her burden with someone else, if only for a few minutes. Abish's eyes widened in horror as Isabel told her everything that had happened.

Well, not everything. Isabel kept her newly discovered feelings about Ammon to herself. That was too personal to share with anyone else. Even Abish.

"And then I came back here." Isabel finished up her tale. Abish looked like Isabel felt.

"I will come with you," Abish said as she reached out to grab Isabel's hands.

For a moment, Isabel was tempted to accept. She might be able to endure Mahlon better if she had Abish with her. But she could never do that to her worst enemy—let alone someone she loved. "No, you must stay here where it is safe."

"Do you think that I would let you face Mahlon alone?" Abish sounded insulted.

Isabel squeezed Abish's hands in response. "You are my best and dearest friend. You always have been. But I will not let you do this. You know what he will do to you."

"I know what he will do to you. You must have someone with you."

"No." Isabel would not argue. She would not let Abish put herself in that sort of danger.

"There must be something we can do to stop him," Abish said. Isabel wished that she still had that sort of hope.

"We could tell Ammon. He would never let Mahlon do this to you," Abish exclaimed. From her position in the gallery, Isabel could still see into her family's courtyard. Ammon continued to play with her brothers and sisters among Kamilah's orchids and fruit trees.

She permitted herself to imagine what it would be like to race over to Ammon, to tell him everything and, how it would feel for him to take her in his arms to comfort her. She could almost hear his voice telling her that he would protect her, that she would always be safe. But it was nothing more than a wish, and she had no more room in her life for wishing.

"We can't tell Ammon. There's nothing he could do. A war would start and many would die, and if he harmed Mahlon, my grandfather would kill him. I won't let him . . ." Isabel's words trailed off. She thought that somehow it might be easier to be married to Mahlon if she knew that Ammon lived, that he was somewhere in the world teaching his faith. That he was happy. She didn't know how she could bear any of it if Ammon died.

"Besides," Isabel tried to keep her tone light, "I am only his friend and not someone he concerns himself with."

"That is not true," Abish said, but to Isabel's relief she didn't press her point. If Isabel had thought there was even the slightest possibility that Ammon might return her feelings, she didn't know if she could go through with the marriage to Mahlon. It would make everything worse if Isabel could hope, even for a moment, that Ammon might love her. Abish interrupted Isabel's thoughts by saying, "But you have found the true faith. You belong here in Ishmael with others who believe as you do."

"Isabel!"

Her insides twisted as Ammon called out her name. He stood up, shielding the sun from his eyes, and waved to her, indicating that she should come over. Isabel drank the sight of him in. This was how she wanted to remember him—smiling, happy, and surrounded by the people she loved.

A sharp pain throbbed in her heart over what she had lost and could never have.

She stood up slowly, keeping her posture erect and regal. "It no longer matters what I believe," she said to Abish.

Then Isabel resolutely turned and walked away from Ammon.

16

Isabel started her day with a morning run, followed by a half hour of practice with her sling. She hit the target dead center almost every time now. She smiled sadly when she remembered why she had started practicing in the first place—to prove something to Ammon. She wished she hadn't been so suspicious of him then. She wished she could have seen him then as she saw him now so all that time wouldn't have been wasted. Her practicing served only to fill her with a heavy sadness as it reminded her of the loss of any future she might have had with Ammon.

When she returned to the palace, Ammon seemed to be everywhere despite her best efforts to avoid him. She'd avoided him for several days, and even though she knew she couldn't stay away from him forever, she didn't feel ready to see him. Isabel feared that it would take very little to convince her to pour her soul out to him and confess the truth of her situation. She wanted to confide in him so badly. So, consequently, she didn't trust herself to be alone with him.

Her plans of avoiding Ammon were altered when her father announced that he had organized a ball game for Ammon's benefit. Apparently Ammon had never seen the game played, and, declaring this a great tragedy, the king commanded his regular team and their alternates to prepare themselves for a demonstration.

Once word had been received that the players were ready, the royal family led a procession out to the ball court. Isabel walked behind the king, keeping her mouth pressed in a line and her gaze off of Ammon. Ammon walked alongside her father, asking him questions about the game. It didn't take long to arrive at the court, as it was not far from the palace.

Isabel looked at the arena as Ammon must be seeing it. There were so many things she could have rediscovered with him. The court itself was I-shaped. Parallel masonry walls enclosed the central alley where the game would be played. The plastered walls sloped up from the playing field in a diagonal direction and were colored in bright yellows, oranges, and reds. The walls and the field had been made perfectly smooth in order to prevent the ball from going in any direction but what the players intended.

Along the top of the walls were several stone markers that had birds, jaguars, monkeys, and other animals carved into them. She heard her father explain to Ammon that they were used to mark zones on the field and also to keep score. Other markers were embedded into the field itself to further delineate the zones. A vertical stone ring hung on each respective wall, but it was rare that someone got the ball through the ring. The last time someone had done so, Isabel had been six years old. She smiled at the memory and excitement of that day.

Her thoughts were soon drowned out by the music and noise from the crowd. She heard Ammon exclaim, "It's so loud!"

Isabel remembered when her father had taken her here at a very young age to show her the special sound qualities of the field. He had placed her at one end and then raced to the other. He had whispered to her, and Isabel had been able to hear him as clearly as if he had been standing next to her. She had in turn brought her younger brothers and sisters to the court to show them the same trick.

So when people yelled out their excitement, and when the musicians struck up their drums, whistles, flutes, and conch-shell trumpets, the sounds were nearly overwhelming.

Isabel allowed herself one peek at Ammon, but he didn't seem overwhelmed. Instead, he grinned at the commotion.

Dancers moved to the music on the field, their elaborate costumes swishing and swaying in time to the rhythm. Acrobats performed their tricks next to the dancers, careful to stay out of the dancers' way.

Her family ascended the stone stairs behind the stands, which were situated right above the field's walls. Temporary scaffolding had been set up at each end zone to allow even more room for spectators. Typically, more people would come to see the match, but there had been no time for faraway farming families to arrive as the notice had been so minimal.

Isabel followed her sisters to their front-row seats. As everyone seated themselves, King Lamoni motioned for Isabel to come closer. He indicated an empty spot next to Ammon.

"Here, you must sit and explain the game to our visitor," Lamoni said with an oh-so-innocent expression on his face. Isabel suspected her father was up to something, but she wasn't certain what.

Everyone stared at her as she stood there, and Isabel saw that she had no choice. She had to sit next to Ammon or risk trouble. She couldn't defy such an explicit command from her father.

"Your father can't explain it as well as you?" Ammon teased. He had to lean in for her to hear, and his breath tickled her ear. This, somehow, made all her insides melt.

Be strong, she reminded herself.

She turned to say back in his ear, "My father takes his gaming very seriously. He doesn't like to be distracted when he's watching an event."

"Oh, I understand," Ammon said with a twinkle in his blue-gray eyes. "That's how my father feels about watching corn grow."

Isabel had to stifle the urge to laugh. Somehow, being here on this beautiful day, surrounded by her family, and sitting next to Ammon, Mahlon and his demands seemed far away. Perhaps she could enjoy herself. Maybe she could have this one last game, this one last time with Ammon, to keep as a precious memory. She should relax and forget her troubles.

Ammon turned then and smiled at her again. He certainly made it easy enough to forget.

The dancers, musicians, and acrobats left the playing field. The game's four judges came out. Then the ten players came on the field, and everyone stood to cheer for them as they waved up to the crowds.

"Who are we rooting for?" Ammon had to yell to Isabel.

Isabel pointed out the five members of her father's official team. Ammon bent his head next to her mouth so she could explain what a great honor it was to be on that team. The players were given many privileges, rights, and wealth. They also had a place at court. The alternate team, if they could defeat the official team, would have the opportunity to compete for a place on the official team and to receive the same honors. It would be an exciting and well-matched game with extremely motivated competitors.

This was the first game Isabel had watched without any ceremonial rituals taking place beforehand. Usually the players would wear stone yokes around their waists, covered with decorative stone hachas. Everyone would wear elaborate feathered headdresses. Not this time.

Now the players wore only their regular equipment. Each competitor had a yoke on his waist made from fiber strips. They wore protective guards on their shins, knees, and forearms, made from quilted cotton or animal hide, held in place by a thin piece of wood and strong, sisal fiber ropes. They wore thick leather helmets on their heads.

Isabel explained the differences in this game to Ammon telling him that in the past the games had been highly ritualistic and significant. The ball was meant to represent the sun, and its movement in the game were like the heavenly bodies in the sky. The game showed the battle between the sun, the light giver, and the moon and stars, the harbingers of darkness. These opposing forces each had a place in the game, each symbolically representing dark and light, good and evil, life and death.

But with Lamoni's conversion, the before-game rituals had been removed. Now it would just be a game. Ammon seemed pleased with this information. Isabel, however, felt a sudden sense of shame and regret over what she had previously seen on this court, the rituals she had participated in just by being here. She thought of all the blood that had been shed on the field.

Then she thought of how many more ball games she would attend that would carry on those sacrifices and symbolism when she married Mahlon.

She shut the dark thoughts out. She would live in this moment, in this day, and she would enjoy herself.

"Have you truly never seen a game before?" Isabel asked.

"Alma's father used to live here in the highlands, and he told us of the game and how it was played. But my father thinks such things are frivolous, and so we have no ball courts in Zarahemla."

The players moved into position, each team going to their half of the field. They got into a straight line between the center dividing line and the end zones. One of the game's judges stood on the center line, and, once he ascertained that both sides were ready, he threw a six-pound rubber ball into play.

"Look at how high it goes!" Ammon called out in amazement. "I can't believe how high it bounces!"

It had never occurred to her that the Nephites might have balls different than the Lamanites. "Do you not mix your rubber tree sap with morning-glory vine juice?" Isabel asked. Ammon said they didn't, so Isabel explained that it was the juice that made the balls bounce so high.

"I'm going to have to take some of those balls back with me," Ammon said as he watched the ball bounce off one of the walls. "Once I show one of those to Aaron . . ." He trailed off and laughed. "Perhaps my brothers and I will be able to convince my father to build a ball court."

His words struck her, but then, of course Ammon would go home at some point. He had said he wished to remain in Ishmael, perhaps for the rest of his days, but realistically he couldn't stay here forever. Why would he? Once he had established his church, there would be nothing to keep him here. Isabel would miss Ammon. In a sense she missed him now. But in Zarahemla he would be safe. It would be better for him to be there. Surprisingly, Isabel found she could let him go if it meant knowing he would stay alive.

Isabel explained the rules of the game as it happened. The teams had to stay on their own side of the playing field. The goal was to be the first team to score eight points. Points were scored when an opposing team accidentally used an illegal part of their bodies—the players could only use their hips, forearms, and legs to hit the ball. If someone used their feet or hands, the other team scored a point.

"Can they use their heads?" Ammon asked.

"They wouldn't want to," Isabel replied.

"Why not?"

Ammon's question was answered when one of the players took a shot to the face. The solid rubber ball smacked hard against the player's chin, knocking him to the ground. The spectators groaned in sympathy when he was hit. Despite his split lip and the quickly forming bruise, the player jumped back to his feet to keep playing, and the crowd roared their approval at his fortitude.

Isabel told Ammon that points could also be scored if the ball was knocked out of reach from the other team so that they could not return it, if it bounced more than once before it was returned, or if it failed to cross the center line when being hit back. The scoring was extremely complicated, as points could not only be accumulated but lost. Games could possibly go on for hours.

"What if someone gets it through the ring?"

"It never happens," Isabel told him. "It is so difficult that the team would automatically win for getting it in."

Now that Ammon understood the game, Isabel saw that he had become totally absorbed. He was so interested in everything, so excited by it. It felt amazingly good to sit next to him, to be part of that. Usually a ball game would enthrall Isabel—she was her father's daughter, after all—but now all she could concentrate on was Ammon's hand resting so near hers, almost touching. Or the way that his leg accidentally bumped into hers several times. This hyperawareness rendered her nearly incapable of focusing on the game.

But then one of her father's team members made a spectacular move, sliding down on his knees to save a ball, and the crowd went wild cheering for him. Isabel jumped up and clapped along with everyone else.

The ball went back and forth, bouncing between the two teams. The players mainly used their hips to return the ball, as the yoke protected them best there. The ball bounced on the field and on the two walls, and whizzed back and forth so quickly it was hard to keep track of it.

The game got more and more intense, with each side scoring and losing points. The alternate team gained another point, which caused the score to be tied. Isabel thought she might go hoarse, she yelled so loudly. Ammon stood next to her, cheering just as loud.

Her father's team broke the tie when the team captain whacked the ball with his right shin and his opponents failed to reach the ball in time, causing it to bounce twice. That made the score seven to six.

Then, to everyone's shock, the impossible happened.

The ball came back into play, and, on the first serve, one of Isabel's father's players hit the ball with his forearm toward the wall . . . and it went right through the opposing team's stone ring!

The crowd went into a frenzy and then started running for the stairs. Isabel laughed with delight and turned to see her father and mother also laughing as they picked up her younger sisters and headed for the back of the stands.

Ammon looked adorably confused. "What's happening?"

Isabel just grabbed Ammon's hand and pulled him toward the stairs. "We have to run!"

She was laughing so hard that it made it difficult to breathe. But Ammon followed her, his hand gripping hers tightly.

"Why are we running?" he asked once they had cleared the ball court.

"If someone makes a shot through one of the rings," Isabel said over her shoulder as they ran, "that player has the right to go into the crowd and collect everyone's jewelry and clothing. So we have to run before he and his friends can catch us!"

This made Ammon laugh as well, and he sped up so that he ran right beside her.

"Come on," she said as they moved away from the crowd. "I know of a place where we can hide."

* * *

"How old were you again when you found this spot?" Ammon asked uncomfortably.

"I was six the last time someone hit the ball in. There was a lot more room then."

He imagined there must have been, as they had no room at all now. They had just barely managed to squeeze into the copse of thick pine trees. At first Ammon had noticed the heavy pine scent that seemed to surround them, but now all he could think of was that Isabel had worn her hair down today, that she had laughed and laughed, and that she had never seemed more beautiful to him.

It did not help matters that she was pressed flush against him. Ammon tried to think of something that would take his mind off of it. Squishing a frog. His sister's pet monkey flinging his droppings at the family during dinner.

Nothing worked.

Isabel started to giggle just as Ammon heard a commotion near the copse. It could be the players looking for stragglers.

"Shhh," he said, putting his hand over her mouth. She continued to giggle behind his hand. Ammon tried hard not to laugh himself.

But his desire to laugh faded away when he realized how soft her lips felt under his hand. Ammon quickly withdrew his hand, but the damage had already been done.

Isabel looked up at him questioningly, the laughter still in her eyes.

Ammon had so many reasons not to kiss Isabel. He tried very hard to remember them. Oh yes—he had a mission. That had to be his focus. He couldn't afford any distractions at all. A woman had already nearly cost him his salvation. He couldn't let it happen again. But suddenly, he didn't care. All his concerns slipped away from him, becoming meaningless and unimportant. All he wanted to do was kiss Isabel. Frighteningly enough, nothing else mattered.

His hands came up to rest on her shoulders as he watched her mouth. The still-functioning part of his brain realized that if he did kiss her the way he wanted to, it would be nothing short of a marriage proposal. But he didn't care.

After all, he rationalized, Lamoni was trying to make a match between Ammon and Isabel. On the way to the game he had told Ammon that his offer still stood, that Ammon could be a son instead of a servant.

This could work. And, he reminded himself, this situation was different. Isabel was not a shady woman from his past. She was his here-and-now. Ammon knew she believed in the things he taught—not only because he had sensed it but because Abish had confided in him several days ago that Isabel had said she knew they were true. He had been waiting for her to come to him. He could be patient and let her take all the time she needed to decide to be baptized.

Isabel could be baptized, he could continue his mission, and then they could marry, and he would get to kiss her as much as he wanted. All in all, this was shaping up to be an incredibly fantastic idea.

He wondered why he hadn't thought of it before.

"Isabel." Ammon murmured her name, almost in warning of what he was about to do.

She seemed to understand his intention, and her eyebrows flew upward in what looked like shock or disbelief. That didn't do much for his ego.

Regardless, he had to kiss her.

He moved his head down, but before his lips could meet hers, Isabel put a hand on his chest. "Wait."

17

WAIT? HE DIDN'T WANT TO. But it forced him to consider the possibility that she might not want him to kiss her. "What is it? Do you not feel the same way I do?"

"I feel . . ." Isabel faltered.

"What? What do you feel, Isabel?" he pressed. He had to know, had to hear her say whether she had the same confusing feelings that he did.

"Being with you is like when I'm running. No, it's better than when I'm running—and I didn't know that there was something better than that."

Ammon felt a sense of satisfaction and immense joy. He leaned in again to kiss her, but she again stopped him.

"We can't."

"Why not?"

"I am betrothed."

Nothing could have shocked Ammon more. He released her shoulders and tried to back up in the small space but couldn't. Betrothed? How was that even possible?

"Since when? To who?" Ammon demanded.

"I can't tell you," Isabel whispered, her eyes filling with tears.

"You can tell me anything, Isabel. Tell me what's happened," Ammon said.

She shook her head. "I want to tell you, but I can't."

"You can," he repeated. Why hadn't anyone told him? Why hadn't he heard that Isabel had become betrothed to another? Had he been so singleminded in his desire to establish the Church that he had somehow missed this announcement completely?

Then she started to cry. Ammon hated that she was crying, hated that he couldn't do anything to stop it. He took her in his arms, saying soothing things against her soft hair.

"Please tell me," he said.

Isabel pulled back to look up at him. "If I tell you, you have to make me a promise first."

He wanted to say, "Anything," but her behavior was so unlike Isabel that it made him hesitate. He felt wary of making a promise he couldn't keep, because he always kept his word.

"What sort of promise?" he finally asked.

"First, you have to promise you will tell no one what I'm about to tell you. Second, you would have to promise me that no matter what I tell you, you won't challenge Mahlon."

"Why would I . . ." Ammon's words trailed off as he figured out the situation. So it was Mahlon. An anger unlike any Ammon had ever felt before possessed his entire body. Mahlon. How could she marry Mahlon?

"What has he done to you?" Ammon demanded.

Isabel began to cry again. "Promise me, or I can't tell you."

While he did feel some jealousy, that wasn't the reason for his reaction. Ammon had heard too many stories from the servants about Mahlon. He couldn't let Isabel marry a man like that.

From the expression on Isabel's face, Ammon saw that she knew exactly the sort of man Mahlon was. Yet she had agreed to marry him. Why?

The only way he would discover the truth was to promise. He could waste time pleading with her to explain, but she might not tell him anything if he didn't promise not to challenge Mahlon.

"Why do you require a promise?" He hoped it might prompt Isabel to tell him what had happened, but she didn't.

"I know that nothing I can say will make you break a promise. You have far too much honor for that."

Ammon clenched and unclenched his jaw several times before he finally said, "I promise."

Then Isabel poured out the whole story, giving Ammon every excruciating detail of what Mahlon had put her through and what he had threatened her with. He saw the fading bruise on Isabel's arm where Mahlon had roughly grabbed her, saw the faint marks on her wrists where Mahlon had tied her with ropes. Only a few minutes earlier he hadn't thought it possible to feel any more anger than he had at that moment—now he realized that he was capable of a good deal more. He wanted to destroy Mahlon for what he had done to Isabel.

"You don't have to marry him."

Isabel sighed, a deep and heartbreaking sigh. "Yes I do. My father would lose everything. No land, no food, no home. He wouldn't even know how to take care of himself or my family."

"I could help you," Ammon said.

"No." Isabel shook her head. "You have to leave me alone. You have to let me go."

"I don't think I can do that anymore."

"You have to," Isabel insisted again. "Let me do this, Ammon. Let me be selfless, for once in my life. Let me do this for my father. For my family. Let me repay them for everything I've put them through in the past."

Ammon wanted to grab her and shake some sense into her head. But he kept his hands balled up at his sides. "No one would want you to sacrifice yourself."

"There's no other way."

"There is always another way. Let me talk to your father. Perhaps if he spoke to your grandfather—"

Isabel let out a strangled cry that sounded like half laughter, half sobbing. "My father is terrified of my grandfather. I'm surprised that he ever stood up to him. My grandfather is a bully and a tyrant. My father would give in. At least this way it is my decision. I can choose to protect them."

Ammon had never felt so helpless before—not when he had been locked up and death seemed imminent, not when he had questioned whether anyone would ever listen to his message and he had proceeded on faith alone. It frustrated him that Isabel wouldn't even consider any other options, that she had already declared herself a martyr and thrown herself on the altar.

"How can you do this?" Ammon asked, hearing the anger in his own voice.

But Isabel didn't shrink away from it. She stood tall and looked him in the eye, reminding him very much of their first encounters. "I will bend. I will adapt. It's what I do. It's what my people have always done."

"It's not too late," Ammon said in desperation. "We can stop him."

Isabel put a calming hand on Ammon's forearm. "It is too late. You don't understand how my grandfather adores Mahlon and how, in the end, my family will lose all that they have. This is the only way to stop him."

"I refuse to accept that."

"You have to."

Isabel then left their hiding spot, wriggling her way through the vines and the gray-brown tree trunks until she got clear and stood on the other side.

Ammon felt as if his heart were being wrenched from his chest. He had refused to recognize how important Isabel was to him, that he did love her and wanted to marry her, even when Jeremias had pointed it out to him. Now his obstinate and narrow-minded vision had cost him the person that suddenly mattered most in the world to him. If only he hadn't been so stubborn, so unwilling to recognize the truth!

His pain was exacerbated when Isabel turned to him with the same pain and sadness evident in her eyes. "If only you'd said yes to my father the first night we met."

Isabel then ran away as if her feet were on fire. Ammon didn't chase after her despite wanting to. She was betrothed to another. He had no more right to interfere in her life.

And it was his own fault. His determination to stay on course had cost him his future happiness.

* * *

Everyone seemed to take notice of Ammon's dark, unhappy mood. He didn't know if anyone else noted Isabel acting the same way. Ammon tried to behave as he always had, but he found it impossible.

At night, when Ammon couldn't sleep for thinking about Isabel,

Jeremias fortunately didn't probe. Jeremias simply offered Ammon his support and promised to render any assistance that Ammon might need. He didn't ask what had happened, and Ammon felt grateful for the reprieve. He didn't want to break his word to Isabel—his promise to tell no one.

Ammon felt guilty praying over the situation. He knew he shouldn't feel that way, but this was a mess he had gotten himself into. He had never once bothered to ask the Lord about Isabel previously. What if the Lord had pointed him in her direction? He didn't feel as if he should now ask for help for a complicated situation that was of his own making.

But despite not praying about it, help still arrived in the form of Isabel's father. King Lamoni summoned Ammon and explained that he would like to take him to the land of Nephi to meet his father. Lamoni explained that since he had not attended his father's feast, he had to go to the city himself and give King Laman an explanation as to why he had missed it. Ammon also understood that since Lamoni had changed his religious beliefs, it would be necessary for him to make a full accounting to his father, as it might alter the political relationship between the two men. If what Isabel had said about her father fearing her grandfather had been correct, this could not have been an easy decision for King Lamoni.

But it meant gaining a private audience with King Laman. It meant the possibility of saving Isabel from Mahlon. It was as if the sun finally shone after weeks of storms. Ammon grinned and agreed to go.

While Ammon didn't know yet how he would convince King Laman to reverse his decision that Mahlon marry Isabel, at least now he might have an opportunity to rectify this situation.

Because of his lapse in not praying about Isabel when he should have, Ammon rededicated himself to knowing the will of the Lord—particularly since the more he thought over the trip, the more trepidation he felt. It was strange—he had initially been thrilled by the idea, but as time progressed, he felt more and more concerned without understanding why.

So Ammon got on his knees and asked the Lord why he felt that way. The answer was distinct and clear—if Ammon and King Lamoni went to the land of Nephi, King Laman would try to kill Ammon.

Then the Lord revealed to him that Ammon and Lamoni were to go to a place called Middoni because Aaron was being held prisoner there, along with his traveling companions, Muloki and Ammah.

Ammon's heart dropped into his stomach with worry for his twin. He knew what it was like to be held in a Lamanite prison. He hoped the change in plans wouldn't upset King Lamoni too much, but with or without the king, Ammon had to free his brother.

He had gone from having hope of helping Isabel to realizing that he now had to pass on his one chance. Part of him still wanted to go with Lamoni, but the Lord had told him to save his brother. It was a horrible decision to have to make, and it tore him apart to make it.

He quickly located the king outside the palace, where he had begun preparations to visit his father. Servants loaded tributes and offerings to appease King Laman into large woven backpacks, putting the tumpline over their foreheads. The king and his massive entourage seemed ready to leave. Ammon approached King Lamoni and said, "My brother and our friends are in a prison in Middoni. I have to go there to free them."

The king considered Ammon's announcement for a moment before he said, "I know that God gives you the power to do all things. But I will go with you to the land of Middoni, for the king of Middoni, whose name is Antiomno, is an ally of mine. I will negotiate with him so that he will let your brethren out of prison." King Lamoni paused as if to judge Ammon's reaction. Ammon worried what it might mean for King Lamoni if he didn't make an appearance in King Laman's court, but he felt grateful for the help. It would certainly expedite the process if King Lamoni could personally intervene with King Antiomno.

Lamoni interrupted his thoughts by asking, "Who told you that your brethren were in prison?"

"No one has told me save it be God."

When Lamoni heard this, he told his servants to leave behind the gifts for his father and to instead make ready to go to Middoni. "Then I think it best that I go with you down to the land of Middoni, and I will plead with the king to release your brethren."

Not knowing what the outcome of Lamoni's negotiations with Antiomno might be, Ammon decided to prepare himself as well. He informed Jeremias of the situation, and Jeremias volunteered to come along. King Lamoni insisted that Jeremias and Ammon carry weapons, as the journey could be dangerous. He gave Ammon an impressive sword. The wood center had multiple carvings and engravings with scenes of battles won; the black obsidian rectangles embedded all around the sides shone brightly. Ammon tucked it into a drawstring pouch, along with a black-bladed hunting knife. He also carried his sling, which he slipped into the belt at his waist. Jeremias had a spear and a bow with a quiver of arrows.

They set out immediately, King Lamoni being carried on his chariot while Ammon and Jeremias walked alongside him. The procession did not move as quickly as Ammon would have liked, but he understood that a political statement regarding Lamoni's power and circumstance had to be made when they entered Middoni.

Middoni lay in a southeasterly direction from Ishmael, at a lower elevation. They walked through high grass fields interspersed with groves of gnarled nance trees blooming with orange and yellow flowers. They descended until they reached a large plateau called Midian. Lamoni pointed out the valley where Middoni was located. Ammon saw a narrow and fertile-looking valley placed between two large volcanic mountains. *Not too far now.* He thought of Aaron being in that valley, tied up in a Lamanite prison. Ammon worried over what Aaron had to deal with, but he knew that the Lord would keep His promise to their father and that he would find his brother alive.

Then one of the servants called out that someone was coming. Everyone turned to look, and Ammon saw a procession nearly twice the size of Lamoni's. "My father," Lamoni said in a low voice. He ordered his chariot to be put down.

Ammon walked forward to gain a better view of King Laman as his entourage rapidly approached. Once King Laman had caught sight of King Lamoni's group, the older king had apparently commanded his servants to increase their pace.

Something's wrong. Ammon's instincts in these sorts of situations were rarely off. He took his sword out of its drawstring pouch, sensing trouble. King Lamoni stood a ways off from his caravan, and Ammon joined him, standing a few feet back at a respectful distance. King Lamoni looked terrified, and Ammon felt worried for him.

King Laman stepped from his chariot and with quick strides reached the spot where Lamoni awaited his father.

Lamoni began to bow and properly greet his father, but Laman interrupted him. "Why did you not come to the feast I held for my sons and my people?"

Ammon knew that by missing the feast when expected, King Lamoni had given his father reason to question his loyalty and allegiance. The feast had been held to strengthen the ties between King Laman and his under kings, and Lamoni's absence had been nothing short of treasonous.

Ammon wondered if King Laman could be reasoned with, but it was easy enough to make out King Laman's character. He struck Ammon as a hard-hearted and powerful man used to getting his way.

King Lamoni tried to explain, but Laman again cut him off. "Where are you going with this Nephite, who is one of the children of a liar?"

This time Lamoni was permitted to speak, and he explained to his father that they were going to Middoni to free Ammon's imprisoned brethren. Ammon had never seen Lamoni like this, with such fear and hesitation in his voice. Isabel had not been exaggerating her father's relationship with her grandfather. He sensed that Lamoni couched his words carefully, so as not to offend the mighty king.

Then, to Ammon's surprise, King Lamoni told his father the exact reasons why he had stayed behind in his own kingdom instead of coming to the feast.

King Laman did not react well. His face turned red, and his voice boomed across the plateau.

"Lamoni, you are planning to deliver these Nephites, who are sons of a liar. Nephi robbed our fathers, and now his children are coming among us that they may, by their cunning and their lyings, deceive us, that they again may rob us of our property."

"My king, you don't understand—"

"I understand perfectly!" King Laman shouted. "You will not go to the land of Middoni, but you will return with me to Ishmael where we will straighten matters out. Now, I command you to take your sword and slay this traitorous Nephite."

Lamoni kept his gaze on the ground. Ammon could see that he had balled his fists behind his back so hard that his knuckles had turned white. King Lamoni shook, whether from fear or anger Ammon didn't know.

Isabel had explained how her father had lost his lands to Mahlon because of his two previous acts of rebellion. If Lamoni refused his father now, he would surely lose what land he had left.

"No."

The word was so quiet that Ammon wondered if he had imagined it.

But from the look on King Laman's face, he realized he hadn't.

"What did you say?"

King Lamoni lifted his face to meet his father's furious gaze. "I said no. I will not slay Ammon, and I will not return to the land of Ishmael. I am going to the land of Middoni that I may release the brethren of Ammon, for I know that they are just men and holy prophets of the true God."

"Do you realize what you are saying?" King Laman bellowed the words at Lamoni like smoke rising from a volcano about to erupt.

Ammon certainly understood what Lamoni had said. King Laman had, in effect, ordered Lamoni to declare his allegiance by making a choice. By choosing to defend the Nephite, King Lamoni had broken all ties with his father. This would be viewed as a treacherous act that might lead to the loss of all his possessions and his own life. Yet Lamoni stood strong in his friendship with Ammon and in his new faith. Ammon had never admired or respected him more.

King Lamoni did not respond to his father's question. With a mighty roar, King Laman withdrew his sword.

Ammon stepped in front of King Lamoni. "You will not slay your son, even though it would be better that he should fall than you, because he has repented of his sins. But if you should fall at this time, in your anger, your soul could not be saved."

"You dare speak to me with such disrespect? I am the greatest of all the Lamanite kings! I will not be spoken to that way by someone like you!"

King Laman stepped forward, and Ammon put his sword out in front of him. "It's best that you stop, for if you slay your son, him being an innocent man, his blood would cry from the ground to the Lord his God for vengeance to come upon you, and perhaps you would lose your soul."

Despite his anger at King Laman's desire to kill his own child, Ammon stayed calm and said his words clearly and succinctly. He wanted King Laman to understand the eternal implications of his temperamental actions.

"I know that if I should slay my son, I should shed innocent blood—for it is *you* that has tried to destroy him."

King Laman undid the knot at his shoulder and let his cloak fall to the ground. "So it is you that I will kill."

Two of King Laman's personal bodyguards rushed forward to help their king. But King Laman held his hand up. "Stay back. I wouldn't be much of a king if I couldn't take care of one Nephite."

"I don't want to fight you," Ammon said as he lifted his sword in a defensive posture, "but I will not let you kill anyone here."

King Laman scowled as he approached. "We will see."

18

"AMMON, HE IS MY FATHER," Lamoni said at Ammon's shoulder.

"I will not slay him," Ammon tried to reassure the king. But as he had said, he would not let King Laman kill Lamoni or anyone else.

There was no hesitation in King Laman's attack, no looking for weakness or attempts at intimidation. The older man came at Ammon with full force.

Ammon defensively lifted his own sword to block the king's blows. Ammon slipped into the same state that he had been in during the battle over the flocks. He couldn't have explained it to anyone else—it was an utter state of calmness, of calculating his opponent's next move and fighting accordingly. His mind cleared, and his body seemed to move of its own accord with his practiced and well-honed skills.

King Laman was an extremely fit man, a very worthy warrior, but he was also much older than Ammon. Ammon didn't want to harm the king or to kill him, so he thought instead to wait the fight out. Surely King Laman would tire before he did—especially if the king kept on the way he was. The king swung at Ammon viciously and repeatedly. Ammon realized his plan would be much easier if he had a shield to help deflect the attacks.

They were caught up in a deadly dance, where the king lunged at him, thrust his sword at him, and Ammon moved out of the way or used his sword to parry if needed. The king came a bit too close with one massive swing aimed at Ammon's torso, and Ammon had to quickly inhale, pulling his stomach inward to keep the sword from hitting him.

Ammon could see the older king's frustration growing as he realized that Ammon had not made any offensive moves. King Laman became angrier and increased his onslaught. It required Ammon to move faster than he had before.

After several more minutes, King Laman showed signs of tiring, and Ammon felt relieved that it was nearly over. The king continued to aim blow after blow at Ammon, but Ammon's skill was superior, his endurance and stamina apparently able to outlast the king's.

After Ammon deflected yet another swing, King Laman staggered backward, breathing heavily. He held his sword in front of him as his chest heaved. The king bent slightly at the waist as he tried to gain control over his breathing.

Ammon saw movement behind King Laman—several of his personal guard had stepped forward to flank their king. Ammon now had to watch the king's bodyguards to make certain that they wouldn't ignore their king's command and step in to protect him. Ammon could see they wanted to.

This new distraction was what kept Ammon from realizing that King Lamoni had come up on his right and asked his father to stop the fight. Ammon heard the worry in Lamoni's voice, just as he realized the danger the king was in. Ammon shouted at him to get back.

Apparently still infuriated over the choices Lamoni had made, King Laman went after his unarmed son. Ammon realized that the fight had to end. Now.

Ammon leapt in front of Lamoni to block King Laman's path. Ammon moved from a defensive posture to an offensive one. King Laman looked surprised at the change in tactics. Now the king had to try and defend himself against Ammon's attacks. Ammon moved swiftly and surely, probing for a weakness in the king's defense.

And there it was. The king didn't properly protect his sword arm. With a slicing motion, Ammon cut the king just above his elbow. King Laman cried out in pain and dropped his sword to the ground, clutching the wound Ammon had just inflicted.

Before anyone could react, Ammon took out his hunting knife and held it to the king's throat.

"Ammon," he heard Lamoni say in alarm.

Though Ammon had no intention of harming King Laman, he decided that no one else needed to know it.

King Laman went wide eyed with surprise and fear. All of his earlier bravado faded as King Laman began to plead for his life. Ammon kept the knife to the king's throat and raised his sword in the other hand so that it was level with Laman's head. "I will smite you except you grant that my brethren be cast out of prison."

"If you will spare me I will grant whatever you ask, even half of the kingdom."

Ammon bit the inside of his cheek to keep from smiling. Only half the kingdom? He should be insulted. For all King Laman knew, Ammon was about to strike him down. And if he did, then Ammon would gain control of the entire kingdom. King Laman was being more miserly than Ammon would have imagined.

Putting aside his desire to tease, Ammon recognized that he did have the king in his hands and could gain whatever favors he wished for. His mind flashed to thoughts of Isabel. Perhaps he could make a difference now. Ammon tried to keep his voice stern and serious when he said, "If you will grant that my brethren are freed from prison, and also that Lamoni may keep his kingdom, and that you will not be displeased with him, but let him live as he desires, I will spare you. Otherwise I will smite you to the earth."

"That is all you would ask for?" King Laman looked confused and relieved at the same time.

Ammon lowered his sword and took the knife away from the king. "Yes."

King Laman looked from Lamoni to Ammon. "You must be a great friend to my son."

Ammon said nothing; it should be obvious to anyone that he cared for King Lamoni.

"Because this is all you have desired, that I release your brothers and allow my son Lamoni to retain his kingdom, I will grant unto you that my son retain his kingdom from this time and forever. I will govern him no more. And I will also grant that your brothers be cast out of prison."

Ammon couldn't have asked for more. Lamoni would now retain his kingdom no matter what. Too many witnesses had heard King

Laman's declaration. Mahlon could never take the kingdom away from Lamoni. Isabel wouldn't have to marry him. Ammon allowed himself a little smile. He couldn't wait to tell her.

"When you say *kingdom,* do you include the return of those lands that King Lamoni has lost?" Ammon wanted to clarify.

"Of course." King Laman nodded as if that was already understood. Mahlon would now cease to be a threat to Lamoni's family in every way. King Laman was also more generous than Ammon had initially thought. He had granted Lamoni political freedom. King Lamoni would no longer have to pay tribute to his father or be under his control. King Laman would let the people in Ishmael worship as they wished. Ammon had not asked for quite such an overwhelming gift, and the gesture was not lost on him.

He thought again of the prayers he had not let himself say aloud, the prayers he had carried in his heart regarding Isabel, and saw that they had just been answered.

Ammon called for bandages to be brought. Jeremias appeared next to him, the clean bandages in his hand. As always, Jeremias seemed to read his mind and knew what Ammon would ask for before he asked.

Jeremias greeted the king and asked permission to treat his wound. With a still somewhat dazed expression, the king permitted it. Jeremias quickly and expertly tended to the wound and wrapped the bandages around it. Ammon had cut the king where he wouldn't be permanently damaged.

While finishing up with the king, Jeremias muttered to Ammon in their native language, "You certainly took your sweet time with that fight."

Ammon grinned. "You knew I would win."

"Yes, but it was still annoying having to wait. We could have been halfway to Middoni by now," Jeremias said dryly.

"The next time I try to take down the leader of a nation, I'll be sure to be quick about it."

"That's all I'm asking for," Jeremias said as he tied off the king's bandage.

King Laman moved to return to his chariot but stopped before he reached it. He turned to Ammon and said, "I wish for you and your brothers to come to me in my kingdom, for I greatly desire to see you. I wish to know more of the things you have taught my son."

"I will come to you as quickly as I can," Ammon said as he bowed. Miracle after miracle seemed to be occurring in rapid succession. It amazed him how the Lord had softened King Laman's heart. In a short time, Ammon had secured all of King Lamoni's kingdom, eliminated Mahlon as a threat, and freed Isabel to marry him—Ammon would have to make sure to ask her father's permission as soon as Aaron, Muloki, and Ammah were safe. And now King Laman, the king over all these lands, wished to learn more about the gospel? Ammon didn't know what he had done to earn such blessings from the Lord, but he was profoundly grateful for them.

King Laman nodded at Ammon's response and took his place on the litter. He was lifted up, and his group turned around to go back the way they had come.

The happiness in King Lamoni's eyes was unmistakable. Ammon understood—the king's future was now secure. He had defied his father in the most unimaginable way, and still retained his life, his kingdom, and the ability to govern himself. There would be nothing stopping any of them from worshipping as they wished now.

"Let's go rescue your brethren," King Lamoni said joyfully.

That made Ammon smile. He couldn't wait to tell Aaron about everything that had just happened, particularly the invitation to go and teach King Laman.

* * *

Isabel sat in Kamilah's embroidery circle and realized just how much she would miss it. She thought of all the times she had tried to get out of it, how she had hated sitting here. She still didn't enjoy embroidering, but she would miss the gentle, fun conversations the women had.

She wondered how many more times she would be able to attend. Did she have days? Weeks? Months? She wished for years but knew Mahlon would be far too impatient for that.

Isabel tried to absorb every detail of the circle surrounding her, the way the women's voices lilted and laughed, how she felt safe and secure being a part of it. Perhaps she could start a circle of her own when she joined Mahlon's home.

A loud commotion in the courtyard outside broke into their little sanctuary. Moments later, Mahlon stormed into the throne room surrounded by his personal guards.

"What is the meaning of this?" Kamilah demanded as she stood.

Several of the women stood as well, but Isabel couldn't move. Not now. Not so soon! But Mahlon wouldn't be so bold otherwise.

"This is none of your concern," Mahlon snapped dismissively at Kamilah. "I am here with news for Isabel."

Isabel could only sit paralyzed on the ground, unable to do anything but blink at him.

"This is an outrage!" Kamilah said as she moved protectively in front of Isabel. "Guards!"

Several soldiers made their way over to Mahlon's band, who had already pulled out their own weapons. They would fight and spill blood here in her father's house. Isabel couldn't let that happen.

"Kamilah," she said in a weak voice.

"I am here to claim my bride," Mahlon said as the soldiers closed in on them. "Isabel and I are to be married in the morning."

Isabel heard the queen's sharp intake of breath. Mahlon's statement seemed to render Kamilah temporarily speechless.

"You can't just—" she finally sputtered, but Mahlon interrupted. "I can and I will. King Laman has granted his permission, and Isabel has already agreed, haven't you?"

The queen turned to look at Isabel with questioning eyes. "Isabel?"

Her father's soldiers continued to press in on Mahlon's men, awaiting the queen's word to attack. Isabel had to stop them. No one else should have to suffer because of Mahlon. "What he says is true," she finally admitted in a low voice.

This shocked all of her father's courtiers, except for Mahlon, who grinned viciously.

The queen knelt down at Isabel's side. "Your father has not given his permission," Kamilah said. "You don't have to marry this creature."

"Yes, I do." Isabel couldn't meet Kamilah's eyes.

"Yes, she does. Tomorrow morning," Mahlon reconfirmed.

Tomorrow morning? Nothing could be prepared in that amount of time—no feast, no wedding clothes, no decorations. Isabel felt an overwhelming desire to delay the ceremony for as long as she could. She had to convince him to wait.

"That is too soon," Isabel said. "My father isn't here. I can't marry without my father's blessing. Can't we wait until his return?"

"This is not a negotiation," Mahlon said. "It isn't my concern who is or is not here."

"But surely King Laman would want to be here for this wedding," Isabel tried again. "There are many relatives who will feel insulted at not having been invited."

Mahlon ignored Isabel's entreaties. "I will return in the morning for the wedding. I suggest you be ready."

Isabel understood all too well the threat in Mahlon's voice. She had no idea what Mahlon might do to the family that remained behind without protection from her father or from Ammon. She thought once more of what it had felt like to be held and comforted by Ammon and how she had so desperately wanted to believe his words that another way could be found to stop Mahlon. It felt like a dream, as if her time with Ammon had happened to someone else. Part of her wished he hadn't left so that she could lean on him for help. But Ammon wasn't there.

Isabel needed to worry about the innocents who were there. She would do what she had agreed to do.

"I will be ready."

With a nod and victorious smile, Mahlon and his men left the way they had come in.

"What is happening?" Kamilah asked in a worried tone. Isabel shook her head, keeping her mouth closed. "Let me help," Kamilah said. Isabel didn't respond. No one could give her any comfort or hope. She had to face the decision she had made on her own.

The queen sent for Abish, though Isabel wanted to tell her there was no point. Abish already knew, but she had been sworn to secrecy. Isabel didn't need a confidant. She needed courage.

"Why are you doing this?" Kamilah asked as she wrapped her arms around Isabel's shoulders. "You don't have to marry him."

"I can't explain," Isabel said in a dull voice. "But tomorrow morning, I will marry Mahlon."

* * *

Mahlon and his guards shoved people out of the way as they left the palace to return to their encampment just outside the city. Mahlon wanted to stay here in Ishmael, where he could keep an eye on things. He no longer trusted his underlings to do an adequate job of this, although, admittedly, his spies in Ishmael had been correct that both King Lamoni and Ammon had gone to Middoni to free the imprisoned Nephites.

Mahlon had recently received an epistle from Antiomno, which laid out their agreement of the reward Mahlon would pay him. It never ceased to amaze him how greedy people could be.

Antiomno had also mentioned that according to Mahlon's desires, portions of Mahlon's plan had been discussed openly in front of the Nephite prisoners. That part had made Mahlon smile. He wanted Ammon to know what he was doing while Ammon was away. He wanted Ammon to suffer, to know that there was nothing he could do to stop Mahlon from marrying Isabel. He had seen the way the Nephite looked at his future wife. Ammon obviously cared for her, and Mahlon delighted in how much pain it would cause him when he returned to find Mahlon and the princess already wed. As soon as Mahlon had received the epistle from Antiomno, he had waited to make certain that Ammon had left.

Mahlon entered his hut and sat down on his pallet to reread the epistle, to make certain he had not missed anything. As he sat thinking over the situation, it did disturb him somewhat that Lamoni had chosen to go with the Nephite. That seemed like such an odd thing for a man of his stature to do, and if Mahlon had wagered on it, he would have bet that the king would have stayed behind. He didn't understand it, but it seemed unimportant at the moment. All it had done was speed his plan up. He didn't have to wait for Ammon to be captured and for the king to leave to secure his release. Now they were both gone, and there was no one left to stand against him.

However, he also felt a bout of uneasiness over the fact that none of his men had actually told King Lamoni and Ammon about the imprisonment in Middoni. They had left on their own, before Mahlon had sent anyone to tell them. He wondered how it had happened. Who had told them? It couldn't have been Antiomno. He was far too weak a king, his kingdom of too little consequence, that he would ever dare risk offending Mahlon in that way.

Mahlon decided it didn't matter. What mattered now was that after ten years of plotting and planning, murdering and scheming, everything was finally about to come together.

He would soon be king.

19

IT TOOK THE ENTIRE NIGHT for King Lamoni to secure the release of Aaron, Ammah, and Muloki. Ammon had stayed outside Antiomno's small palace, as Lamoni had thought that Ammon's presence might complicate matters.

Finally, at dawn's first light, King Lamoni emerged to take Ammon over to the prison. Ammon started to ask the king what it had cost him for the negotiations so that Ammon could somehow repay him, but King Lamoni held up a hand and refused to discuss the matter. Ammon took some comfort in the thought that, due to King Laman's grant, King Lamoni was about to become a much wealthier man.

King Lamoni mentioned to Ammon that Antiomno had had difficulty believing that King Laman himself had ordered Ammon's brethren to be released. Antiomno had wanted to send runners to Nephi, but Lamoni had worried about how the Nephites would be treated while they waited. He thought it best to have the release accomplished as soon as possible, and so the lengthy negotiations had started. King Lamoni thought that Antiomno still planned to send messengers to Nephi to make certain that King Laman had authorized the release, but thankfully, Antiomno was willing to let them take the Nephites now.

Lamanite guards led King Lamoni's group to just outside the prison. The soldiers told them to wait.

"King Antiomno offered to have them brought to the palace, but I thought it would be better for us to retrieve them here," King Lamoni told Ammon.

A few minutes later, Ammon understood why. The three Nephite prisoners stumbled out into the early morning sunlight, their wrists still bound, the markings on their ankles showing that they had been tied there as well. All three were naked, and their bodies were covered in marks, lashes, and bruises that showed where they had been beaten.

Ammon felt angry and sick all at the same time.

Aaron saw Ammon and grinned. "Ammon! Little brother! Do you think that next time you could get here before the beatings? I'm much too handsome to have my face permanently scarred."

"That's gratitude for you. I come all this way, and all you can worry about is your precious hide," Ammon teased, blinking back the hot, thick tears at his brother's condition. He pulled out a knife and busied himself with cutting Aaron's bindings. King Lamoni's servants brought over capes to cover the men, and the king sent several other servants into the palace to have Antiomno give them clothing and to gather food from the kitchens.

"Are you all right?" Ammon asked in a more serious tone as he pulled the ropes from his brother's arms.

"This new way of fasting and suffering the Lamanites have taught us did wonders for our humility." Aaron rubbed his wrists.

"We should have a healer look at you," Ammon told his twin, hoping he communicated his need for Aaron to be serious about his health.

Aaron held his arms out in front of him for Ammon to see. "I don't have any broken bones, open sores, or wounds to worry about, nor do I think Ammah and Muloki have any. I managed to convince the Lamanites to administer the majority of the beatings to me. Apparently, I have quite a mouth on me."

Ammon shook his head. He understood why Aaron had antagonized the guards; he would have done the same thing to keep his companions safe.

"But I'm fine. It looks worse than it feels."

Jeremias came up from behind Ammon to throw his arms around Aaron. Aaron laughed and thumped Jeremias on the back. "You must be so glad to see me after being stuck with Ammon all this time."

But their cousin didn't play along. "I'm glad you're safe," Jeremias said as he released Aaron.

"I should have known better than to let my younger brother go off on his own." Ammon sighed. "Obviously you still need my protection."

Aaron let out a guffaw of disbelief. "Younger brother? And which of us was chosen by the voice of the people to be king? Oh, yes, that would be me."

"I hardly think the bad taste of our people qualifies your claim to being the eldest," Ammon retorted with a smile.

King Lamoni approached them, standing near Ammon's elbow.

"At least I had the maturity not to fall in love with some girl," Aaron said as he accepted the clothing given to him by one of King Lamoni's servants.

Ammon had been about to introduce King Lamoni when this statement made him stop. He glanced at the king's surprised face before he said, "What? How could you possibly know . . ."

Aaron quickly dressed and gratefully accepted the food offered him. In between bites of a flat corn cake, he said to Jeremias, "I'm assuming she has nice hair. You know how Ammon is about hair."

"This is not a time for jokes," Ammon said as he tried to understand what Aaron had just said. "How did you know about Isabel?"

Aaron's face sobered at Ammon's reaction. He gulped down the rest of the cake he had been eating. "We were imprisoned here at the request of a man named Mahlon. He wanted to overthrow a king, and somehow we were part of that plan."

"King Lamoni?"

"Yes, that was the name."

Ammon turned and pointed to the king. "Aaron, this is Lamoni."

Aaron looked slightly embarrassed at not having relayed the information earlier. "I didn't realize."

"Why would they discuss their plans in front of you? And specifically mention Mahlon's name?"

"They spoke not only of the king but of you, Ammon. They said that Mahlon would marry a woman you cared for when you were out of the way. I didn't think much of it. I thought it to be some sort of ruse, because I knew you would never again allow yourself to care for . . ." Aaron's words trailed off in disbelief as he looked at Ammon's face.

A thousand knives pierced Ammon's heart as his throat closed in, making it nearly impossible for him to breathe. After the encounter with King Laman, Ammon had thought that he and Isabel would be safe to start their lives together. He had never even considered the possibility that Mahlon could still ruin everything.

Jeremias said, "It seems to me that Mahlon wanted you to know that he was going to marry Isabel and that you'd be unable to stop it."

A sudden surge of energy burst to life inside of Ammon. "That's where he was mistaken. I am going to stop it."

He turned to King Lamoni. "I will need waterskins. I am going to run back to Ishmael to stop the wedding."

Lamoni nodded and called for his servants to bring the requested supplies, along with extra weapons. *Of course,* Ammon thought, seeing the wisdom in the king's command. It was possible that Mahlon would be expecting them to return and that they'd have to fight their way through.

Ammon pulled out his sword and set about repairing some of the blades that had broken in his fight with King Laman.

He heard Jeremias ask Aaron, "So other than the imprisonment, how have things been?"

"The usual. We've been cast out, beaten, driven from house to house and place to place, until we got here and had the chance to enjoy the luxurious accommodations. And you?"

Jeremias briefly recounted the success they had had in Ishmael and what had happened on their journey here to Middoni.

"Ammon was always the luckier twin." Aaron was impressed at King Laman's request for Ammon and his brethren to come and teach in the land of Nephi. "You'll have to tell me more about King Laman later. For now, tell me about this Isabel that we're going to save."

Jeremias told Aaron what Isabel had done their first night in Ishmael. Aaron chuckled loudly with a laugh that sounded to Ammon just like his own. "Oh, I like her. Made your life difficult, did she?"

"You can't begin to imagine," Ammon said as he finished up with his sword. He swung it a few times to make sure that the blades were properly embedded in the sides. He'd spend the rest of his life chasing after Isabel if he had to. He wanted only to keep her safe and to let her know that she was loved. Not only by him, but by all of her family. She deserved happiness. He wanted to be the one to make her happy.

Ammon knew it was not only the sort of husband Mahlon would be that concerned him, but Isabel's eternal salvation as well. Abish had told him that Isabel desired baptism, and, for the first time, Ammon understood why Isabel hadn't come to him. Mahlon would force her to continue the Lamanites' murderous practices—the rituals and sacrifices. He understood the misery and guilt this would bring her in light of her new knowledge.

I will prevent this, Ammon vowed.

The servants returned with the water and the weapons which they began passing out. "What are you doing?" Ammon asked when he turned and saw the king.

King Lamoni had removed all the trappings of his office—his high, carved, wooden and green-feathered headdress; his kingly cloak; and the ornaments encircling his waist, neck, ankles, and throat. "I'm going with you. I may not look it, but I was quite the runner in my day. Where do you suppose Isabel gets it from?"

"And of course Jeremias and I are going as well," Aaron said as he strapped several skins across his chest.

"You're not well enough. Stay with the others," Ammon told his brother, although he knew Aaron would never stay behind. Injured or not, his twin would come.

Aaron snorted. "What's wrong? Worried you can't keep up with me?"

But before Aaron had uttered his last word, Ammon had already started to run. He heard the other three men fall into line directly behind him; the servants and Ammah and Muloki followed at a slower pace.

He didn't look forward to running up the plateau they had just descended, but he would scale any mountain, endure any obstacle, if it meant keeping Isabel safe from Mahlon.

As he ran through the grasses in the open fields surrounding Middoni, Ammon thought of how much time he had spent running away from Isabel. The irony of his running toward her now, when he might be too late, was not lost on him.

He simply couldn't consider the possibility that he would be too late. He had to be fast enough and strong enough to reach her in time.

Ammon prayed for strength, for endurance, and for the opportunity to stop the wedding. He wished he had some way of communicating with Isabel, a way to let her know that if she could put Mahlon off, he would be there to help her.

Isabel, wait for me.

* * *

Isabel could only wait for the inevitable. It kept her from sleeping. How could she sleep under the circumstances?

Abish had stayed the night with her, telling her stories about Isabel's mother and tales from her childhood that she had not heard in many years. It gave her some comfort as they passed through the darkness together.

Every time she thought of her impending wedding, Isabel felt like she might throw up. That gave her a slight smile—the image of her vomiting throughout the entire ceremony. It would certainly be an accurate embodiment of her feelings.

She knew she should start getting ready. It would take a long time to dress in her mother's wedding clothes, prepare her hair, paint her face, and put on her mother's jewelry.

But Isabel found herself repeatedly struck by a desire to put off the wedding for as long as possible. Obviously it was the worst event of her life, but there was something else . . . something deep within her . . . But what did it matter if she married Mahlon now or hours from now? It didn't make sense.

Despite not making sense, the feeling persisted. She had already made her decision. She would see it through. It was understandable that she would have regrets, but there was nothing to be done. She had to marry Mahlon to save her family. But the overwhelming urge to do nothing won out. Neither she nor Abish said anything about the ceremony, and neither did anything to get Isabel ready.

Their do-nothing state continued until one of Mahlon's men, his new captain, Elam, barged into her room. It outraged Isabel that he didn't even have the decency to look apologetic at having intruded.

"I am here to escort you to the wedding," he told her before she could protest his actions.

"As you can see, I'm not ready," Isabel told him casually. "Return in an hour or so."

Elam looked confused. "My orders are to escort you now."

"Do you think Mahlon will be pleased if I arrive looking as if I just woke up?" Isabel stood and put her hands on her hips, hoping she looked intimidating.

"He told you that you would marry this morning."

"Yes, but he never told me at what hour. You will have to tell him to be patient."

"He will not be patient long," Elam said. "And I will return in an hour to take you to the ceremony regardless of how you look."

Isabel caught the implied threat. None of Mahlon's men had ever been very subtle. Elam did not want to be punished by Mahlon, and if Isabel continued to thwart him, Elam would force her to comply. She had no doubt he would drag her to the wedding naked in order to save his own skin.

Ideally, it would have taken much longer than an hour to get ready, but Isabel and Abish did what they could.

It certainly didn't help matters that Isabel kept bursting into tears, making the paint on her face run so that Abish had to keep fixing it. Most of last night and all of this morning Isabel's thoughts had turned again and again to Ammon. She told herself that she had to stop thinking about him. Soon she would be another man's wife, and she would never see Ammon again. It was a waste of time and emotion to think of him so often.

But she couldn't wipe the look on Ammon's face from her memory—that mixture of despair, grief, and disbelief when she had told him she would marry another. She hated that he had been so hurt. She hated even more that she had been the one to hurt him.

After the hour passed, it was not Elam who came into Isabel's room unannounced. Mahlon strode in angrily. He jerked Isabel to her feet. "Let's go."

Over Mahlon's shoulder, Isabel saw Elam, whose left eye had been blackened, presumably by Mahlon's fist. Mahlon forced Isabel into the courtyard just beyond her room where two of Kamilah's servants stopped them. "Princess, please. You must come with us. The queen has become very, very ill."

Isabel shook off Mahlon's grip, and, before he had a chance to react, she followed the servants into Kamilah's room.

Kamilah lay on her cushioned pallet. Her hair was damp and matted to her head. Beads of sweat dotted her forehead. She moaned and clutched her stomach.

"What's wrong?" Isabel said as she knelt next to the queen. "Where are the healers?"

An immediate change came over Kamilah. She stopped writhing around and opened her eyes to smile at Isabel. "The healers are all out finding rare herbs to cure me."

"But you're not sick. Why are you pretending to be sick?" Isabel whispered in confusion. Suddenly Kamilah let out a loud groan, and Isabel looked to see Mahlon entering the room with his arms crossed.

"Water," the queen gasped. "I need water."

Isabel poured the water herself from the low table at the queen's bedside and put the clay cup to the queen's lips. Kamilah raised herself up to sip at the water and to speak in low tones to Isabel.

"I know what you said yesterday, and I woke up this morning intending to honor your wishes, but something happened. I'm not certain I can explain why, but I feel as if we should try to delay things."

"I had the same feeling," Isabel said quietly.

"Then the illness must continue until the healers can return. Sprinkle some of that water on my forehead when he isn't looking." Kamilah lay back down and moaned.

"It seems the queen will live," Mahlon said as he approached the two women. "Time to get married."

Isabel stood to face him. "The healers have gone to fetch a cure for the queen. I will have to wait for them to come back. I can't get married thinking my mother might have a serious illness." It wasn't technically a lie; she truly wouldn't want to get married if she thought Kamilah was sick. That she happened to know Kamilah wasn't ill didn't matter if it would gain her some time.

Kamilah stopped groaning behind Isabel and went very still.

Mahlon let out a short bark of laughter. "She's not your mother."

"She's been like a mother to me for the past ten years. I will not wed without knowing she will be taken care of."

Isabel knelt back down, deliberately turning her back on Mahlon.

"Fine," Mahlon finally grunted. "We will wait for the healers to return with their medicines and not a moment longer. You can't put me off forever."

Isabel knew she couldn't put him off forever. But she wanted to try.

20

MAHLON WAS AS IMPATIENT AS ever. He had sent his own guards out after the healers, and had they found the men lounging by the waters of Sebus. The guards had hurried them back, and the healers had concocted their "cures" for the queen. Fortunately, Mahlon only suspected the healers of laziness instead of being part of a conspiracy.

For a conspiracy it had become, on a scale that Isabel only realized when she finally agreed to leave with Mahlon to go to the altar where the ceremony would be performed. The processional moved slowly, with happy music that made her heart want to break. They had not gone far outside the palace walls when suddenly they were surrounded by what must be all of her father's flocks.

Peccaries, turkeys, and deer ran about with great abandon. Her father's hunting dogs gleefully snapped at any animal that got too close. Isabel was inundated with the sounds, sights, and smells of dozens of animals running amuck.

Mahlon yelled at the members of the processional to continue on, but no one responded. Everyone tried to avoid the rampaging flocks. Isabel backed up to the wall outside of the palace to stay out of harm's way.

"You better catch them," Isabel shouted at Mahlon. She knew of his greed and his desire to be king over all of Ishmael. "That's most of my father's wealth running about."

That made Mahlon order his men to start rounding up the animals. Despite her grim circumstances, Isabel couldn't help but laugh at the sight of these war-hardened soldiers rendered panicked and helpless by the stampeding flocks.

Isabel noticed that while at first glance it appeared that the servants "helped" to gather the animals, they were in fact further riling the flocks up. The chaotic confusion masked their true intent.

She didn't know how much time had passed, but finally the majority of the animals were driven back to her father's stables. Isabel covered her nose when Mahlon came back to her side. Mahlon now reeked of scared peccary. It was a horrible smell.

The processional continued, slowed even further by the now-exhausted soldiers and servants. They all looked bedraggled and worn down, and the stench was intensified when they gathered together. Isabel thought she might pass out.

Then, suddenly, there was another scent that filled the air around her. "Do you smell that?" she heard Elam ask.

"Fire!" someone else screamed.

Here, outside the palace's walls, a fire could mean the loss of nearly the entire city, as most of the outer buildings were made of wood.

It couldn't be a coincidence. Isabel wondered which servant was responsible for the fire. She would certainly take advantage of the situation.

"Hurry!" Isabel called. "The fire must be put out before the whole city is lost!"

Mahlon couldn't let the city burn to the ground. She could see the frustration in his face as his desire to marry continued to be thwarted. He had no choice. He had to put the fire out before the wedding could proceed.

Again, her father's servants seemed to be helping but only exacerbated the problems. They "accidentally" knocked water containers over just as they reached Mahlon's men. Mahlon sent some of the servants to fetch more water, they didn't return. Instead of using blankets to suppress the fire, they used them to fan the flames.

"That was harder than I thought it would be," Abish said as she materialized at Isabel's side.

"You did this?" Isabel said as she watched the sky darken with smoke.

Abish nodded, a feverish excitement in her eyes. "Don't worry, that entire area has been evacuated, and a breakline has been created near the wall's outer limits to contain the fire in that section."

"All those homes," Isabel said.

"We can build more homes. We only have one Princess Isabel," Abish told her. Isabel turned to hug her sooty and smoky friend.

On their own, and despite the servants' best efforts to the contrary, Mahlon's men eventually managed to contain the fire and extinguish it. Mahlon returned with his chest heaving. Smoke and ashes had left black streaks all over his face and arms.

"You're a mess," Isabel informed him. "You should go and bathe."

"No more delays," Mahlon said through gritted teeth. "You'd better hope nothing else happens."

"Have you considered that these might be omens from the gods?" Isabel tried hopefully.

But apparently Mahlon didn't care. He grabbed her and made her practically run toward the altar.

He pushed her down so that she knelt, and then he knelt down next to her. "Where's the priest?" Mahlon shouted.

"He's coming," one of the king's servants responded. "There."

Isabel had to cover her mouth to keep from laughing at Kamilah's choice for a priest.

The high priest, Zedekiah, shuffled down the street, accompanied on either side by younger priests. He held on to a walking stick to keep himself upright.

Zedekiah had married her parents. It was rumored that he had married her grandparents. No one knew for certain how old he was, but Isabel's father had told her that Zedekiah had already been ancient when he'd been born. Isabel knew that despite his appearance Zedekiah had an extremely sharp and quick mind, but Mahlon didn't.

"Go get that doddering old fool," Mahlon told his men.

Isabel watched as two soldiers went over to Zedekiah in an attempt to hurry him along. Zedekiah ineffectually beat on the men with his walking stick. "Get away from me. Have you no respect for your elders? I'll get there when I get there."

The two soldiers backed off as Zedekiah refused to pick up his pace.

"This is all your doing," Mahlon hissed at Isabel.

She looked at him with wide, innocent eyes. "I have no idea what you're talking about."

"No matter what you do, this wedding will go forward. And you will have to suffer the consequences of your actions when it is over," Mahlon threatened.

That managed to take the smile off Isabel's face. She could only imagine what Mahlon might do to punish her.

Zedekiah moved slower than a sloth; he seemed to take one small step every few minutes. As he came closer, she noticed that he intentionally shook as he walked, causing his stick to tap against the stone floor of the dais where the altar had been constructed.

After what must have seemed an eternity to Mahlon but felt like only a few moments to Isabel, Zedekiah finally stood in front of them.

Zedekiah cleared his throat several times. He asked one of the younger priests to fetch him a cup of water to drink. The whole crowd waited for Zedekiah's drink to arrive. When it did, Zedekiah drank the entire cup and asked for another.

Mahlon pulled out one of his short obsidian knives and pointed it at Zedekiah. "No more water. Proceed now."

The high priest had no reaction to Mahlon's command other than to cough again and to wait for another drink. After taking a few sips from the second cup of water, Zedekiah handed it back to the younger priest. Zedekiah cleared his throat.

"It is certainly a beautiful day today. It reminds me of a time many years ago, when I was a boy. I went fishing on a day like this . . ." Zedekiah began a long, rambling story of a childhood memory involving a large fish that got away.

Isabel thought Mahlon might actually explode. His body vibrated with tension.

"Get on with it!" he finally snapped when Zedekiah reached a stopping point. The high priest glared at Mahlon before he said, "Marriage is a serious commitment, and much will be expected of you both. When I married Isabel's parents many years ago, it was the day my favorite dog died. His name was Stump because he'd been born without a leg. That dog went everywhere with me. I remember once when he—"

But before Zedekiah could go off on another tangent, Mahlon took out his wicked-looking sword and stood. "Do this ceremony right, do it now, or I will strike you down."

"It is not wise to start a marriage so angry," Zedekiah reprimanded him but showed no fear. "I have a point to my tale, if you will only be patient enough to listen. It is my obligation to instruct you on your roles and responsibilities in your married life."

But Mahlon refused to hear it. He started arguing with the high priest. Isabel wanted to clap her hands over her ears to block out the sound. She looked up at the clear blue sky and saw that the sun had begun its descent. Kamilah and her servants had managed to delay the wedding for many hours.

Mahlon yelled for another priest to be brought to perform the wedding. One of Zedekiah's attendants told Mahlon that no other priest would dare insult Zedekiah by displacing him at this royal ceremony. That only served to further infuriate Mahlon.

Isabel closed her eyes for a moment in an effort to block out the picture of a sooty, black-streaked Mahlon arguing with the priests, threatening them with death if someone didn't finish the ceremony right then.

She wondered where Ammon was, what he was doing. Had he managed to free his brethren from prison? Where would Ammon go after she married Mahlon? Would he stay here in Ishmael or would he continue his travels? Isabel said a little prayer then, asking God to continue to bless Ammon's life. She had nothing but a lifetime of misery in front of her. She hoped Ammon wouldn't suffer a similar fate.

Mahlon ended the argument with Zedekiah by ordering his guards to capture all of the priests. In a short amount of time they were rounded up. Mahlon threatened to kill one of the priests every time Zedekiah tried to further delay the proceedings. Kamilah appeared then, but even she couldn't say anything to stop Mahlon.

The expression on Zedekiah's face, a sort of bewildered befuddlement, immediately disappeared. He had no choice. Isabel wouldn't want any of her father's priests harmed. She nodded slightly at Zedekiah, signaling that she understood. He looked at Isabel with apologetic eyes before he started the ceremony properly.

Mahlon knelt back down next to her, a triumphant smirk on his face. "I see that the queen has made an amazing recovery," he said snidely, but Isabel refused to acknowledge him. Soon she would be his wife, but for these last few moments she was still her own person. She would ignore him if she wanted to.

Isabel wondered why she had felt the need to delay. It hadn't done her any good. Here she was, going through the motions of the ceremony, exchanging goods with Mahlon to show that they understood their roles as husband and wife. All the delaying had only made Mahlon angrier. She supposed she could look forward to a night filled with the physical evidence of his anger.

For a moment Isabel let herself imagine that it was Ammon who knelt next to her. She imagined how happy she would be, the love she would feel.

But it would not happen. She had to let the imagined future with Ammon go.

Because this was how her life would end. Here, with this wedding.

Mahlon turned to face Isabel as he drank from the steaming chocolate drink spiced with vanilla and chili pepper. He passed the cup to Isabel. She had to face him in return. She would drink, and this portion of the ceremony would be over. She would be considered his wife, and the ceremony would be cemented by eating food from his home as they traveled back there.

Isabel wished she could see Ammon one last time.

"Drink it," Mahlon ordered.

She started to lift the cup slowly to her lips when it was knocked from her hand, spilling the brown liquid all over her wedding clothes.

Like something out of a dream, Isabel turned to see Ammon standing at the edge of the courtyard, his sling in hand. Isabel stood up. "Ammon," she whispered. This couldn't be happening.

"I hope I'm not interrupting."

* * *

"Good thing he didn't miss," Aaron said. But Ammon barely heard his brother.

Ammon had reached new limits in his anger at the sight of Isabel kneeling next to Mahlon. It had taken every ounce of self-control he possessed not to thrash Mahlon on the spot.

Mahlon stood. "What do you think you're doing? Isabel is marrying me of her own accord. There's nothing you can do to stop it." He told one of his guards to procure another drink so that the wedding could be completed.

Isabel stayed rooted in her spot, staring at Ammon like a deer who had just been discovered by a predator. Ammon smiled at her, wanting to tell her everything so that she would never have to fear again, so she would never have to worry about Mahlon being part of her life.

"She does have very nice hair," Aaron said in their language as he stood next to Ammon. "I approve."

Ammon turned to glare at his twin. "Stop looking at her like that."

"Like what?" Aaron said too innocently. "Worried, are you?"

"Why would I be worried? I'm older and better looking."

"Shouldn't you be off fighting to save the woman you love?"

Aaron was right. Ammon anticipated that Mahlon wouldn't allow him to explain the situation without a fight. So he took out his sword.

Behind him, Jeremias also pulled out his sword. Jeremias nudged Aaron. "Aren't you getting your sword out?"

"Why? I could hardly claim Ammon as a relation if he couldn't manage to take down this Mahlon character."

"Quite right." Jeremias put his sword away.

"Besides, if he's foolish enough to get himself killed, we can step in then and take care of things."

"I'm not going to get myself killed," Ammon grumbled as he advanced on Mahlon. If anyone was going to die, it certainly wouldn't be him.

But King Lamoni stopped Ammon by putting a hand on his shoulder. "This is my fight," the king said. "Let me finish this."

Ammon knew he was right. Lamoni was Isabel's father. He was the one Mahlon had plotted against. As much as he hated it, Ammon knew he had to stand aside.

He tried to hand King Lamoni his sword, but the king refused it. "As angry as I feel right now," he said, "I fear what I might do to Mahlon with it. I can never take up another weapon in anger."

Ammon felt immediately chastised for his own angry impulses, while feeling great pride in how far Lamoni had come in such a short time.

Mahlon had called his guards together, and Ammon saw that King Lamoni's men had started to assemble around them. King Lamoni had his citizens, his servants, his entire army here. Mahlon did not. Ammon realized that Mahlon must have felt awfully certain his plan would work, since he had come without most of his army.

But Ammon didn't trust Mahlon to avoid harming the king. If King Lamoni would not take a sword, then Ammon would take his. He shadowed King Lamoni as he made his way to the altar.

"This stops now," King Lamoni said. "You and your men will leave. There will be no wedding."

"Isabel has made this marriage agreement of her own free will," Mahlon said.

"You did not seek my permission, and you did not perform any of the proper protocols for a betrothal. This entire ceremony is invalid."

"Ask her," Mahlon sounded a little desperate in light of King Lamoni's confidence.

King Lamoni walked to Isabel, taking both of her hands in his. Ammon saw Isabel's lower lip tremble as her father looked lovingly at her. "Why would you marry this man?"

"I didn't think you would say no to Grandfather again," Isabel said with a shaking voice. "Mahlon said it would cost you everything you had left if I refused him."

"You meant to sacrifice yourself for us?" King Lamoni sounded incredulous. "My Isabel, my precious jewel, don't you know that I would give up everything for you?"

King Lamoni took her in his arms. Then Isabel cried great, soul-rending sobs.

It made Ammon's desire to hit Mahlon in the face even stronger.

Mahlon would not let the king ignore him. "King Laman wants this marriage. You wouldn't dare defy him."

King Lamoni slowly released Isabel by passing her to Ammon's waiting arms. Ammon held her tightly as she continued to cry, promising himself that he would never let her go again.

King Lamoni turned to face Mahlon. "Your spies are not nearly as clever as you think. If they were, you would already know that my father has granted me not only my kingship for the rest of my life, but has returned all of my lands to me. All," he repeated. "And he has said that he will no longer rule over me or my people."

"He freed you from tribute? I find that difficult to believe."

"What you believe is irrelevant. If you are foolish enough to try and fight for the lands you once possessed, you will be declaring war on a land that has the full support of King Laman, since this kingdom was created by his express command. Whose side do you think he will take?"

"Lies." Mahlon spat the word out. "Laman would never—"

"You may go to Nephi and find out for yourself," King Lamoni interrupted him. "Or I will forward you a copy of the notes my scribes took from the conversation I had with my father in Midian. For now you will take your men and leave, or I will force you out of my kingdom. I will give you one week to collect your men, supplies, and belongings from my lands, which is more time than you gave me when you took them from me. After one week you are banished from stepping one foot inside of my borders."

Ammon saw Mahlon's frustration as all his carefully laid plans tumbled down around him. He saw that Mahlon wanted to fight, but even Mahlon had to know he couldn't possibly win.

Finally Mahlon signaled to his men. "I will leave. But this isn't over."

"Yes, it is." King Lamoni said to him. "This is over, and we will never see you again."

21

KING LAMONI CALLED TO HIS guards, asking them to escort Mahlon out of the city walls.

Ammon continued to hold Isabel tightly, though she had stopped crying. He could feel her murmuring something against his tunic front. He pulled back from her. "What are you saying?"

Her brown eyes sparkled with unshed tears. "You're here. I can't believe you're here. You stopped Mahlon. I don't have to marry him."

"Of course I'm here. We came as soon as we heard what Mahlon had done. We ran the entire way back from Middoni. I would have done anything to stop this. I would have given my own life if it meant I could save you from him."

Isabel didn't react the way he thought she might. She just looked at him. She didn't ask him why he had been so desperate to stop her wedding, as part of him had hoped she would. It would have made what he had to say easier.

"Isabel, I . . ."

Ammon wanted to say it. He needed to say it. He would have preferred not to have an audience, but this is how it was.

Taking a deep gulp of air, he said, "Isabel, I love you."

Her face softened into a mixture of wonder and happiness. "Ammon, I believe in Jesus Christ."

Ammon heard Aaron let out a loud guffaw of laughter before Jeremias made him be quiet.

Red-hot embarrassment flooded through him. "That's not quite how I imagined this conversation going."

"No," Isabel said, holding onto his arms as if to prevent him from leaving. "I want you to know before you make any other plans or declarations. I want you to know that I'm not like her. I believe. I want to be baptized."

Relief replaced his humiliation. "Isabel, I've never loved anyone the way that I love you. I was so focused on what I thought I had to do, I almost missed out on creating one of the most important relationships in my life. I want to marry you. I want to be your husband."

When Isabel said nothing in response, Ammon suddenly realized that she hadn't specifically said she had feelings for him.

Suddenly feeling very foolish, Ammon started to backtrack. "Of course, if that's not what you want, I completely understand . . ."

His words trailed off as Isabel threw her arms around his neck. "There's nothing I want more!"

Ammon grinned. "So you do love me then?"

Isabel pulled back to look at him. "Of course I do," she said as if he were simpleminded.

"Then say it!" Ammon wanted to hear the words coming from Isabel's lips.

Isabel flashed him a dazzling smile that made his stomach flip. "Ammon, I love you."

Ammon had completely forgotten the crowd of people gathered around them, watching and listening, until King Lamoni put his hand on Ammon's shoulder. Ammon immediately released Isabel and turned to face her father.

"I suppose this means I can no longer allow you to be a servant in my home," King Lamoni said good-naturedly.

"I know that I have done this all wrong. I didn't properly ask for your consent—"

King Lamoni held up one hand to stop Ammon from speaking further. "I don't see a need for that. I had a good feeling that things would go this way when I saw your determination to return and stop Isabel's wedding to Mahlon. It gives me great pleasure that you will no longer be a servant, but will live here as a son."

Ammon still felt some mortification over his mishandling of the situation. "This is wrong. I have nothing to offer you or Isabel as wedding gifts. No lands to speak of, no way to make a living to provide for her."

"My son," King Lamoni said. "You have given us the most incredible gift of all, a knowledge of our Savior. No earthly wealth could ever compare to it. And let me worry about providing for you and Isabel. You have another work to do, and the Lord has made certain that I'll be able to well afford it."

The queen had come up to join this circle. She smiled and said, "I fear I'm not quite as selfless as my husband. I'd like grandchildren as soon as possible as my gift."

Isabel flushed several different shades of red as she looked down and away while Ammon tried not to laugh. "Yes, well, we'll see what we can do about that. If you'll excuse us for a moment."

Aaron called out, "She didn't mean right now!"

Several people nearby laughed as Ammon shot his brother an I'll-deal-with-you-later look. Ammon took Isabel by the hand and pulled her away from the crowd.

"There's something important I need to tell you," Ammon said.

"Something more important than you love me and want to marry me?" Isabel teased. Ammon couldn't help but smile back. He never thought he'd see the day when Isabel would tease him, when she would laugh with him the way she had, when she would look at him with such love in her eyes.

But he had to focus. "I need you to know that I must continue with my mission. I worry that it might be difficult to balance everything. But it's very important to me that I continue to do the Lord's work."

He worried what her response might be. What would he do if she said she wanted him to cease his labors?

She regarded him with a quizzical look. "I wouldn't love you very much if I tried to keep you from your work. It's important to me too. There are so many people who need to hear your message."

"Our lives won't be normal." Ammon wanted to make certain that she understood what she was agreeing to.

"Nothing has been normal since you came into my life, and I wouldn't have it any other way."

"Would you just kiss her?" Aaron shouted from behind them. Several cheers and whistles went up.

"For once, I think my younger brother is right," Ammon informed his future bride just before he kissed her, much to the crowd's delight.

Kamilah announced that it was time to return to the palace. A celebratory dinner had to be prepared to honor Isabel and Ammon's betrothal. She came and collected Isabel, telling Ammon there would be time for kissing later. Isabel had to get ready for the celebration.

Ammon tried to protest, saying Isabel was already the most beautiful woman in Ishmael. She didn't need any sort of preparation. He was rewarded with a kiss on the cheek from Isabel, but the queen insisted.

He hated being parted from her, even if it would be only a matter of minutes until he saw her again.

"My little brother falling under the wiles of another woman. Well, at least you converted this one," Aaron said as he slung his arm around Ammon's shoulders.

"Just wait," Ammon smiled. "It will be your turn soon."

Aaron let out a sound of disgust as they both watched Isabel leave. She kept sneaking glances at Ammon, giving him little smiles that made him want to chase after her and plead with her to marry him right then and there.

"As your elder brother," Aaron started to say, but Ammon interrupted. "You're not the eldest."

"Father thinks I'm the eldest."

"Father also thought we should marry to spread the message," Ammon said pointedly. "Do you plan on doing that?"

The expression on Aaron's face was his answer. "That's what we have you for, isn't it? To marry Lamanite princesses. And we have me to go see King Laman."

"What?" Ammon said. "But I wanted to go and see him."

"I know you did, but I think you'll have things to take care of here, if I'm not mistaken."

"You don't even know how to get to Nephi," Ammon said.

"That's what faith and the Spirit are for," Aaron replied. "We'll make our way there and teach anyone we can find along the way."

"We?"

"Muloki wants to come with me. Ammah wants to stay here with you. Something about needing a break from prisons and torture. So we'll leave tonight."

"Tonight? So soon?"

Aaron shrugged. "Why not? You're the one who said it, little brother—there is so much work to be done out there. The field is ripe; we will thrust in our sickles and reap with all our might to gather the sheaves."

"I meant me, not you."

"Jealous?" Aaron grinned.

Ammon caught one last fleeting glimpse of Isabel. "No, not jealous. You're right. There is much to be done here. King Lamoni wants to start building synagogues so that we can assemble the people together."

"Then I'll go, and you'll stay. If King Laman is really mad about you not coming, I can go out and come back in and just pretend to be you."

Ammon laughed as he thought of the many times in their youth when they had exchanged identities. "I'm not certain that will work. But don't leave tonight. Stay for the celebration. Get some rest."

Aaron made a demurring sound until Ammon added, "You should stay and try to fill that bottomless pit you call a stomach."

"Why didn't you say there was food involved?" Aaron grinned as his stomach rumbled loudly. "I suppose we can stay for a day or so."

Feeling happier than he had for a long time, Ammon walked with his brother to the palace. In such a short amount of time, his life had been completely changed, and it thrilled him. Ammon looked forward to the missionary work he would continue to do, to the life he would build with Isabel, and to the children they would have someday.

It put Ammon in an extremely generous mood. "You know," Ammon said to Aaron, "I hope if Isabel and I have a son he'll be just like you."

"The world would be a much better place with more people like me in it," Aaron agreed seriously.

Ammon laughed, hugged his brother and then went inside the palace to get ready for the feast.

* * *

To my younger brother, Aaron:

Now that I finally know where you are, I'm excited to send you this epistle to catch you up on my life and to make plans for the near future.

It's hard to believe that the last time I saw you was at my wedding. What a busy and glorious day—I baptized Isabel in the morning, and in the afternoon she became my wife. It is the best decision I ever made, and I've tried my hardest to make sure Isabel knows how important she is to me. Even if, as you told her, she deserves better.

I'm so impressed by the strides you've made with King Laman and his people, and that he asked you to accompany him to the wedding. And contrary to what you might think, a great work has gone on here in Ishmael since your departure back to Nephi. King Lamoni told his people they were free from King Laman's rule and that they would have the liberty of worshipping the Lord as they wished, wherever they wished. I wish you could have seen the way they rejoiced! I've spent my days preaching to the people of King Lamoni, and never in my life have I seen a people who are so zealous in keeping the commandments of God.

I have traveled as you have, thanks to the proclamation King Laman sent among all his people. I agree that it is much nicer to teach people when you don't have to worry about being bound or put in prison, spit on, hit, cast out, or having stones thrown at you, etc. I have heard through secondhand accounts much about the work you have been able to do—and now we have thousands converted in Nephi, Ishmael, Middoni, Shilom, Shemlon, Lemuel, and in Shimnilom.

King Laman used to come often to visit us, and he told us of his people's desire to select a new name to reflect the changes in their beliefs. I heard you were instrumental in helping to select the name of Anti-Nephi-Lehi for them as a group and as the name for their new king, Laman's eldest son.

It's still difficult to believe that King Laman has passed into the next life. I know the news must have been especially hard on you—I know how close the two of you had become. But I do rejoice that he died in the knowledge of Jesus Christ and that the king could return to Him again.

And that is part of the reason why I write you now—King Laman's death has destabilized the kingdoms to the north. The Amalekites and

Amulonites plan to take advantage of it to install their own king, despite the fact that Laman named Anti-Nephi-Lehi as his successor before his death. King Lamoni's spies tell us that the Amalekites and Amulonites have recruited Lamanites to their cause and that they make preparations to come to war against us. I sense that our good friend Mahlon may have something to do with this.

So I think it best for all of us to meet in Midian, since it is a convenient midway point for us to gather. I think you should bring with you all of those you've converted. It will soon become necessary for all of the people of the Lord to live together as a form of protection. After we meet in Midian, we should return here to Ishmael to make plans with King Lamoni and King Anti-Nephi-Lehi on how to defend ourselves against the invasion. I am concerned because King Anti-Nephi-Lehi has already stated that neither he nor his people will take up arms against their brethren and that none of them have any intention of making preparations for a defense. Perhaps we can convince him otherwise.

I have sent runners to find Omner and Himni and to find everyone who came out of Zarahemla with us so that they may also join us at the meeting in Midian.

I look forward to seeing you again, my brother. My son—and your namesake—is especially excited to meet you. He asks on an almost daily basis when you will come. Unfortunately, he hardly believes anything I tell him about the sorts of things you've done in the past. You are some sort of paragon of virtue in his eyes. But he is only three. We can't expect him to know better.

But in all seriousness, if my son becomes even half the man you are, I will consider myself a success as a father.

Isabel is with child again and seems convinced that it is a girl. Perhaps the babe will be born during your time here so that you may properly greet her. I am looking forward to meeting your wife and hearing from her own lips the unusual circumstances that brought the two of you together. And to remind you both that you owe me a nephew named after me.

It is difficult to believe that the years have passed so quickly. How is it even possible? I suppose when you're doing work that you love, when you're surrounded by people that you love, time ceases to have much meaning.

I can't express the smallest part of which I feel in how the Lord has blessed all of us. I know that I can never truly be a profitable servant to Him, but how I long to spend the rest of my days trying to be!

May God keep you and bless you always.

Your elder brother,

Ammon

22

Six months later

"EVERYONE STOOD HERE, RIGHT ON this spot," Ammon said, holding his arms out wide. "Your great-uncle, Anti-Nephi-Lehi, spoke to the crowd. His voice was filled with power as he promised that if the people would make the oath, that they would keep their swords bright."

Little Aaron nodded, enthralled. He had heard this story so many times before, but he never seemed to tire of it. "An oath is a special promise."

"That's right. An oath is a special promise. And as part of their promise, the people dug a great pit into which they threw all of their weapons. Swords, knives, daggers, bows and arrows, spears—the pit filled up quickly. They covered the weapons with a huge mound of dirt so that none of them would be tempted to dig them up again. Then everyone took a sacred oath. They promised that they would never again use weapons to shed another man's blood. They made covenants with God that they would give up their own lives rather than take someone else's."

"But why all the weapons?" Aaron pressed. "What if they needed to defend themselves?"

Ammon smiled at his son as he crouched down next to him. "Because of the murders and sacrifices they had committed in the past. They feared that if they gave themselves over to shedding more blood, they might never find their way back. They also did it to show God how sorry they were for what they had done in the past."

Ammon looked over to see Isabel sitting on a nearby log, listening to Ammon's tale as she wove a garland of pink-and-white flowers for herself. Her very large stomach gave her an excellent place to keep the flowers, her own table. Ammon had learned early on not to comment on how adorable he found such things.

He had tried to impart some of this wisdom to his brother, since Aaron's wife was also great with child, but his brother had refused to believe him until Aaron had been forced to spend a night sleeping outside.

"Do I have to bury my weapon?" little Aaron asked his father with a worried expression on his face. He held the sling that had once belonged to Isabel.

"No, you don't have to bury your weapon," Ammon said as he ruffled his son's hair. Satisfied, Aaron tucked the sling back into his belt in exactly the same way Ammon would put his away.

"We should head back," Ammon said as he went to help his wife get to her feet. They had spent the entire morning outside.

"I'm hungry," little Aaron asked.

"He does have a stomach like your brother," Isabel said as the trio walked back to the palace in Nephi. Aaron held both his mother's and father's hands and swung in between them with delighted shrieks as they lifted him off the ground.

Isabel didn't waddle as their sister-in-law did, despite the fact that Isabel was slightly further along. Ammon didn't know if it was her height or her love of running, but she seemed to carry her pregnancy easily. She still went for long walks every morning, as she could no longer comfortably run.

They had come to Nephi with the hope that there would be safety in numbers. Many of the other recent converts had come here as well. It seemed that the Amulonites and Amalekites still planned to install their own king over the Lamanite lands, and it had turned into a waiting game. Ammon and his brothers had tried to organize the Anti-Nephi-Lehies to help construct some defenses, mostly walls and pits, but the work was slow going.

"What is that sound?" Isabel asked suddenly.

Ammon shushed little Aaron and stood still to listen. He heard a dull roar coming from somewhere near the palace. It sounded like a far-off thunderstorm. Or, Ammon feared, like a battle. Isabel came to the same realization as they exchanged worried glances.

He picked Aaron up and reached out to take Isabel by the hand. He moved as quickly as he dared, knowing how difficult it must be for Isabel to hurry. But he had to get them to safety.

As they reached the palace in Nephi, Ammon saw that the east wall had collapsed. Their suspicions had been right—Nephi was being invaded. They must have come from the foothills up through Shemlon, or else there would have been some sort of warning of their coming. His brothers would be at the other walls, doing what they could to keep the city safe. The majority of the invading army seemed to be entering at the flattened wall.

First he had to take care of his family, and then he would go and do what he could to stop this fight. But he didn't know how to get them into the palace without running through the attackers.

Perhaps he should hide Isabel and Aaron in the wilderness. He said as much to Isabel, but she shook her head. "My family is in the palace. I have to make certain that they are all right. If they die, if Kamilah dies never knowing how I . . . if I never told her . . . we have to find them!"

"There's no way of getting into the palace."

"This way!" Isabel said as she tugged on Ammon's arm. She took him to the back of the palace where there were no entrances.

"What are you doing?" he asked.

"My father's palace is based on the exact same design as my grandfather's. There are secret passages back here. We can use them to get in."

And then these passages could be used to evacuate his family if it came down to that, Ammon thought. At least inside the palace they would be surrounded by stone walls and people that he knew would give their lives to protect them.

Isabel plunged them into a dark, musty hallway filled with bugs and spiderwebs. Little Aaron whimpered once and hugged his father tightly, burying his face in Ammon's neck. "You are such a brave boy," Ammon whispered, trying to calm his son as they went through twists and turns. Isabel's steps never once faltered. She seemed to know exactly where she was going.

They burst into the throne room, where all of Isabel's extended family had gathered. They were praying and singing. An air of peace and calm filled the entire room.

"Isabel!" King Lamoni said as he ran over to hug his daughter. "We were so worried about you being outside the city."

Ammon handed Aaron to Kamilah. He came over to kiss and hug his wife good-bye.

Isabel's eyes widened as she realized what Ammon was doing. She grabbed the front of his tunic. "Where are you going?"

"I have to go help," Ammon said as he took Isabel by the wrists to release her grip.

"Ammon, don't go. Please. They'll kill you."

Ammon kissed her hands. "I have to try, Isabel. I have to try to stop them."

"You can't face an entire army by yourself!" Her voice sounded shrill and anxious. "I can't lose you," she said as her eyes filled with tears. She put a hand on her stomach. "*We* can't lose you."

Ammon put his hands on Isabel's upper arms, making certain that she looked directly at him. "I swear to you that I will come back to you. Have some faith in me."

"Ammon," she tried again.

"Isabel," he responded. "Do you trust me? Do you trust the Lord?"

"Yes." The word was little more than a whisper.

"Then believe, Isabel. I will come back."

"You can't fight," little Aaron interjected from Kamilah's arms. "What about the oath?"

"Daddy didn't make the oath," Ammon told him.

He kissed his precious wife on the forehead and ran out of the room. Ammon went to their rooms to retrieve his weapons. He dashed outside the palace and stopped short when he realized what was happening.

He saw bodies everywhere, people he recognized and loved. How many? Hundreds? Thousands?

And standing over those bodies he saw Lamanites, Lamanites who had been stirred up to anger by the Amulonites and Amalekites. But the Lamanites were no longer attacking. Many of them stood mournfully over the bodies of those they had just slain. Those Anti-Nephi-Lehies who had not been killed called out in prayer to the Lord. They had prostrated themselves on the ground, simply awaiting their fates. They would rather die than fight back. The Anti-Nephi-Lehies had offered no resistance to the aggressors.

He saw some Lamanites dropping their weapons to the ground and falling upon their knees to beg forgiveness from those they had almost killed.

The sounds of war began to dissipate as more and more Lamanites simply stopped what they were doing. This was not a fight. It was a slaughter. There was no resistance.

Ammon realized that not every Lamanite had the same reaction to the Anti-Nephi-Lehies' failure to fight. Many of them had stopped simply because they had nothing to gain by continuing to kill people. Warriors who did not fight back or at least try to run away would bring the Lamanites no honor. They couldn't be taken as war captives to become sacrifices, a necessary part of the ceremonies required to install a new king.

The fighting seemed to taper off as more and more Lamanites ceased their attack. However, those who fought next to banners indicating that they were Amulonites or Amalekites did not stop.

And at the forefront of those groups, Ammon saw Mahlon. Just as he had suspected. Apparently Mahlon's greed now extended beyond becoming king of Ishmael to becoming king of the entire Lamanite nation.

Gripping his sword tightly, Ammon knew exactly how to end this fight.

"Mahlon!" Ammon yelled the man's name as he ran toward him.

Mahlon looked over and saw Ammon. He gave Ammon a wicked grin. "It is very foolish of you to come running over here like this. I could kill you."

A squadron of Mahlon's men moved into position to attack Ammon at Mahlon's command. Ammon gripped his sword tightly. He'd rather fight just Mahlon to stop this battle. But he would fight anyone he had to in order to end this.

"They could try," Ammon taunted. Mahlon's face darkened as his men reacted to Ammon's declaration. "But are you really such a coward that you're afraid to face me yourself? Call off your men. Let this be between you and me."

Mahlon seemed to consider Ammon's offer, but Ammon knew what Mahlon's response would have to be. He couldn't afford to seem weak now in front of his army. They'd displace him as leader and the fight would end. Mahlon had to accept Ammon's challenge. Mahlon nodded once and then approached Ammon. He called out for his troops to stop. The battle would now hinge on the outcome of this fight. Ammon couldn't lose.

"I've been looking forward to this for a long time," Mahlon told him.

Ammon heard the men behind Mahlon buzzing at this turn of events.

"It's that Nephite. The one who can't be killed."

"Every man can be killed. Especially a Nephite."

"They say the Nephite god protects him."

"Our gods are more powerful. He will be defeated."

"He is like a god himself. I was at the battle of Sebus."

Such superstition would certainly work in his favor with this fight. If he could defeat Mahlon, Mahlon's troops would leave, as in their minds it would indicate that the gods favored Ammon and that any further attempts at fighting would be doomed.

Not that anyone seemed overly concerned with this possible outcome. The soldiers began making wagers on the fight, and it sounded as if the odds were being cast in Mahlon's favor.

Mahlon's men called out taunts and threats at Ammon while Mahlon smiled. But Ammon had no more time to waste. He would not wait for his opponent to come to him.

He ran at Mahlon, his sword out in front of him. This would be a fight unlike any other Ammon had experienced. He would not be trying to draw things out. He would not be taking on multiple opponents. He would fight Mahlon, fight him hard and fast, until it was finished.

Mahlon was ready for him. Mahlon fought well, which did not surprise Ammon. A man in Mahlon's position would have to be a great warrior to have gained favor with King Laman and to have such respect from his men. But what Mahlon fought for was greed, revenge, and to satiate his own bloodlust and desire for power. Ammon fought to protect the faith of the Anti-Nephi-Lehies. He fought for his brothers. He fought for his newfound royal family. He fought for the safety of his son and his unborn child.

And he fought for Isabel.

He had made himself a promise to always protect her from Mahlon. He would not fail her now.

Their swords clashed against each other, the sound of wood cracking against wood echoing across the strangely silent battlefield. Everyone around them watched the struggle between Ammon and Mahlon as they waited for the outcome.

Mahlon swung wide, and Ammon circled to his right to stay out of range. Ammon quickly brought his own sword down in a slicing motion, his dangerous obsidian blades angled toward Mahlon's body. Mahlon threw both arms up and jumped backward just in time to avoid being hit.

This made Mahlon go slightly off balance and gave Ammon the opportunity to cut at Mahlon's stomach. The wound was mostly superficial, but Mahlon staggered backward in surprise, his hand going to his stomach, where it was quickly covered in blood. He blinked several times at Ammon before he growled and launched another attack.

Back and forth the two men went, both refusing to give any ground. Ammon concentrated to make his movements smooth and deliberate. He slipped into a state of being so focused that he moved as one with his weapon, never faltering, never letting up.

Mahlon, perhaps in desperation, turned his sword the wrong way so that his blades became embedded into the body of Ammon's sword. Ammon wrenched his sword away, which ripped several obsidian pieces away from Mahlon's weapon.

"Surrender," Ammon said.

Mahlon growled in response, wiping the sweat from his brow.

The battle resumed, and Ammon couldn't help but smile when he and Mahlon arrived at the same realization at the same time—Mahlon would lose. Mahlon fought in the style of the Lamanites. He fought to take captives and sacrificial victims. He fought to wound, to inflict enough pain to immobilize his opponent. There would be no honor in taking a life, only in capturing a prisoner.

But Ammon fought, as the Nephites had been forced to do for so many centuries—for survival. He fought to protect his family and his beliefs.

He would win, and Mahlon knew it.

Mahlon frantically tried to adjust his own movements, but it was too late. Ammon cut Mahlon on both arms and wounded him in the chest. Ammon slammed into Mahlon, forcing him to drop his weapon. The motion knocked Mahlon backward, and he lay on the ground with his chest heaving from the exertion.

Ammon took the chance to whip out his hunting knife and hold it against Mahlon's throat.

"Do you surrender?" Ammon said.

"No! Give me a weapon!" Mahlon called out to his men. But no one would even look at their fallen leader. He had dishonored and disgraced them. The siege against Nephi was at an end. As Ammon had hoped, they had taken Mahlon's defeat as a sign that there would be no victory today. They left Mahlon to his death as they began to retreat.

"Come back!" Mahlon yelled at them from his place on the ground. "Cowards! Come back!"

Ammon pushed the tip of his knife against Mahlon's neck, which made him return his attention to Ammon. "I suppose you will kill me now?" Although Mahlon's voice was flat, Ammon could see the fear in his eyes.

Part of him wanted to bury the knife in Mahlon's throat. His fingers curled tightly around the blade's handle. He wanted to permanently remove Mahlon as a threat. He knew Mahlon would not have given him any reprieve if the circumstances had been reversed. But if he did this now, if he gave into his baser instincts, he would be no better than Mahlon. He was a man of God, and he needed to remember that. He didn't need to kill him. There was another way.

"I will spare your life only if you swear an oath that you will leave the Lamanite lands and promise never to come to battle against King Anti-Nephi-Lehi or any of his relations or his alliances."

Mahlon's heavy breathing had finally ceased. He looked at Ammon for several moments before he said, "I will make the oath if you will put down your weapons as a token of trust."

Ammon considered Mahlon's offer. Mahlon had no sword or weapon available to him. His soldiers had departed, and the two men had been left alone on the battlefield. If it meant ensuring Isabel and her family's safety, he had to do it. He had bested Mahlon once. If Mahlon meant to fight him without weapons, Ammon didn't doubt that he could win again. Mahlon was powerless.

It seemed a reasonable request. Ammon had not made any oaths or promises to not hurt Mahlon, and Mahlon had no reason to believe that Ammon wouldn't strike him down.

Ammon saw Mahlon's eyes roll back in his head, but Mahlon fought the weariness, waiting for Ammon's response. So Ammon threw his weapons to the side, removing those in his belt as well. He held his hands out, palms up, to show that he had no other weapons.

Mahlon nodded once. He rolled to his side with great effort, groaning as he turned. He then said in a low voice, "I swear an oath that I will never again fight with the king of Nephi or any of his family," and then he promptly passed out.

It was done. Ammon needed to find his brothers, to check on their condition. Ammon turned toward to the southern wall. He would begin his search there. He wanted to return to Isabel and their family, but this had to be taken care of first. He did not worry for their well-being, as none of the armies had reached the palace.

Ammon did worry over what the future now held for all of them. Mahlon might have led the first wave, but it would not be the last. There would be others who would try to take over the kingship, particularly now that many men would be vying for the leadership position Mahlon had just lost. The Anti-Nephi-Lehies would not be able to stay here forever.

He wondered what could be done to better shore up their defenses while they remained in these lands. As he planned ways to prevent today's events from ever happening again, he heard Isabel calling his name in a panicked way that made his heart stop.

Despite the distance, he could see that she wasn't looking at him. She was looking over his shoulder, and Ammon turned to see Mahlon easily standing with a victorious grin, about to throw Ammon's own hunting knife at him. Ammon quickly searched around for an available weapon. *There.* A spear had pinned someone to the ground. If he could only reach it in time . . .

But even as he ran, he knew he would never make it.

23

THE QUIETNESS HAD CONCERNED HER.

Where minutes before there had been the stomach-turning sounds of war, of men yelling and screaming in pain, the clashing of weapons, the groans and cries of the dying, now there was only a strange silence. Isabel didn't know what it meant, and the stress was almost more than she could bear.

Was Ammon safe? Had he and his brothers somehow stopped the army? Would he come back to her as he had promised?

She held her hands protectively over her stomach. Would Ammon live to see this baby come into the world?

She hated this. She hated worrying and wondering. She had to do something. She had to help. But how?

Isabel decided to follow after Ammon. Twice in her life she had cowered when Ammon was in danger, too frightened to do anything but watch. Not this time.

She approached Kamilah, who still held little Aaron in her lap. "Would you lend me the sling for a while?" The only weapons Isabel knew of in the palace were in her and Ammon's rooms, but Ammon had presumably taken those. She would have only this sling to protect herself. She hoped it would be enough.

Her son didn't hesitate, immediately giving Isabel her sling back. "Will you use it to fight like Daddy? Or did you make the oath?"

Isabel held the sling tightly in her hands. "No, Mommy didn't make the oath either."

"Isabel." Kamilah reached out to grab Isabel's wrist. "What do you think you're doing?"

"He's my husband," Isabel said. "You can't expect me to stay and just wait. It sounds as if the fighting has finished. I have to know that he is all right."

Kamilah looked over at Isabel's father and then back at Isabel. Her expression indicated that she perfectly understood Isabel's need. "Please don't do anything foolish."

Isabel wondered how she would leave without arousing the suspicion of every person in the room. She knew Kamilah wouldn't betray her intentions, but her father would never allow her to go.

She decided to slip through the secret passages. She could ease her way over and simply disappear inside. Hopefully no one would notice.

Isabel kissed Aaron and hugged him tightly. He growled in response, having recently decided he was too old to be coddled by his mother. "Do you know how much your mother loves you?" she had asked Aaron.

"I know, I know," he said in a voice laced with disgust at her overt display of affection.

She did not consider herself a fool and did take into account how badly things could go. Ammon might already be dead. She might die. But she could no longer stand by and hope for the best. She had to take action. However, she realized that this might be the last time she would ever see Kamilah. She shouldn't have waited so long. Isabel should have told Kamilah years ago how she felt. This could be her last chance to do so.

"I'm so sorry," Isabel said.

Kamilah looked up in astonishment. "Sorry? Whatever for?"

"For everything. For everything I've done and said. I am so, so sorry."

Kamilah looked at Isabel with such kindness in her eyes that Isabel had to fight back her tears. Kamilah reached out to cup one side of Isabel's face with her hand. "There is nothing to be sorry for."

"I need you to know that . . . that I . . . I . . ." Isabel's voice caught. Why could she say these words so easily to Ammon and to their son and not say them now when it mattered so much?

"I understand," Kamilah had answered with a soft smile.

It somehow gave her the strength to finally say it. "I am fortunate to have had two mothers that I love."

Kamilah reached out to hug Isabel, and Isabel held on tightly. Aaron again protested at being squished between the two women, and in a mixture of laughter and tears, the women released each other.

"Be careful," Kamilah said.

"I will."

Isabel got unsteadily to her feet, willing herself not to keel over from her balance problems, and began to edge her way toward the passages. Now to sneak from the room without calling attention to herself.

She saw little Aaron turn to look at her. He put his hand out to wave and opened his mouth. *No, no, no*, Isabel thought. She knew what was coming next, how he would call out his good-bye to her. He would alert everyone there to what she was doing.

Suddenly, her very pregnant sister-in-law gasped and stood up. "My waters have started."

The entire room was thrown into an uproar as the women rushed to her side. Isabel took advantage of the chaos. She heard little Aaron calling behind her, "Good-bye, Mommy!"

His words were swallowed up in the confusion, and Isabel slipped out.

She hurried through the passages that would give her access to the front of the palace, where the fighting had been. Isabel didn't know if it was the thick stone that muted any sound or if the battlefield had become even quieter. The sick, queasy feeling in her stomach increased, and the knot of fear tightened inside her.

The sunlight blinded her momentarily as she ran outside. Isabel stopped and blinked, adjusting to the light. A wave of revulsion threatened to overcome her. There were bodies everywhere. While Isabel had grown up hearing and knowing of battles, this was the first time she'd had such a personal experience with it. Was Ammon among them? How would she find him?

As she carefully made her way onto the field, she searched the faces of the men who lay on the ground. So many dead. So many wives had lost their husbands, and so many children had lost their fathers.

The smell of blood and bile made Isabel cover her mouth and nose. How would she go on if she found Ammon among the dead? She had to believe in his promise that he would return. She had to believe that he was all right, because the possibility of his death was more than she could bear.

Movement at the periphery of her vision caused Isabel to look up. She saw a man slowly walking across the battlefield. *Ammon.* It was Ammon. She nearly collapsed in relief. He was headed toward the southern wall. He was safe.

But behind him she saw someone else moving, a man who had been lying down. The man stood up, and Isabel saw the sun glinting off of a dark obsidian blade that he'd raised to throw at Ammon.

It was Mahlon. Ammon had his back to Mahlon. He wouldn't even see the attack coming.

"Ammon!" Isabel screamed. Ammon looked up and saw her and then turned to see Mahlon, his weapon poised. But instead of attacking, Ammon ran.

Making himself a moving target would make it harder for Mahlon to hit him, and Isabel saw Mahlon's hesitation as he tried to compensate for Ammon running. Why hadn't Ammon tried to fight?

She didn't have time to try and make sense of it. Isabel pulled out her sling. She ignored the sharp pain in her side as she leaned over to pick up a rock.

Everything seemed to slow down around her as she fit the rock into the sling. She found herself praying for Ammon's safety and for accuracy.

The sling made a whizzing sound as it circled past her head, and with a jerk Isabel let the rock fly.

The rock soared through the air and found its mark. It hit Mahlon in the face, temporarily stunning him before he could throw the knife.

Ammon wrenched a spear from the ground and threw it at Mahlon. It caught Mahlon in the torso. Mahlon staggered from one foot to the next, clutching at the spear. He swayed backward and then collapsed. He did not move again.

Mahlon was dead.

* * *

Ammon rushed to his wife, whose face had turned a sickly shade of green. He gave Isabel a fierce hug. "I can't believe you did that."

"What were you thinking?" he demanded as he pulled away from her, gripping her shoulders. He hugged her again, holding her closely to him. "I could have lost you both." His voice was choked with emotion.

But she showed no signs of guilt or remorse for running onto a battlefield nine months pregnant. She steadily met his gaze. He could see that she didn't regret her decision. Ammon hugged her a third time. "Where did you learn to use a sling like that?"

"You taught me." Isabel's voice was muffled against his shoulder. He released her to let her speak. "I used to practice every day."

"Why?"

"You know what your father says. You never know when it will be useful. Besides, you saved me with your sling. It was the least I could do to return the favor." Ammon gathered her up again, ignoring her teasing. He was just relieved that she was all right.

Isabel let out a small groan of pain, and Ammon let go, fearing that he had hugged her too tightly. But before he could ask, he heard Aaron calling his name.

His twin had streaks of blood on his arms and his face, and he was helping support their brother Omner, who was limping.

"Where's Himni?" Ammon asked.

"He stayed in the field to help the wounded and to gather up the surrendered Lamanites who said they wanted to know more about what the Anti-Nephi-Lehies believed."

Ammon and Aaron helped Omner to sit. Omner's leg had been severely damaged. The bandage covering it was already soaked with blood. With Aaron's help, Ammon changed the bandages and cleaned the wound as best he could. He focused on helping his brother and missed the increasing gasps of pain coming from Isabel. The wounds were bad enough that Ammon feared his brother might never walk again.

"We should administer to him," Aaron said quietly.

"Yes, soon, please," Omner said in a strangled voice.

After they finished blessing him, others came to help, and a healer took charge of Omner.

Once he knew his brother would survive his wounds, Ammon pulled Aaron aside to speak with him. "How many dead?"

"At least a thousand," Aaron informed him grimly. "Perhaps more." They both looked over the battlefield that had started to fill with family members looking for loved ones, the sounds of their keening and grieving surrounding them.

"These men sacrificed their own lives rather than take the lives of their enemies because of the love they had for them," Aaron continued. "Has there ever been so great a love in all the land?"

"No, there hasn't, not even among the Nephites," Ammon replied.

"We won't be able to stay here much longer. We have some time, because they'll have to go somewhere else to find sacrifices to crown a new king. But they will be back."

Aaron was right. They wouldn't be able to stay in the Lamanite lands. Ammon wanted to stay, to continue teaching the gospel to the Lamanites, but the decision had been taken out of his hands. It wasn't safe. "Perhaps we can bring everyone with us to Zarahemla."

Himni arrived then with Jeremias and with some of the men who had come up from Zarahemla to teach the Lamanites. "We came back for supplies and to gather up able bodies to help find the wounded and bury the dead."

"I'll come," Aaron said, and Ammon quickly agreed until he heard Isabel call his name.

He turned to see her clutching at her stomach. He recognized the look on her face. "Now?"

"Now," Isabel said as she clamped her teeth together. "And Aaron, you must come as well."

Aaron looked alarmed. "I don't particularly want to see that."

"No," Isabel said. "Your wife began her labor just before I came out here."

Aaron's surprise turned into eager but worried anticipation. Ammon understood all too well. "But we're needed here."

Himni shook his head. "There are others who can help. Go, be with your wives. Give us something to look forward to after our work here is finished."

Aaron didn't have to be asked twice. He ran off to join his wife. Ammon hurried to Isabel's side and gently helped her get to her feet. She nearly tumbled over when another wave of pain hit, and despite her protests, Ammon swept her up to carry her back to the palace.

"I can walk."

"No, you can't. Now stop arguing."

Isabel, for once, was too tired to disagree with him. Ammon worried that she might fall asleep as her eyelids drifted shut and she let out a soft moan.

"Still think it's a girl?"

Isabel's eyes opened. "I know it's a girl."

"What if you're wrong?"

"Me? Wrong?" Isabel asked, breathing heavily. "When has that ever occurred?"

Ammon wanted to laugh with relief. It felt wrong to laugh after so much tragedy and loss though. Too many had died this day. But he reminded himself that he did not have to worry over the fate of those who had fallen in battle. They went this day to their Lord and Savior without blemish. He thought of what Aaron had told him, how many of the invaders had stayed behind to learn more of what the Anti-Nephi-Lehies believed. He thought of how those who had sacrificed so much had turned the hearts of their attackers. A great good had been rendered despite the awfulness of it all.

It forced Ammon to think of his own mortality, that he could be taken from this world at any time. It renewed his desire to do all he could to teach the words of the Lord. He too wanted to return without fault or sin.

Isabel groaned again, and Ammon held her tighter. "Not much further," he tried to reassure her.

Despite the death that surrounded them, he held life in his arms. Ammon would mourn those who had fallen, but he would continue to appreciate every day that he had on this earth. He would remind his family how much he loved them and would never take anything he had for granted. The laughter would return, and their lives would be filled with joy again.

"Everything will be all right," Ammon told Isabel. And he realized that it truly would be. Things might not go the way he anticipated, but in the end, everything would be all right.

So he decided to worry about the future on another day. He would have faith that the Lord would help him handle any obstacles that came their way. For now his only concern would be greeting his newborn child and welcoming her to the world.

He couldn't wait to meet her.

About the Author

Sariah S. Wilson grew up in California. She graduated from Brigham Young University with a degree in history and currently lives in Cincinnati, Ohio, with her husband, Kevin. She is the oldest of nine children and is the mother of two sons and a newborn daughter. You can contact her via her website, www.sariahswilson.com, or go online and drop in at sixldswriters.blogspot.com where Sariah blogs with five other LDS authors.